Advance Praise for Hap a

"Seven laid-back adventures, one of them brand new, for 'freelance troubleshooter' and good old boy Hap Collins and his gay black Republican partner Leonard Pine. . . . No one currently working the field demonstrates more convincingly and joyously the deep affinity between pulp fiction and the American tall tale."
—*Kirkus*

"As Mr. Lansdale might say, 'This was more fun than rolling down a hill with a bunch of armadillos.'"
—*Horror Novel Reviews*

". . . it's great to have all of these wonderful stories together in one nifty volume."
—*Horror Drive-In*

"Highly entertaining."
—*Sons of Spade*

Praise for Joe R. Lansdale's Hap and Leonard series

"Hap and Leonard function as a sort of Holmes and Watson—if Holmes and Watson had had more lusty appetites and less refined educations and spent their lives in East Texas. . . . Not only funny, but also slyly offers acute commentary on matters of race, friendship and love in small-town America."
—*New York Times*

"Lansdale reveals the human condition—our darkest secrets and our proudest moments, all within the unlikely confines of an East Texas adventure featuring the two scruffiest protagonists in modern crime fiction."
—*Booklist*

"As usual, the dialogue is deadpan tart and the action extreme but convincing. . . . Lansdale once again proves he's the East Texas master of redneck noir."
—*Publishers Weekly* (on *Hyenas*)

Praise for Joe R. Lansdale

"There's no bullshit in a Joe Lansdale book. There's everything a good story needs, and nothing it doesn't."
—Christopher Moore, author of *Secondhand Souls*

"[Joe Lansdale has] a folklorist's eye for telling detail and a front-porch raconteur's sense of pace . . . a considerable literary intelligence at work."
—*New York Times Book Review*

"Joe Lansdale is a born storyteller."
—Robert Bloch, author of *Psycho*

"Joe Lansdale simply must be read."
—Robert Crais, author of the Elvis Cole and Joe Pike novels

"Read Joe Lansdale and see the true writer's gift."
—Andrew Vachss, author of *Shockwave*

"Among the best fiction writers in America today, Joe Lansdale turns on the juice and cuts the damn thing loose. Enjoy the ride!"
—Kinky Friedman, author of *Ten Little New Yorkers*

"Hunter S. Thompson meets Stephen King."
—Charles de Lint, author of *The Onion Girl*

HAP AND LEONARD

JOE R. LANSDALE

tachyon | san francisco

Interior and cover design by Elizabeth Story
Interior photographs courtesy of SundanceTV LLC; copyright © 2015 by James Minchin III and Hilary Gayle

Tachyon Publications LLC
1459 18th Street #139
San Francisco, CA 94107
415.285.5615
www.tachyonpublications.com
tachyon@tachyonpublications.com

Series Editor: Jacob Weisman
Editor: Richard Klaw
Project Editor: Jill Roberts

ISBN 13: 978-1-61696-191-6

Printed in the United States by Worzalla
First Edition: 2016

9 8 7 6 5 4 3 2 1

Also by Joe R. Lansdale

For Lowell Northrop.
Thanks for your determination and dedication.

Contents

INTRODUCTION:
AN APPRECIATION OF JOE R. LANSDALE

Michael Koryta

DIFFERENT WRITERS have different goals, but there are—or should be—some constants. Here are a few: memorable characters, original voice, stories that make the reader feel something.

I can think of many writers who have achieved those things. Then I think of Joe Lansdale, who has achieved them, lapped them, and redefined them. This wonderful collection of the tales of Hap Collins and Leonard Pine is—somehow—just a taste of the Lansdale oeuvre, but it is a delicious one.

Memorable characters? Meet Hap, a former social activist and a "white trash rebel," and Leonard, a black, gay, Vietnam veteran and Republican voter. In the hands of many writers, this mix would be disastrous, an overwrought pairing designed to conceal inauthentic storytelling. In Lansdale's hands, not only does the duo work, but they seem natural together, playing off each other in beautiful fashion. The dialogue exchanges between these two, as typified in the novella "Hyenas," are filled with more gems than a jewelry store:

"Well," Leonard said, "in cases like that, the gut is often right. We still know a shark when we see one. That's why we crawled

1

out of the water and became men in the first place. Only thing is,
some of the sharks crawled out after us."
"That would be the lawyers," I said.

There's a smile on every page and an outright howler on every other, but it's in the momentum of the stories that I've always found the true genius. Hap and Leonard do a lot of chatting, sure, a unique patter that seasons their adventures, but they're always in motion, and the dialogue is truly in service of the story, not the other way around. A lot of writers with a gifted ear for dialogue—and Joe has one of the best ears around—can get caught in a trap built by their own abilities, creating wandering exchanges that don't do much except show off. Joe's stories are constantly in motion, and the dialogue reflects that:

"Ready?" I said.
"I was born ready," Leonard said.
"Scared?"
"I don't get scared."
"Bullshit."
"Okay, I'm a little scared. Let's get it done before I get more
scared."
We started walking.

There you go—they started walking. They're going somewhere, these two, and you'll find yourself turning pages at paper-cut speed to keep up, watching a remarkable feat where Joe Lansdale balances violence and humor, tension and howling laughter, in a way that feels organic, unforced, and perfectly original. Each story or novel seems to begin in mid-sentence, with the sense that you'd best hustle along and catch up or you're going to be left behind. There's a confidence to the prose that is simply masterful, a trust in both voice and reader.

There is also—and I think this is overlooked in the Hap and Leonard stories—a hell of a lot of wisdom. Amid the fun and between the punches, there's the voice of a writer who at times resembles Twain himself—and, yes, I really mean that, and, no, I do not say it lightly or easily.

In "The Boy Who Became Invisible," a story of Hap in his early years, Lansdale does more than make the reader feel something—he makes you hurt. The early pages, a story of seemingly casual schoolyard bullying, show the making of the man we will know as Hap.

That hit me pretty hard, but I'm ashamed to say not hard enough, Hap thinks of his own role, his moral acquiescence to something beneath him. His one-time friend, Jesse, is becoming a target of ridicule, and what Lansdale has to say about it speaks not just to schoolyard torment but to the dangers of group think, of what happens when you compromise personal integrity to just go along with the flow. When the kids laugh at Jesse, you'll hurt for him, and hurt for Hap, I assure you. But better than that, and more impressive—you'll hurt *because* of Hap. And because of yourself. That is when the character-reader bond has reached an emotional height, and it's a special experience.

When Jesse spoke to me, if no one was looking, I would nod.

We all carry memories of shame, embarrassment over our own conduct. Lansdale isn't directing you to examine them; he's too good a writer for that. The reflection is a product of the story, and all the great things—laughter, fear, profundity—that come from his work will *always* come from the story. While many writers repeat the *show don't tell* cliché, Joe Lansdale lives it. If you don't believe me, wait until you get to the last line of "The Boy Who Became Invisible." See how long that one lingers.

Again, this is merely a taste of a remarkable body of work. That's staggering to consider, and inspiring.

I just have a knack to aim at something and hit it, Hap reflects on his shooting ability in "Hyenas," and that's the way reading Lansdale feels—effortless talent, a knack so natural that he just leans back in his chair, puts his feet up, and spins a yarn. Meet him in person, and you'll leave thinking the same thing, that this stuff comes easily, that he shares great storytelling as naturally as most of us exhale.

And I'm here to tell you it's bullshit.

Does Joe Lansdale, like Hap Collins, have one hell of a lot of natural talent, a "knack" for hitting stories out of the park and dropping one-liners that are the envy of professional comedians? Sure. Does it come easily? No. It comes from a lifetime of dedicated work, a man committed to craft, a man so aware of how story works and why that he can fool us into thinking it's effortless. William Blundell once said, "Easy writing makes hard reading. Hard writing makes easy reading."

I think of that line when I read Hap and Leonard, and when I read Joe Lansdale in general. I think about how smooth these stories go down, each line so razor-edged, each action scene so perfectly choreographed, and I think—this guy has worked awfully hard so the reader doesn't have to.

You have in your hands a collection by a master. Enjoy it, treasure it, and as you breeze through with a smile on your face and some head-nodding over bits of polished wisdom, be damn grateful that Joe Lansdale has put in the work to deliver it so well. I assure you, the writing is not easy.

But the reading? It's an absolute joy. You'd best get started. Hap and Leonard are already in motion, I assure you, and you're going to want to catch up.

Michael Koryta is the *New York Times* bestselling author of eleven suspense and horror novels.

HYENAS

"The hyenas are hungry—they howl for food."
—*King Solomon's Mines*, H. Rider Haggard

WHEN I DROVE OVER to the nightclub, Leonard was sitting on the curb holding a bloody rag to his head. Two police cruisers were parked just down from where he sat. One of the cops, Jane Bowden, a stout woman with her blonde hair tied back, was standing by Leonard. I knew her a little. She was a friend of my girlfriend, Brett. There was a guy stretched out in the parking lot on his back.

I parked and walked over, glanced at the man on the ground.

He didn't look so good, like a poisoned insect on its way out. His eyes, which could be barely seen through the swelling, were roaming around in his head like maybe they were about to go down a drain. His mouth was bloody, but no bloodier than his nose and cheekbones. He was missing teeth. I knew that because quite a few of them were on his chest, like Chiclets he had spat out. I saw what looked like a chunk of his hair lying near by. The parking lot light made the hunk of blond hair

5

appear bronze. He was missing a shoe. I saw it just under one of the cop cars. It was still tied.

I went over and tried not to look too grim or too happy. Truth was I didn't know how to play it, because I didn't know the situation. I didn't know who had started what, and why.

Jane had called and told me to come down to the Big Frog Club because Leonard was in trouble. Since she didn't say he was in jail, I was thinking positive on the way over.

When Leonard saw me, he said, "Hey, Hap."

"Hey," I said. I looked at Jane. "Well, what happened?"

"It's a little complicated," Jane said. "Seems Leonard here was in the club, and one of the guys said something, and Leonard said something, and then the two guys inside—"

"Inside?"

"You'll immediately know who they are if you go in the club. One of them actually had his head shoved through the Sheetrock, and the other guy got his hair parted with a chair. He's behind the bar taking a nap."

"Ouch."

"That's what he said," Jane said.

"So . . . I hate to ask . . . but how bad a trouble is Leonard in?"

"There's paperwork, and that puts me off of him," Jane said, "but everyone says the three guys started it, and Leonard ended it, and, well, there were three of them and one of him."

"How come this one is out in the parking lot?" I said, pointing to the fellow with his teeth on his chest.

Leonard looked over at me, but didn't say anything. Sometimes he knew when to keep his mouth shut, but you could put those times on the head of a pin and have enough left over to engrave the first page of the King James Bible and a couple of fart jokes.

"Reason that guy's here, and the other two are inside," Jane said, "is he could run faster."

"But not fast enough?" I said.

"That's where we got a little problem. You see, that guy, he's knocked out so hard his astral self took a trip to somewhere far away. Maybe interplanetary. He's really out of here, and he hasn't shown signs of reentry."

No sooner had she said that then an ambulance pulled up. A guy and a woman got out and went over and looked at the guy on the ground. The male attendant said, "I guess clubbing doesn't agree with him."

"Either kind of clubbing didn't agree with him," the female EMT said.

It took me a minute to get what she meant. To do their job, I guess you have to have a sense of humor, lame as it might be.

They looked him over where he lay, and I was glad to hear him come around. He said something that sounded like a whale farting underwater, and then he said, "Nigger," quite clearly.

Leonard said, "I can hear that, motherfucker."

The guy went silent.

They loaded him in the ambulance.

"Don't forget his shoe," I said, pointing at it. But they didn't pay me any mind. Hell, they worked for the city.

"We got a bit of a problem here," Jane said. "You see, once this guy ran for it, and Leonard chased him, it couldn't quite be called self-defense."

"I didn't want him to come back," Leonard said. "I was chasing him down because I was in fear of my life."

"Uh-huh," Jane said.

"He turned on me when I caught up with him," Leonard said.

"Just be quiet, Leonard," she said. "Things will go better. You see, the part that's hard to reconcile, as we in the law business say, is Leonard turning him around and then beating him like a bongo drum. Leonard grabbed him by the throat and hit him a lot."

"A few times," Leonard said. "He called me nigger."

"You called him asshole," Jane said. "That's what the witnesses said."

"He started it," Leonard said. "And there's that whole deep cultural wound associated with the word nigger, and me being black and all. That's how it is. Look it up."

"No joke," she said. "You're black?"

"To the bone," Leonard said.

Jane turned her attention back to me. "A guy watching all this," she pointed to a fellow standing over by the open door of the club, "he said Leonard hit that guy a lot."

"Define a lot," I said.

"After the nose was broke and the cheekbones were crushed, and that's just my analysis, Leonard set about knocking out his teeth, said while he was doing it, according to the gentleman over there, and I quote, 'All the better to suck dick with, you sonofabitch,' unquote."

"So, Leonard's going to jail?"

"What Leonard has going for him is yon man in yon ambulance—"

I looked to see it drive off with the lights on, but it wasn't speeding and there wasn't any siren.

"—hit Leonard with a chair first, and he did call him the Nigger word."

"You mean the N word. When you say Nigger word, well, you've said nigger."

"Did I say the Nigger word instead of the N word?"

"You did."

"If you're quoting someone said Nigger, isn't that different?"

"I think so."

"Hey," Leonard said. "Sitting right here."

"Well, hell, I've pulled two shifts," Jane said. "Another hour on the job and I'll be calling everybody sweetie baby. Anyway, back to Leonard. Somewhere between the N word and him chasing the track star out into the lot, he hit one of the other attackers with a chair and slammed the other guy's head into the wall. Ralph, that's my partner, he's in there right now trying to get the fellow's head out of the wall without breaking something. Either wall or victim."

"Actually," I said, "Leonard had to have been provoked. He's normally very sweet."

"No shit?" Jane said.

"No shit."

"I don't think so. But here's what we're going to do. You bring Leonard by the station tomorrow morning, not the crack of dawn, but before lunch, and we'll fill out some papers. I won't be there. I'll be snoozing. But I got my notes and I got statements, and I'm going to turn those in, so they'll be there. And, just as a sidenote, I really did enjoy seeing that fellow's head stuck in the wall. Before you go, you need to go in there and take a peek, if they haven't got his head loose. They haven't, then you don't want to miss this. It's a fucking classic."

I did take a look inside the Big Frog Club before I drove Leonard home, and the cop trying to work the guy's head out of the Sheetrock was snickering. He looked at me and lost it, made a spitting sound, and let go of him and wandered off, bent over and hooting.

Another cop, smiling, went over and, without a whole lot of conviction, pulled one of the guy's ears—the other one wasn't visible—said, "Come on out, now."

The guy's head was pretty far through the wall. It was poking into a bathroom. He must have turned his back to escape and found a wall, and then Leonard shoved the back of his head, pushing the front of it through the wall and into the bathroom. He was all scratched up, like a cat had been sharpening its claws on his face.

The bathroom walls had never really been laid out, just Sheetrocked, so it hadn't been too hard to push the guy's head through. I took a good look at him. His chin had locked behind a support board, and the back of his head was locked behind another. He had fit in there easily enough, but in such a way he couldn't get out, and the cops didn't seem to be working that hard to release him.

I said, "You had some antlers, we could just leave you there and tell folks you're a deer."

"Fuck you," he said, but it was weak and without conviction, so I didn't take offense.

I used the urinal, which was just under him and smiled as I peed. I didn't flush. I went back in the main room and saw the back of the guy. He was bent slightly with his butt in the air, standing on his tip-toes, probably getting a good bracing from the piss in the urinal.

I went over to the bar, leaned and peeked over. The other guy Leonard had hit was awake and had his back against the bar. A broken chair was on the floor next to him.

I said, "You put your dick in a beehive, my friend."

"Tell me about it," he said. "We was just funnin'."

"Yeah, how fun was it?"

"Not so much," he said.

I got Leonard and drove him home.

When we were at my place, I sat Leonard in a chair in the kitchen. Brett, my gorgeous redhead, came downstairs. She was wearing a pair of my pajamas and she looked cute in them, as they were oversized. She was barefoot and her red painted toenails stood out like miniature Easter eggs. She came over and looked at Leonard.

"Anyone check you over?" she said.

"Wouldn't let them," he said.

Brett made him move his hand and the bloody rag. She checked out the wound. She's a nurse, so she was the right one to do it.

"It's not as bad as it looks," she said. "I think you can get by without stitches."

"Yeah, well, it feels bad," Leonard said.

"Would some vanilla cookies and cold milk make it feel better?" she said.

"Hell, yeah," Leonard said. "Maybe after the milk, a Dr. Pepper."

"That can be arranged," Brett said, "but first, come in the bathroom and let me patch you up."

When that was finished, Leonard came in with a bandage on his head. Brett got him a plate with some cookies on it and a big glass of cold milk. Leonard sat and smiled and dipped the cookies in the milk.

I said, "So, what happened?"

"They called me a queer."

"You are a queer," I said.

"It was their tone of voice," he said.

"How did they know?" Brett said.

"I made a very delicate pass at one of them," Leonard said.

"How delicate?" I asked.

"I merely asked him if he was gay, because he looked it, and then the shit hit the fan."

"Actually, you hit a guy with a chair, shoved another guy's head through some Sheetrock, and beat the cold dead dog shit out of the other guy in the parking lot. No fan was involved."

"Yeah, that was pretty much it," Leonard said, and bit into a cookie.

Next morning we went down to the cop shop. They sent us in to see the chief. He was in his office. There was a cop I had never seen before in there with him. They had a bunch of photos spread out on the desk, and the cop was laughing.

I glanced at the photos. They were of the guy with his head through the Sheetrock.

The cop was trying to get hold of himself, trying to quit laughing.

The chief said, "You can't act professional, you can just leave."

The cop went past us and out of the room. He was giggling as he went, trying to hold it in, making a sound like a kid spitting water.

"Have a seat," said the chief.

There were two chairs on our side, and we took them. The chief said, "We can't have this, fellows. It's keeping all my officers from doing their jobs. They keep coming in here to look at the crime scene photos."

He held up one of the photos.

It was of the guy's face thrust through the Sheetrock.

"This one," he said, "is especially precious."

I made the spitting water sound the cop had made.

"And then," he said, "there's this one."

This was an extreme close-up of the fellow's face, casting a baleful eye out at us.

The chief even laughed this time. He put the photo down on the desk.

"Everyone in the department had copies made. Officer Jane Bowden took them, in the name of efficiency and coverage of a crime scene."

"Do you have any wallet size?" I asked.

"No, but we're having some made up. Listen here, Leonard. You're lucky. Witnesses said they started it and you had to defend yourself. Bar owner is pressing charges against them. Thing is, them starting it, that's probably right, but sometimes, it don't hurt to walk away."

"It was the chair upside my head kept me from walking," Leonard said. "It knocked me down for a minute, and then when I got up, I was perturbed."

"Point taken," said the chief. "Not only were there witnesses, but one of the three you whipped is a witness himself. In your favor. He's going to have to pay a fine and some repairs at the club, but he's admitting they started it."

"Which one would that be," Leonard said, "Mr. Sheetrock?"

"No."

"I'm betting it isn't Toothless," I said.

"That would be a good bet."

"So, that leaves the one I knocked over the bar with a chair," Leonard said.

"Bingo."

When we went out, we saw the guy who had been knocked behind the bar. He was sitting in the waiting room. He hadn't been there when we came in.

Leonard touched two fingers to the edge of his eyebrow in salute as we passed.

The guy was about thirty, blond, and in good shape. He might be nice looking when he healed up. His left eye was closed and swollen and black, his lips were red and meaty like rubber fishing worms. As he followed us out into the parking lot, he had a limp.

We were about to get in my car when he came toward us.

Leonard turned, said, "You and me not finished?"

The man held up his hands. "We are. Mr. Pine—that's right isn't it? Pine?"

Leonard nodded.

"I want to apologize," the man said.

"Accepted," Leonard said. "Good-bye."

"Wait. Please."

I had been at the driver's side, about to get in, but now I went around on Leonard's side and we both leaned against the car.

"My name is Kelly Smith. I want to hire you." He was looking at Leonard when he said it.

"Hire me?" Leonard said. "What for? You like to take beatings?"

"Nothing like that. I have this problem. That's why I was at the bar."

"Drinking problem?" I said.

"No," he said, looking at me. "And who are you?"

"A friend," I said.

He nodded, spoke to Leonard. "Could we talk private?"

"You got something to say, say it," Leonard said. "Me and Hap can hear it together and no one will cry. We're not criers."

"I don't know," I said. "There was that movie. You know the one."

"Oh, *The Last Airbender*," Leonard said. "Yeah. That sucked. That could make anyone cry. And what was up with that 3-D? It should have been in Smell-O-Vision."

Kelly stood there while we went through our act. When we finished he said, "What I need is someone to do something tough that's a little against the law."

"How little?" Leonard asked.

"Well," he said, "maybe a lot more than a little."

We went to a coffee place and got a table near the back wall. There was music playing, and there were a few people at tables, and a nice-looking woman in very short shorts came in. Never been a fan of the heat, but for some things, you had to love summer.

Leonard said, "Hap, pay attention."

"Right with you," I said.

"I'll tell Brett," he said.

"I'm back, just watching the scenery, not trying to move it around."

Kelly had been looking at her too. Now he looked at us. He said, "I wasn't really with those guys last night."

"Sure looked a lot like you," Leonard said.

"I know," Kelly said. "I meant they aren't friends."

"You fought like they were your buddies," Leonard said.

"We didn't fight well," he said. "You kind of walked through us."

"I staggered a little," Leonard said. "That chair hurt."

"You went down and you came up like a jack-in-the-box," Kelly said. "When you did that, I thought you were fucking Dracula."

"Actually, I would have been Blacula. Ever see that old movie?"

Kelly shook his head.

"Never mind," Leonard said. "Look, it's nice, you buying us coffee and a Danish—"

"I'm having an apple fritter," I said.

"Okay," Leonard said. "Danish and fritters, but if you've got something to say besides I'm sorry and let me buy you coffee, then let's move on. Me and Hap are busy men. We got places to go, things to do, and people to see."

"Not really," I said. "Our day is pretty open."

Leonard gave me a sour face.

"I'll pay you to help me out," Kelly said.

"We talking about moving a piano?" Leonard said.

"No," he said. "We're talking about maybe you having to rough someone up."

"First off," Leonard said. "Why? And how much?"

"It's my brother, Donny. He's in deep doo-doo," Kelly said.

"What kind of doo-doo?" I asked.

"He got in with these fellas that rob armored cars," Kelly said.

We all sat there for a moment and let that statement hang between us like a carcass.

"This is starting to sound like doo-doo that's too deep," I said.

"It's deep all right," Kelly said. "He's only twenty-one. Good kid, really."

"Except for wanting to rob an armored car," I said. "I would consider that a possible blemish on his character."

Kelly nodded.

I said, "He's twenty-one, you're like, what, thirty? You guys are some years apart, aren't you?"

"Thirty-one, and yeah, he was like a surprise," Kelly said. "Dad wasn't all that good about hanging around anyway, but that little surprise, Donny, it was more than he could handle. He took the car out for an oil change, and just kept going."

"So what's this got to do with me?" Leonard asked.

"You know that robbery took place in LaBorde last year, the armored car guards at the bank?"

"Yeah, I remember," Leonard said. "They got the guards when they were transporting the money out of the bank to the truck. Just walked up with masks on and had guns and locked the guards in the back of the truck. It was maybe, what, two hundred thousand dollars they got?"

"About four hundred thousand," Kelly said. "They must have had someone waiting that drove up, picked them up, and took them away. No one knows. All they know is they were there with Halloween masks on one minute, then they had the money, and then they were gone. That was it. Took the guards' guns and put the guards in the back of the armored car and put plastic cuffs on them. Fastened one cuff to their left ankle, one to their right wrist. Then had them put an arm behind their back and fixed it there and pulled the plastic down to the other ankle, linked it from behind. That way they couldn't move well, damn sure couldn't run."

"That's cute," I said.

"Was your brother one of them?" Leonard asked.

"No, but I think he's about to be."

"And, pray tell, why do you think that?" I asked.

"Because in his room he's got some articles about the heist," he said.

"That doesn't mean anything," Leonard said. "Hap has books about Satan, but he ain't a Satanist. At least, as far as we know."

"Those damn books and that rap music," I said. "They can change a man."

Kelly ignored me. Sometimes it's all you can do. He said, "Yeah, but Donny, he has these friends come around, and they lock themselves in the back room for hours. I know they're smoking dope. I can smell it. But what I really worry about is I think these friends are the robbers and they want to pull my brother in."

"That's a big guess," I said. "Any reason to have it?"

"These guys, they're a real tough bunch," Kelly said. "And as you can know, I'm not so tough."

"You take a good fall, though," Leonard said.

"You still don't have any serious reason we should believe your brother is about to be part of a robbery."

"I heard them talking. I was sort of sneaking around, and I heard them say they needed a driver. The guy talking was the one Donny calls Smoke Stack. That's the name they all call him. I guess 'cause he smokes all the time. I don't allow it in the house, but he smokes anyway. I asked him not to once, and he just lit up and smiled at me, went in the back room with Donny. Hell, even Donny is tougher than me. He grew up different. He grew up tough. I can almost guarantee you these guys are going to rob another armored car, and they're going to pull Donny into it."

"Still a little lame," I said. "But, if you think you got something, go to the police. We know the chief over there. I'm not sure he likes us, but he did get some humor out of the photos of your buddy with his head through the Sheetrock. So right this minute, he sees Leonard as a comedian."

"I go to the police, they're going to run Donny in, and he's a good kid, really. He was living at home, and our mom died. A heart attack. She was overweight, didn't take care of herself. Went to hell after our dad ran off with another woman and went up North somewhere. She died, I moved back home. But I wasn't able to do it right away. I had a job in Austin, and I had to find another one up this area. I work at the university, doing janitor work."

"What did you do before?" I asked.

"I was a computer specialist, and I made half a mil a year. Now, I got just enough to buy gas for the car and bread for the table. I kind of thought Donny wasn't doing so good and needed me here. Last time I saw him, before Mom died, I could tell he was making some bad decisions. But the bottom line is these friends of his, I don't like them, and I'm sure they're the guys."

"That's your instinct?" I said.

"Yeah."

"Well," Leonard said, "instinct is all right, but it can be you telling yourself something and thinking you're enlightened. Gut instinct tells people to believe lots of things, and most of them are wrong. And, Kelly, this isn't our problem. It's a police problem."

He shook his head. "No. The police pick up Donny, his life is ruined."

"He robs an armored car, a bank, he might get a bullet through his head," Leonard said. "That ruins things too."

"Yeah, that can cut a career short," I said.

"Last night, I went to that bar looking for help. I didn't tell the details to those guys, but I said I was looking for someone could do a little roughhouse work. Those guys were recommended to me by a fellow I know. And then there was that whole thing about one of them calling you a name, and it all getting started . . . I think they started it just to show me how tough they were. Next thing I knew, I was in it with them, you know, part of the pack, and then I'm down, and one guy's got his head through the Sheetrock, and you're chasing the other guy outside. And you're older than them."

"Watch it," Leonard said.

"All I'm saying is, after I saw that, I decided maybe you were the guy instead of them."

"I don't know," Leonard said.

"Donny, he really looks up to this Smoke Stack. He wants to impress him. The guy's got muscles on muscles and he's just mean. Just mean."

"The gut instinct again?" Leonard said.

"Yeah."

"Well," Leonard said, "in cases like that, the gut is often right. We still know a shark when we see one. That's why we crawled out of the water and became men in the first place. Only thing is, some of the sharks crawled out after us."

"That would be the lawyers," I said.

"I told Smoke Stack and his buddies not to come back, but it doesn't matter," Kelly said. "They come around anyway, and if they don't, Donny goes to meet them. Him being twenty-one, I can't legally tell him squat."

"You wouldn't know where he goes to meet them, would you?" I asked.

"No," Kelly said. "And I'm embarrassed to tell you, I'm afraid to follow. I'm afraid they'll catch me. I think Smoke Stack and those guys would do anything."

"What about the other guys, his pals?"

"Three of them. They're followers. It's Smoke Stack runs the program, that's easy to see. I don't know their names, anything about them. Hell, I don't really know anything about Smoke Stack."

"Say we looked into it, found Donny was just smoking dope, or maybe he was selling drugs. What then?"

"I don't know. Maybe you can discourage him. It's such a mess. I wanted to be a big brother to him, but he doesn't care what I think. This Smoke Stack, I think he's like a tough father figure. And he looks like he could wad up a wrench. Again, I think he's like a father for Donny."

"Fathers just need to be tough in will," I said. "It don't hurt if they can bend a tire tool over their knee, but it's not part of the job description."

"Yeah," Kelly said, "but Donny doesn't know that. Look, really, he's a good kid. He's just got to get straight. He gets into this, his life is ruined. I got some money. It's from my savings, saved up before I moved here. I'll give you ten thousand apiece."

I looked at Leonard. He sighed.

I said, "Look, for right now, hang onto your money. Let us think about it, maybe look things over, and then, if we think we can help, we'll talk. If not, we'll still talk. But you might not like the conversation."

"Sure," Kelly said. "Sure, that's all right. That's good."

That afternoon, we went over to the gym to work out. Our gym sucks. It's small and it's hot and it has a small mat room. The mat is thin as paper and smells like sweaty feet. The owner isn't someone who is much into gym work himself. He's a guy with a physique akin to a rubber apple. He sits on a stool by the door so he can get some wind from outside, meaning there's no air conditioning. The door's always open, except dead of winter. Flies are always fluttering about.

He sits there to check memberships. The only advantage his gym has is his memberships are cheap, and he's not that far from the house. The only conversation I remember having with him was him saying, "That'll be thirty dollars a month, apiece."

But, it's all right. We bring our own gloves when we spar. When we spar we use fists a lot, but in real situations I like to use an open hand along with fists. You can use open hands with the gloves we have, but we're friends, and that kind of business can sometimes be worse than fists. Nothing says, "Oh, shit," like sticking a finger in your buddy's eye.

We moved around a little, flicking punches, throwing kicks. We were gym fighting, not really fighting. The two should never be confused. The first is like a swim in a heated pool, the other is like being dropped into a stormy, shark-infested ocean.

So, we were moving around, getting a workout, popping each other a little, and I said, "You believe him?"

"I don't know," Leonard said, pausing a little, putting his hands on his hips, taking a deep breath. "Maybe. A story like that, it's so stupid it's bound to have some reality about it. I mean, a guy has a problem with his younger brother hanging with thugs that might be bank robbers, so he goes into a bar to get someone to beat the robbers up."

"You think that's all he wanted?"

"I don't know. Maybe he wants us to do something more permanent with these guys."

"That, I don't want to do."

"We may not need to. Here's the thing, Hap. I think the guy is serious about being worried about his brother, but maybe we can look into it and solve it better than him. We don't, he's going to hire someone like that guy I left in the parking lot. Then things will turn messy, and before it's over Kelly and his brother both might go to prison."

"Usually, you're talking me out of stupid shit like this."

"Does it ever work?"

"Not so much. This guy got to you a little, didn't he?"

"A little."

We moved around some more. Leonard hit me a good snap

on the forehead. I hooked low, then switched to an overhand right and caught him on the cheek.

He said, "Ouch, I've had enough for the day. That was right on my wound."

"That was your cheek," I said.

"I don't mean the taped part of my head, I mean the bruise. I am so wonderfully black you just can't see it."

"If you say so."

There was no place to take a shower, and as part of our workout, we had jogged from my house, into town and to the gym.

As we jogged back to my place, I said, "We can check into things, see the lay of the land. If it's not lying right, and we don't like it, we can step out. Call the law if we choose."

"Then we'll have some explaining to do."

"We say we thought the guy was full of it, and just wanted us to straighten his brother out."

"You think these guys really are bank robbers?" Leonard said.

"I don't know," I said. "Anything is possible. Say they are robbers. Kid comes along, they see a new recruit. Someone to drive the car is my guess. They start buttering him up with all their King Robber stories, tell him how he'll be rich and his own man, that kind of stuff. The kid, not having a father around and his mother dead, his brother not being around before, maybe not having the relationship they could have had, Donny's ripe for bad business."

"Sure, it could be like that."

We jogged along, silent for awhile. I could tell Leonard was thinking things over, and I let him.

Finally, I said, "So, are we going to check it out?"

"Say we take it easy. We determine if the kid really is in trouble. If these guys really are robbers, and if there's anything we can do about it without getting locked up. I reckon we ought to do that much."

"That's how it is then," I said, and we bumped fists.

We got our friend Marvin Hanson to come in with us. He runs a private investigation agency, and he was once a cop. Sometimes we work for him. Last job we did was simple and we didn't get paid because the client didn't like the outcome. He didn't pay Marvin, so Marvin couldn't pay us.

Because of that, Marvin owed us a favor.

We had him meet Kelly. We had him watch Kelly and Donny's house, see where the kid went, and when he went, and if he went with some guys that looked tough.

When he finished a shift, I took over, and then Leonard took over. We had been at this for a couple of days. We were posted down from the house twenty-four seven, near an empty soccer field with grown-up grass and missing goal nets.

So, it was Marvin's watch, and I'm home with Brett, and we're upstairs in bed reading, and Leonard is snoozing on the couch downstairs, having finished his shift watching Kelly's place not too long back. I put the Western I was reading down, glanced at the clock. Twelve midnight.

I was about to turn in, get some sleep before I went on at eight a.m., and the doorbell dinged. I don't like it when the doorbell dings that late.

I got my automatic out of the drawer by the nightstand, and Brett got her revolver.

"I'll check," I said. "Leonard's down there, and if it's anything nasty, you call the cops."

I went downstairs, but the door was already open. Leonard was letting in Marvin.

I said, "Man, that was a short shift."

"Yeah," Marvin said.

Marvin has a limp and a cane. He was quick to find a chair. He took off his hat, which had once belonged to a friend of ours, and rested it on his knee. He said, "Things went a way I thought maybe you ought to know about."

"So, about nine thirty I'm sitting in the car, thinking I'd like to be home in bed with the wife, when I see a car pull up at the curb. Four guys get out. One of them looks like he lifts weights. Lots of weights, big weights, heavy weights."

"That would be the loveable Smoke Stack."

"Yeah, for all that muscle business, he's smoking like the proverbial smoke stack."

"Oh, Marvin," I said. "That is good. Him smoking like a smoke stack and having the name Smoke Stack. You are so clever."

"Yep. They go around back, and then coming back from around the house I see all of them again, and this younger guy that I figure is Donny. They got in the car, tight as coins in a miser's wallet, and drive away. I followed. They went out to the warehouse district, and I went with them, but sneaky like. They never saw me. They went down where the rentals are. It's one of those cheap places. No cameras, no security gate. You just drive in and take your padlock off your shed. I couldn't follow them in, so I drove across the street and looked. I could see through the fence and I could see them park, and I could see which storage building they opened. I could see a car in there. An older car, a muscle car. Something that could run like a spotted-ass ape if needed."

"Ah, the old spotted-ass ape," Leonard said. "How fast do they run?"

"They are very fast," Marvin said. "So, they're there awhile with the door pulled shut, and I could see they had a light on because it was shining under a crack at the bottom of the door."

"That is some of that ace detective work you're famous for," I said.

"My guess is, if they're planning a robbery, that storage shed is their villains' lair."

"Probably has a basement in there, test tubes and shit," Leonard said. "It's like the evil Fortress of Solitude."

"I got another guess too," Marvin said. "When the other robbery went down, the one with the guards, about a month later they found a guy in a car out in the woods with a bullet through his head. He'd been dead for awhile. At the time it was unexplained. Just a random murder. But, I been thinking maybe the dead guy was their getaway man. And when he got them away, they put him away. My guess is Donny is next on the list. They get some young guy doesn't know squat, they use him for the robbery, for the driving, then they pop him and the cut is bigger. Next time they got plans, they recruit again. Each new driver doesn't know about the other. It works until the word gets out they're finding lots of dead people in stolen cars with false license plates."

"So Donny is just a tool for them to use and then destroy," I said.

"That's my guess. Another thing, I followed them after they left the warehouse. They didn't take Donny home. They drove him to a house on the edge of town. Most of the block there is burned out, and beyond it the town quits and the woods starts. It's a run-down place where the back acres have been sawed over by pulp woodworkers. I parked there for a little while, then drove to the warehouse and got closer to the building they were in. It's number fifteen. Then I came here. I could go back and finish my shift, but I don't know I need to now."

"Probably not," I said. "We know where they keep the getaway car, and we know where they live. And that they may have sold pulp wood."

"That pulp wood money could be the way they financed the first robbery," Marvin said. "Bought the getaway car. Now they got money from the first robbery to pull another. They aren't living high on the hog out there, so they're keeping what loot they got tamped down for now, which is smart."

"Marvin," I said, "your work is done."

"So we're even on what I owe you two?" he said.

"We are," I said.

"Good luck to you," Marvin said, got up, and picked up his hat and cane. "If you need me for anything, even or not, give me a call."

Marvin went out and closed the door.

I looked up and saw Brett was sitting on the top stair looking down, listening. I smiled at her and she waved. She was wearing those oversized pajamas and my bunny slippers with the ears on them.

She said, "How about we have some milk and cookies?"

"Hell, yeah," Leonard said.

We sat at the kitchen table and had our milk and vanilla cookies and thought on the matter. Way we saw it, if we waited until they decided to rob an armored car, it would be too late.

First off, we didn't know when they had their little heist planned, and we didn't know if they might tire of Donny and pop him. We didn't even know if they were actually the robbers, but it sure seemed likely, and we were going to play it that way.

We thought about a number of cool ways to go at it, and we explained them to Brett, and she said, "Why don't you just go over and confront them, tell Donny how things went with their past driver. Otherwise, while you're making your plans, he could already be the wheel man and dead and under some log in a creek somewhere."

"There's a logic to that," I said.

"And it fits what you've done in the past," Brett said.

"You mean strong-armed our way through?" Leonard said.

"Yeah," Brett said. "You guys are smart enough, but you don't have the patience to be masterminds."

"Yeah," Leonard said, "and it's boring, and yucky, and I don't want to do it."

"So there," I said. "If we go over, confront them, and if we convince and save Donny, they could still commit the crime and they could kill another idiot driver. I know that's not supposed to be our problem. Our problem is supposed to be just Donny, but I don't like it."

"If you convince Donny to leave," Brett said, "then you can give an anonymous tip about the car, say it's stolen or something, because most likely it is, and put the cops on it."

"They'll need more proof than that to go take a look," Leonard said.

Brett crossed a pajama-clothed leg, dangled a rabbit shoe from her foot, picked up her glass of milk, and sipped. When she sat the glass down, she had a thick, beaded, white milk mustache that made me smile.

"That's right," Brett said, "they will need more proof, but that tip could start movement in the right direction. After that, you get stuck on what to do, just come to me and I'll figure it out from there."

Next day we went over to the university and drove around for awhile before we could find a visitor's parking spot that wasn't filled, and walked over to the building where Kelly worked as a janitor. On the bottom floor students moved about, and an older woman in a janitor's uniform was pushing a trash cart. She looked about as excited as a corpse.

We asked her about Kelly, and what she told us sent us by elevator to the fourth floor. Leonard wanted to push the button, and I had to let him, or I would never hear the end of it. He likes pushing buttons on elevators. I can't explain it. But every time he gets to do it, for several minutes afterward, I must admit, I feel slightly deprived.

There were no students on the top floor. I went to one of the windows and looked out. I had gone to the university for awhile. I had been a good student. I enjoyed it. I still liked the atmosphere of a university, but I was too lazy to finish up my education, and most likely the classes I'd taken long ago in stalking the woolly mammoth and how to build a fire with flint and steel and a gust of wind were no longer valid.

We looked around a while and found an open door and heard some clattering, went in there and discovered Kelly banging a garbage can against the inside of his cart so it would empty.

Kelly looked up at us. The swelling around his eyes had gone down. He said, "You wouldn't believe the stuff you find in these cans."

I leaned my ass into the desk up front, and Leonard took a seat at one of the standard desks in the front row. Kelly put the garbage can back in place by the teacher's desk, said, "Well."

"We reckon you're right," Leonard said. "Those people Donny is running with, they're not up to any good, and that means neither is Donny."

"Can you do something about it?"

"Maybe," I said. "But here's the thing. We do what we're talking about doing, you might not be safe. You might not want to go home for awhile."

"How long's awhile?"

I shook my head.

"I see," he said. "And you can get Donny out of this?"

"You can't make a man believe what he doesn't want to believe," I said. "But we can try and show Donny that things aren't as good as he might think. In fact, they're really worse than we thought."

"How?" Kelly asked.

We told him about the dead man in the car, what we suspected.

When we finished, Kelly found a desk and sat down. He said, "Shit, how does stuff like this happen?"

"Humans," I said.

"Yeah," Leonard said, "they can be pesky."

"So," I said, "what we're asking is, do we go ahead with things? 'Cause if we do, it might make it hot around the old hacienda. Meaning, you need to not be there. And the job here, I don't know how safe it keeps you."

Kelly nodded slowly. "I got some place I can go for awhile. I mean, I can figure that out. But the job, I need this job. I need it bad. I can't just walk away."

"We can't guarantee your safety, you stay on the job," I said. "We don't recommend it. We didn't have any trouble getting to you, and if they decide to find you, it won't just be to talk."

"I'll leave the house," Kelly said. "But I'll stay with the job. Go ahead and do what you need to do."

"We'll need a photo of Donny," I said.

"I can do that, after work," Kelly said. "But, you will try to save him, won't you?"

"We'll do what we can," Leonard said, "and more often than not, that's a lot."

Marvin was out of it now, and we didn't work in shifts after that. We just drove over together and parked down the street from where Kelly lived. Ever now and then we would move the car to a new position, so no one in a house nearby would call the law on us.

Kelly had followed our advice and found a new place to stay. We told him not to tell us where. That way we didn't have information we didn't need and wouldn't want to accidentally spill.

We also had something else. A last gift from Marvin. Having been a former cop, he had good connections. He got us information on Smoke Stack. Once Marvin knew where he lived, and what his car license was, it wasn't so hard. Marvin wasn't sure about the other guys, but he was sure about Smoke Stack. The license led to the car, and that led to a description, and that led to a rap sheet. I had that with me. And a grainy photo that had been faxed to Marvin and that he gave to us. Smoke Stack's real name was Trey Manton.

Leonard had a small flashlight on and he was using it to look the photo over again and read the rap sheet. We had already done that, but it was a way to pass the time. Leonard spent a lot of time looking at the bad photo. He clicked off the light and closed the folder and put it on the seat between us, said, "Man, that guy looks like he tried to roller skate in a buffalo herd."

"I'm going to guess the buffalo may not have turned out so well. And he's done time for drugs, and he is, shall we say, a violent person, as his prison time shows."

"We are violent ourselves," Leonard said. "But we're the good guys."

"I guess that's one way of looking at it," I said.

"Rather us as tough guys than people like Smoke Stack as tough guys."

"And yet another way of looking at it."

Leonard gave me Smoke Stack's photo. I looked at it again just to have something to do. I gave it back, and took the photo of Donny and looked it over. He looked like the usual, pimple-faced, sassy ass kid. It was a full body shot, and it made me think of the photos I'd seen of Billy the Kid, only without the cowboy hat, the rifle, and the six-gun on his hip. But it had the same attitude about it. The rifle and six-gun had been replaced by sagging pants and tennis shoes that looked too big for his feet. The strings were untied. That's showing them.

As it got dark and they didn't show up, we decided to go to their place and have a chat. Maybe Donny was already with them. With Kelly gone, maybe he no longer saw a need to go home. Next thing was they'd move into Kelly's house and never let him come back. They were the type. I had seen it before.

When we got over to the address Marvin had given us, we parked down from their house in the lot of an abandoned convenience store. It was about three blocks from their house, but seemed the best place to park. Everything there was as Marvin said. The houses and most of the convenience store were burned out and you could smell the dead fire still. Something had set the whole block on fire. Where the burned buildings ended, the woods took over, and up on a hill with some logged-out acres behind it was the house.

I opened the glove box and got out my automatic and gave Leonard his. They were both in black holsters, but the guns themselves did not match. Brett thought it would be cute if we got matching guns with our initials on them.

We got out of the car and Leonard pulled out his shirt and lifted it up and clipped on his holster. He arranged his shirt around it. It was only hidden if you weren't looking for it or you were blind in one eye and couldn't see out the other. I clipped mine to my belt. I was wearing a loose T-shirt, so it didn't cover much.

"Ready?" I said.

"I was born ready," Leonard said.

"Scared?"

"I never get scared."

"Bullshit."

"Okay, I'm a little scared. Let's get it done before I get more scared."

We started walking.

The house had a car out front, and we had to climb up the hill to get there. We stayed to the right side where there was still a line of trees just behind a barbed-wire fence, and then there was a pasture, and more trees, and then the house with the logged-out area behind it.

The house was not well lit and there wasn't much you could

tell about it in the dark, but there seemed to be a sadness that came from it. All old uncared for houses seem that way to me. As if they are living things dying slowly from neglect. It's like they're old people no one will visit, or if they do, it's out of obligation or even spite.

There were a series of walking stones that led from a place near the road to the front porch, but grass had mostly covered them. There were a few shingles lying like scales in the yard; they had blown off the roof in a high wind. The rest of the yard had grass growing tall enough to hide a rhinoceros if he crouched a little. There was a washing machine in the yard, tipped on its side, and it looked to have been a popular model about the turn of the century. An old stone bird feeder was still standing. Grass seeds had gotten in it along with enough blown dirt and dust to make a bed, and blades of grass had grown up in a manner that made it look as if someone had used Butch Wax on them.

There was a thin beam of light escaping from under a window to the right of the door. I went up and bent down and looked through the window. There were three guys on the couch passing a joint back and forth. The light of a television strobed across their faces. One of them was Smoke Stack. He was hard to miss. He took up about a third of the couch. He was wearing a T-shirt with the sleeves rolled up so folks could get a look at his biceps, which looked like bowling balls in tight rubber tubing. There were tattoos on his arms, some kind of Chinese writing. I figured Smoke Stack was doing well to read English, let alone Chinese. The tats looked like they had been made by a blowtorch and a fountain pen.

I didn't see Donny.

I stepped back and Leonard took my place. After he took a look, he said, "Rock and roll."

I went up on the porch and Leonard went around back. We didn't say that we should do this. We just knew it. It wasn't our first rodeo.

I carefully pulled back the screen, which had so many holes punched through it, it might as well have just been a frame. It squeaked a little, like a dog toy.

I waited. No one shot at me through the door. No one jerked the door open. I could hear the TV. It was some kind of music show. Music videos, I guess. The music playing was rap, the only kind of music I can't stand, unless it's bagpipe music, which, with the exception of "Amazing Grace," always sounds to me like someone starting up a lawn mower.

I heard the back door breaking open, and when I did, I kicked the front door with all my might. It hurt my foot a little, but the door sagged back, which spoke not so much for my manliness as it did for the geriatric state of the house.

Rushing inside, I had my gun drawn. I was wearing my badass smile. I know it's bad ass, because I practice it in front of a mirror.

As we came in, me from the front, Leonard from the back, I focused on the three on the couch. As I said, one of them was Smoke Stack. The thugs on either side of him were almost interchangeable. Lanky with pot bellies and greasy hair, arms branded with tattoos, their heads wreathed in cigarette smoke. They looked like the kind of guys that might share a brain, and today the brain had a day off.

Sitting in chairs to the side were Donny and another guy. Leonard was watching them. Donny looked like a dumb kid, thin-faced, big-eyed, his chin bristling with a few hairs and competing pimples. The guy next to him was dark and short and stout and sunburned. He had his hair cut in a military do, probably because the hair on top was as thin as dirty water. Overall, he gave the impression of someone who had lived on a planet with heavy gravity and too much sunlight.

They jumped up and went for guns they had in their pants. Except Donny. He just sat there with his mouth hanging open.

Leonard waved his gun, said, "Who do I shoot first?"

There were no volunteers. They stopped moving.

I had my gun pointed too. I said, "Okay, boys, let's keep standing, and take them out one at a time, starting with you, Smoke Stack. Put them on the floor. And I'm not talking about your dicks."

"Do I know you?" Smoke Stack said.

"No," I said. "But you're about to know a little about me, and my guess is you aren't going to like it."

When they had the guns on the floor, I told them to kick them lightly away. Leonard held his gun on them, collected theirs, and took them outside. I watched through the open door as he threw them under the porch and came back inside.

"Nice night," I said to no one in particular.

Leonard turned off the TV.

"What you guys want?" Smoke Stack said. "We ain't got nothing for you to rob."

"I think maybe you got some money from a bank robbery somewhere," Leonard said.

Smoke Stack looked at Leonard, then me, then they all looked at Donny. They just kept staring, like they were waiting for him to break out into a little dance.

"No, man," Donny said. "I didn't tell them anything. I don't even know these guys."

"He ain't lying," I said. "He doesn't know us. But, we are here for Donny's benefit. We want that you should quit this group, Donny. Come home and quit acting like a gangster wanta-be. Or what we refer to in the privacies of our home as a dumb dick."

"My brother," Donny said. "He sent you. That's it, isn't it? Well, he and you both can keep your nose out of my business."

"Just come home and forget these guys," I said. "You do that, life will be a lot better for you, and so will the air. Man, you guys could use a bath. Or is it because you're shitting behind the couch?"

"Ha!" Smoke Stack said. He looked at us and our guns like he was looking at kids with suckers. "You ain't so much."

"We got guns," I said. "That puts us way ahead of you. We took yours away from you. And you know what? We might not give it back."

Smoke Stack looked at Donny. "Who are these guys, kid?"

"I tell you, I ain't had nothin' to do with them. I tell you, I don't know these guys."

"They know you," he said.

"Actually, we know who he is," I said. "He doesn't know us, and we don't know him. But we have a nice photograph. And we know this. You are planning to pull a heist, and the kid here, you want to get him in on it, and then when it's over, you'll pop him, and we're not talking about with a wet towel."

Smoke Stack let that revelation roam around in his head for awhile. It went on for so long you could see it cross behind his eyes, like someone moving past a window. I glanced at Donny. There was something roaming around in his head as well. Suspicion, I hoped.

"What the hell you talking about?" Smoke Stack said.

"That doesn't sound all that convincing," I said. "The part where you try to act like you don't know what's going on, and you've don't remember how you clowns shot your last wheel man and left him in the woods for the ants."

"What's he talking about?" Donny said, looking at Smoke Stack.

"They don't know nothing," Smoke Stack said. "They're just talking air. Don't pay them no mind. You really don't know them, then just keep your mouth shut."

"What they like to do," Leonard said, looking right at Donny, "is they hire some dumbass to drive their car, and then they kill him and split it between themselves."

"What, for one less split we kill a guy?" Smoke Stack said.

"Yep," I said. "And, hey, you fellas, what makes you think

one of you isn't next? Were you all in on the previous job? Are there some bodies in the woods somewhere?"

I could tell from the way a couple guys looked at Smoke Stack that I had hit a chord.

"You guys don't listen to this shit," Smoke Stack said. "And you, Donny. Ain't I treated you right? I been more of brother to you than your own brother."

"You mean you've kind of let him do what he wants," I said, "because at the bottom of it all, you don't care about him. He's just a pawn. It's tough being a father or mother or big brother, 'cause they got to tell you stuff you don't want to hear, make you do stuff you don't want to do. But you, you can just tell him everything's all right, even when it isn't."

"I ain't got to do nothing," Donny said. "My brother, he ain't much of a man."

"And Smoke Stack is?" I said. "Your brother works his ass off for you. Butt-wipe here steals what he wants and hangs out. Not a whole lot of manly in that."

"I could snap you like a stick," Smoke Stack said.

"No," I said. "No, you couldn't."

"You talk tough with a gun," Donny said. "I've seen what he can do. You ain't so tough."

"What?" Leonard said, grinning at Donny. "Smoke Stack? Tough? With some drunk, maybe? Some poor guy half in the bag. You think he's bad because he has muscles and tattoos and cigarette breath. Hap here, on his worst day, could turn him inside out and make him say how much he likes it."

"Ha!" Smoke Stack said.

I went over and gave Leonard my gun. Now he had one in either hand. I took off my jacket, hung it over the doorknob of the door I'd kicked open.

"Why don't I show you that he's not so tough?" I said.

"That'll be the goddamn day," Smoke Stack said.

"This is, in fact, that day," Leonard said.

Smoke Stack grinned at Leonard. "I get through mopping the floor with him, you're next, nigger."

"Oh, don't make me wet," Leonard said, then he waved the guns at the others. "All you assholes, except Smoke Stack, and you, Donny, all of you over here and on your bellies. Make like fucking run-over snakes."

They did what they were told. They lay on the floor on their bellies by the wall, lifted their heads up to see what was going on.

Leonard looked at them, said, "All you dick cheeses, all you move is your heads, savvy? Donny, you sit on the couch. You get a bird's-eye view."

"Why we doing this?" Smoke Stack said.

"Because we can," I said. "And because you think you're tough as an old saddle."

"You're too old for me," Smoke Stack said to me.

"Yeah, well, I'll try not to hurt you too bad."

"I think tough guy is starting to waffle, Hap," Leonard said. "I think he's looking for a hole to run into."

Smoke Stack said to me, "We get started, it goes bad for you, your man will step in with the guns?"

"He's got the guns to keep your friends in line. It goes bad for me, I'll take my beating, and then we'll leave."

"Shit," Donny said. "Think you can beat Smoke Stack, you're crazy. I seen him whip two guys once, and one of them with a board."

I felt a little nervous right then, because that old adage about how bullies are always cowards isn't true. Sometimes they're bullies simply because they can do what they say they can do, and they enjoy doing it.

Leonard said, "Yeah, but it ain't how many guys he whipped, it's the guys. Hap, he wasn't one of those guys."

"He whips Smoke Stack, hell, I'll go with you," Donny said. "That's how much faith I got in him."

Smoke Stack looked at the kid and nodded.

"All right," I said. "I don't whip him. You stay, and we'll go, and we're out of your life. You rob banks, you fuck goats, you do what you like. We're done."

"You'll be saying stuff to folks you shouldn't, like we're going to rob a bank," Smoke Stack said. "We wouldn't want people believing something like that. You ain't got no proof of nothing that way."

"We'll make it simple for you," Leonard said. "You whip Hap, we'll leave, and then, so you don't cry at night, you can always come and try to kill us before we let the cat out of the bag. We'll give you a whole two days. You got our word, and that's better than yours, I'm sure."

"I whip him," Smoke Stack said, nodding at me, "then I'm coming for you. That's gonna be a treat."

"You don't even know me," Leonard said, then smiled at him. "And you don't want to. But if Hap slips on a banana peel, then I'll put the gun away, and me and you can dance all over this place."

"Hey, Smoke Stack," I said. "You gonna talk us to death, or you gonna show me what you got?"

There was a clearing between the people on the floor and the couch where Donny sat. Leonard was by the open door, pointing the guns. Smoke Stack moved forward, and as he did he crouched a little and put his fists up. He smiled at me, came closer.

He hooked a big right. I could have seen it coming with a bag over my head. I stepped into him at an angle and the punch went around me. I popped a jab in Smoke Stack's eye, hooked him to the throat. He had his chin down, so the hook was a so-so shot. Still, he didn't like it. He stepped back with a sputter, coughed a little, and came at me windmilling. I leaned way right when he was right on me, put out my foot, and caught his ankle as he rushed. It catapulted him forward and into the wall and caused him to knock a hole in the Sheetrock with his head, then to roll on top of his gang members.

When he got himself straight and turned, I kicked Smoke Stack in the balls so hard people in China had heart pains. I stepped in quick and gave him a left-hand Three-Stooges poke in the eyes, hit him with a right cross that came from hell without a bus ticket and that smacked against the ridge of his jaw. He twisted and went down and started to get up, but didn't.

"You waitin' on reinforcements, Smoke Stack?" I said.

"What he needs to get up," Leonard said, "is a fucking winch truck."

Smoke Stack finally got upright, rushed me with his head down, bellowing like a bull. I hooked my arm under his neck as he came and went back on my hips and kicked him in the nuts again and lifted him over me so that he hit hard on his back on the floor. I could hear the breath go out of him, loud as an elephant fart.

I flipped back so that I landed straddling him, slammed my forearm into his nose and chin. Once. Twice. Three times.

He quit struggling. I got up and looked down at him. His face was bloody. He rolled over on his stomach and started crawling away, like a roach that had had its rear end stepped on. Then he collapsed, quit crawling. He was unconscious.

Donny was looking at me with his mouth open so wide you could have turned a semitruck around in there.

Donny said, "Did you kill him?"

"Just his pride," I said. "And maybe one of the two brain cells he had. That leaves him one so he knows how not to shit himself. Now, come on."

Donny looked at Smoke Stack, then at me. "I don't know."

"We had a deal. You can come, or Leonard here will pistol-whip the goddamn shit out of you and we'll take you anyway. You can go without knots and bruises, or we can fix you up. You get to choose. And you get to choose right now."

Donny nodded.

"We'll be taking all your guns," Leonard said. "We're gonna make Donny crawl under the porch and bring them out. He's going to do that without pulling one, so that way we don't have to shoot him. You can check for your pistols at the bottom of assorted lakes, creeks, and rivers. And if you follow us, I will personally shoot holes in your head, and when they find you, your guns will be shoved up your asses."

When we were in the car, with Donny seated in back, he said, "But he was so much bigger."

"David and Goliath," I said. "Ever read that passage in the Bible?"

"No. What's it mean?"

"It means David got lucky," I said.

"Only Hap wasn't lucky," Leonard said. "He was skilled. Smoke Stack, he's got big arms and a big mouth, but he was gonna get you killed, kid. We done you a favor, and you don't even know it."

"I don't believe that," Donny said, but his voice didn't hold a lot of conviction.

"Yeah, well, you can be stupid, or you can be lucky, and right now, you're goddamn lucky," Leonard said.

"I didn't think anyone could do that to Smoke Stack," Donny said.

"Your problem, kid," Leonard said, "is you haven't been doing a whole lot thinkin', just reactin', and you haven't been around long enough to know life ain't like the movies. I get the whole lost your parents thing. Been there. But that don't have to turn you stupid. That's a choice, like wearing green stretch pants. You don't have to do it."

"My brother shouldn't have done this," he said. "He shouldn't have asked you guys to do this."

"Woulda, shoulda, coulda," I said. "We're trying to save you from yourself. But, we got a time limit, boy. You fuck it up later, then we done what we could. You can go back to being stupid and probably shot to death in a car out in the woods. But, for right now, we got other plans."

"What plans?" Donny said.

"Pancakes," Leonard said.

We went to my place and made pancakes. It was late by the time we did, and Brett came in. She was carrying a newspaper. She saw Donny sitting at the kitchen table with a large glass of milk and a plate of pancakes covered in syrup. He was eating heartily. Leonard sat across from him with a Dr. Pepper. Leonard thought Dr. Pepper went with most anything. Brett nodded at Leonard and Donny, said to me, "So, you found a child in the yard and took him in to raise."

"Found him under a rock," I said. "Can we keep him? We'll build him a pen out back."

She smiled at me. "We'll think it over. You got any more pancake batter?"

"Coming right up, banana pancakes," I said. "I should work at IHOP, I'm so good at this."

I went about making her pancakes. While I did, she sat at the table and looked at Leonard for an explanation. Leonard told her all about it.

Brett looked at Donny, said, "Honey, you could have been in some real trouble."

"I just wanted to make some money," he said, and the way he looked at her it was hard to determine if he was seeing a sister figure, a mother, or someone he wished he was old enough to date. Brett had that effect on people.

"So taking someone else's money is okay so you can have some?" she said.

"Smoke Stack said it's not someone's money if they can't keep it," Donny said. "And besides, that bank money, it's insured."

"Someone pays out the insurance, baby boy," she said, "and that might be me if I bank there." She picked up the newspaper and hit him a pretty good whack in the back of the head. "Bad dog. Bad, bad dog."

Donny lowered his eyes, said, "I didn't think about it like that."

"You haven't been thinking," she said. "You been hearing some bullshit, is what you been hearing, and I got to say, for you to take it as fact, you must want to believe it. There's people born stupid, but you're one of those Hap calls the Happily Stupid. They believe what they hear, not what they investigate or think about. They're the ones that don't listen to news, they listen to opinions and editorials and think it's news. Rumors and lies and sometimes the truth. It's all the same to them."

"I haven't had it so good," Donny said.

"So, you're like a special case?" Leonard said.

"Ain't no one matters but yourself," Donny said. "That's what Smoke Stack told me."

"Then that means you don't matter much to him," I said. "He's telling you the truth when it comes to his philosophy. He doesn't care about you or anyone else. You're just a cog in the machine, and he wouldn't mind replacing you with another cog at the drop of a hat."

I put Brett's pancakes in front of her and heated up the syrup a little in the microwave. I brought it to her and then got her a cold glass of milk. I sat down across from her.

When I sat, I put my hands in front of me, clasped together, and Brett said, "You okay, Hap?"

"I cut my knuckles."

I held them out for her to see.

"So you did."

"I think I can use some sympathy."

"We'll talk about it when we go to bed," Brett said.

What we ended up doing was not going to bed right away, but calling Marvin, and getting him out of bed, and pissing him off, but he came over anyway. He came over with the information about the body found in the woods, and in fact, he had gotten a copy of a photograph from one of his cop friends, had it in a big yellow envelope. We didn't look at it right away.

Once he had some of my pancakes, his attitude was better. We went into the living room, and Marvin told Donny some of what he knew. He took the photo out of the envelope and showed it to Donny. It was a clear photo of a man behind the wheel of a car. He had a hole in his forehead, and he was swollen up so bad his shirt collar had rolled into the swell of his neck. Insects had been at him, and a string of ants were clearly visible crawling into his nose.

"No gun was found," Marvin said. "He didn't shoot himself."

"That could be anyone at anytime," Donny said.

"Yeah, it could," Marvin said. "It's a possibility it is someone unrelated to your buddy Smoke Stack. It could be a pumpkin painted up to look like a man. But I don't think so. Timing's right, the description of the car fits."

"There's lots of cars like that one," Donny said.

"You got me there, kid. You're bound and determined to get yourself killed. So have at it. You want to take the chance it's not connected, that's your bailiwick. Me, I'm going home."

Marvin stood up, leaving the photograph on the coffee table.

On his way out, Marvin picked his hat and cane off the back of a chair, said, "Nice knowing you, kid. Next time I see you, it'll be in a photograph like that one."

Marvin went out and closed the door.

"Bullshit," Donny said.

"He's just trying to help," Brett said.

"He's trying to scare me," Donny said.

"Yeah," I said, "he is. I hope it's working. You damn well better be scared. This is some serious business we're talking about. Smoke Stack, he's a loser. He's so cool and important, why's he live in that shithole where he lives and have a bunch of other losers hanging around him, and that includes you. But it doesn't have to."

"He does all right," Donny said.

"Yeah," Leonard said. "Well, he don't keep his left hand up worth a shit."

"Or his right," I said.

That night we put Donny in the little guest bedroom we had built of recent for Leonard. It wasn't very big, but we had built it onto the back of the house. There was a window that Donny could climb out of if he were ambitious. The only thing was, Leonard was sleeping in the bed under the window and near the door. Donny was sleeping on a pallet on the floor. Donny would have had to have been a ninja to get out that window and Leonard not know it.

As we walked him to the bedroom and I laid out his pallet, Brett brought him pajamas and a towel for a shower, Leonard said, "I'm a light sleeper. And if you wake me up, thinking you're going to sneak out, I'm going to beat the hell out of you. That's as simple as I can put it."

Donny looked at me.

"He will," I said.

"Here," Brett said, handing him the towel and pajamas. "Baby, you ought to listen to these boys. They know what they're talking about. Like your brother, they just want to help you."

"My brother is a loser," Donny said.

"Your brother quit a good job to come here and take care of

you," Leonard said. "He went from high living to low living. He's a janitor. Good honest work, but not work of his choosing. He did that for you. He may not be perfect, but he did it for you. That means something."

Donny didn't say anything to that.

Brett said, "You should listen. Those people you were with, hell, not people . . . those beasts you were with. They aren't human. They're hyenas. They might have been people once, but they're hyenas now. You don't have to be one too. You get to choose. That's the difference between you and a natural-born hyena. There's a choice for you. For the animal there isn't, but for humans to choose not to be animals, there is."

"Actually," Leonard said, "I like the hyenas better than humans."

"I don't know what you mean," Donny said.

"That's what scares us," I said.

"He knows," Brett said, and took hold of Donny's chin with her thumb and forefinger. "He's just not ready to admit it. . . . And Donny, honey, be sure and take that shower before you lay down to sleep. You'll sleep better, and you won't stink."

Donny looked as if someone had just stuck a hot shot to his balls.

"Not trying to hurt your feelings," Brett said, "just fact. Girls sure don't want to be around some stinker. And you're kind of cute, if you'd clean yourself up."

"Really?" Donny said.

"Really."

"Smoke Stack said if you got money, you got the girls."

"Did he?" Brett said. "That's like saying if you got corn you get the pigs. Thing is, who wants pigs? Look here, kid. Get a shower, and let's see we can do something about those pimples. You just aren't washing your face good. And I got some stuff you can put on them. Even a natural beauty, a goddamn goddess like me, sometimes gets a bump."

———————

Next morning Brett slept in, and I went downstairs and woke Leonard and Donny. I called Kelly and told him we had his little brother, and that we would try and hang onto him for a few days, to see if common sense soaked in. I didn't offer him any guarantees.

We called Marvin about seeing if he could drop a word to the police about the car in the shed, and so on. He did. They didn't really have enough cause, but they went out and cut the lock anyway. The car inside was gone. The place was empty. They went out to the house where Smoke Stack lived. It was cleaned up and only Smoke Stack was home. He told them the bruises on his face were from falling down in the driveway.

It was an iffy move, putting them on the alert like that, but me and Leonard figured it was best to make them a little nervous.

After we got the news, Leonard said, "Smoke Stack and his swinging-dick friends are done tidying up. There's nothing left for the cops to find. I think we should have shot them all last night. I think we should have shot Smoke Stack twice."

Donny was sitting on the couch, listening.

"That includes you," Leonard said.

"He's just testy," I said. "He hasn't had his morning coffee. And his boyfriend isn't talking to him."

"You're gay?" Donny said to Leonard.

"Yep."

"You don't act gay."

"How do they act?"

"I don't know. . . ."

"Look here, kid. We come in all shapes, sizes, and attitudes. But it's pretty much a given we all have big dicks."

"Yeah," I said, "but he doesn't have an ounce of fashion sense."

"No Barbra Streisand records either," Leonard said. "I just

prefer men to women. And just for the record, I can whip your ass and pretty much anyone else's on any day of the week, provided the moon is in Leo."

"What?" Donny said.

"He's fucking with you," I said. "About the moon in Leo part."

We went to the gym and took Donny with us. When we got there we put the bag gloves on him and showed him how to work the heavy bag. He didn't want to do it at first, but Leonard persuaded him with a threat. After Donny hit the bag a few times, he got into it. He started asking questions on how to throw punches. He had seen us do it, seen how we moved the bag, and he wanted to learn it. I think he was also thinking about that ass-whipping I had given his hero.

Leonard said, "You got to come from the hip. But, you get older, you get more experience, you realize this bag don't mean shit. Hitting a person, you don't have to be able to move this bag. You got to hit a man when he's in the void, when he's stepping, when he's trying to shift or recover his balance. Catch him then, you can take down a big guy with a simple punch, a kick. Catching someone off balance, or controlling their balance, makes them easier to throw."

We spent two hours at the gym, then went back home.

We pulled up in the drive, and I saw the front door was open. Leonard and I were in the front seat. He turned and looked over his shoulder, said, "Donny, you stay in the car. If anyone comes out shooting, or you hear shooting, you run like a motherfucker. But, you don't hear shooting, I come out, and you're gone, I will track you down—"

"And beat the shit out of me," Donny said.

"That's right."

We had guns in the glove box and we got them out. Leonard went around back, and I went up on the porch and moved the open front door wider with my foot, peeked inside.

I didn't see anyone. I moved in slowly, and then I heard the back door lock click, and Leonard was in.

Leonard took the kitchen, and I took his room. We checked the bathrooms. I went upstairs. The bedcovers were pulled back, and the big red T-shirt she had slept in was lying on the floor. On the end of the bed was a note.

I picked it up and read it.

WE GOT YOUR REDHEAD. WE GOT DONNY'S BROTHER. WE GOT YOUR LADY'S CELL PHONE, AND WE GOT YOUR NUMBER. GO TO THE COPS, THEY'RE BOTH DEAD. WAIT FOR OUR CALL.

There's no way to describe the emptiness I felt. I went downstairs with the note and gave it to Leonard. He read it and went upstairs and came down with a shotgun, two pistols, and a single-shot .22 rifle. None of them are registered. I keep them in a special place in the closet where the ceiling tiles can be moved and the guns can be stored.

I sat at the table, stunned, and Leonard went out and got Donny and brought him in.

Donny looked at me, said, "What's wrong?"

Leonard gave him the note, said, "That's your man, Donny. He's got Brett and your brother. That's what cowards do."

Donny put the note down. "Smoke Stack said no one would get hurt. He said we'd just end up making some money."

"Someone will get hurt all right," Leonard said. "Smoke Stack. And anyone with him. If he hurts Brett, we'll kill them all and shit on their graves on a weekly basis."

"Brett didn't have anything to do with this," Donny said.

"Yeah, and that mattered, didn't it?" Leonard said.

I was thinking on what to do next when the cell rang.

When I answered, Smoke Stack said, "All right, bad ass. We got your woman and she's going to drive the getaway car for us. That's ironic, ain't it, asshole? It didn't take all that much work to figure who you guys were, 'cause first off, we got the brother, and it didn't take more than a few burning cigarettes on his chest and he talked right up, told us who you were. How you like that?"

"Peachy," I said.

"We nabbed Donny's brother at his job just before he started to clean a toilet. Now listen up tight 'cause I ain't gonna repeat it. We hit the First Commercial Bank at one thirty today. Anyone should get tipped off before then, or at all, we'll kill the chick and the brother too. What we're gonna have the redhead do is drive the getaway car. Ain't that classic? You take our wheel man, and we take your girl, and now she's our wheel man. Pardon my goddamn fucking manners. Wheel woman. I hope she can drive, 'cause if she can't, got to just go on and pop her."

"She can drive," I said. "Don't hurt her."

"Man, that would be a shame, wouldn't it? Fox like that. She's fine, man. I don't know how you got something like that. I see her, and I see you, I got to wonder you got some kind of Love Potion thing going."

"Just don't hurt her. . . . How do I get her back?"

"You didn't mention getting the brother back. So, we'll keep him. We'll keep him until we're gone for some time. We give the redhead back, you tell who we are, then he's toast. Otherwise, a week from now we'll let him go . . . no. I don't like that. You see, I'm thinking since you didn't even ask about him, he's not such a big worry for you. You get the woman back, then what do you care? We'll do it the other way. We'll keep the redhead and give you the brother. A week from now, we'll let her go. Just so you know, we caught her sleeping. Just sprang the lock and found her upstairs. I made her change, and I watched while she did it. It's good to know she's a natural redhead. It's good to know what she's got under the hood, so to speak."

"Fuck you," I said.

"Don't get rowdy. It might not do to get me mad. And let me tell you something. Other night, you got lucky. I was high as a kite."

"Yeah, and you can't fight either."

"Maybe we'll get another chance and I can show you what I can do when I'm straight."

"Maybe we will."

"Tell you what. We keep her a week, we'll give her back, but in the meantime, we might try and put out that little fire between her legs. I'm a regular fireman."

"You hurt her, you touch her, you're dead," I said.

"I wouldn't talk like that, if I was you. There's all kinds of things can happen between now and then. You could be looking for her for twenty years and not so much as find a hair. That body we left in the woods, in the car, that was a mistake. From now on, there won't be bodies to find. So you better pay attention to me. You sit quiet. We'll hit the bank. We'll leave the brother somewhere, and then we'll let your woman go in a week. That way, we got plenty of time to do what we want and get where we want. You don't believe me, call the police. Show up and cause trouble. You might get me, but you won't get her back. Least not alive. Have a nice fucking day, asshole."

I put the cell away and told Leonard what Smoke Stack said.

I said to Donny, "He won't let your brother go, and he won't let Brett go. He knows we know who he is, and he's determined to pull the armored car job anyway. Out of spite. He's trying to prove he's smart."

"I'm so sorry," Donny said. "I guess I haven't been thinking."

"You ought to be sorry, kid," Leonard said. "You've stirred up the goddamn bees' nest."

"He might let them go," Donny said.

"No," I said. "His pride is what this is about. He knows at some point we'll tell somebody, so I figure he'll do the robbery, then tell us he's going to let the brother go, and we can pick him up at such and such a place, but neither brother nor Brett will be alive by then. And they'll be waiting for us. They'll ask that you come along, like they're gonna take you back. But you know what? They plan to kill us all. No witnesses, and then they're back in business. Cops will know it's them that did it because of circumstantial evidence, but thinking and proving, that's two different things. They could lay low for a year or two and then launder the money somewhere, come out good. And my figure is everyone in that group, except Smoke Stack, will turn up dead. He'll end up with all the money and no one to talk about how things were done."

"You know, it's not a nice thing to say," Leonard said, looking at Donny, "but this is all your fault."

"It is, isn't it?" Donny said.

"Damn straight," Leonard said.

"It's not all your fault," I said. "I was Kelly, I'd have told too. No one is as tough as they show in the movies. I should have thought that angle. We tried to play this one too nice."

"Hap likes being nice," Leonard said. "Me, I don't care for nice."

"Will you go to the police?" Donny asked.

"We could take that chance, but we won't," I said.

Donny looked at the floor, then up at me. "It's not an armored car this time."

"No?"

"They're just going to hit the bank. Two inside, and then they'll come out and the getaway car will be waiting. I wanted to tell you that. He shouldn't have bothered Kelly and Brett."

"I bet Smoke Stack stays in the car," Leonard said.

"Yeah," Donny said. "Him and one of the others. And the driver."

"And now that driver is Brett, and your brother will be in the car too," Leonard said.

"All right," I said. "That doesn't change much, it might make it easier, no armored car guys to worry with."

"Yeah, it really doesn't matter," Leonard said. "But you showed some balls by telling us, by stepping farther away from that asshole Smoke Stack."

"What will you do?" Donny asked.

"What Leonard said earlier. We'll kill them all and shit on their graves."

It was still early in the day. My guess was they would keep Brett and Kelly alive until they were finished with the job. That would be their insurance until they didn't need them anymore. I had to hold onto that idea. It was my only comfort. Still, it wouldn't be long after the job was over that both Brett and Kelly would end up dead.

I called Marvin and told him the situation.

"So, how about I park somewhere where I can see them do the robbery. The asshole even told you the bank."

"He thinks he's untouchable."

"I can be an eyewitness later. Say I saw them. Right after I shoot the living hell out of them."

"Just be a witness," I said. "Don't get involved. Leonard and I will take care of them."

"I know that," Marvin said. "I never thought otherwise. But I can do my part."

"Not for us you won't," I said.

"I didn't say anything about it being for you and Leonard. It's Brett I'm talking about."

"And I appreciate it, but just watch what goes down so you can say you saw them there. If you see us, kind of forget that you did."

"If they call me on the witness stand later and ask if I saw you two?"

"Lie under oath."

"Certainly. I just wanted to make sure we were on the same page."

We met Marvin at a drive-through eatery about noon, had some coffee. I don't remember if I drank mine or not. We were sitting in Marvin's car. Leonard's car was parked beside it. Donny was sitting with us.

"Donny, you stay with Marvin," I said.

"You don't have to worry about me running," Donny said. "I want my brother back. I want you to get Brett back. She was right. I do get to choose."

"Yeah, well," Leonard said, "talk is cheap."

"By the way," I said, "in case you choose wrong, I'm not worrying about you running. Marvin will shoot you."

"I will," Marvin said. "A whole lot."

"Maybe somebody ought to shoot me," Donny said. It was a little dramatic, but right then I think he meant it.

Leonard raised his hand. "Who's for it?"

"Right now you just stay out of trouble, Donny," I said. "This kind of stuff is our business."

"Yeah, like we don't fuck up regularly," Leonard said.

"Not this time," I said.

"But they said for you not to come," Donny said. "That if you did they'd kill her."

"They'll kill her anyway," Marvin said. "So, it's then or not at all."

Leonard and I got in his car. We had put false license plates on it that morning, and we had a roll of false pinstripe to use. It was a stick-on thing you could remove easily, then wipe the sides of the car with some rubbing alcohol and it was like it had never been there. It was a little thing, but it was something that might throw an observer off.

Just to keep the disguise theme going, Leonard and I were going to wear hats.

Marvin was to drive to a spot across from the bank. A hotel parking lot. It would be quite a coincidence, him being at the hotel parking lot at the same time as the robbery, considering he'd turned in information about them earlier. Information that didn't pan out. But, he planned to tell them the hotel had a hell of a catfish buffet, and that he liked to take it in now and again, just happened to be there when the whole thing went down. Donny being there might take a bit more explaining, but in the end, truthfully, I didn't think it would matter. Not with what I had in mind.

We stopped in a lot behind a closed supermarket and got out and quickly put the pinstripes on the car. We put our hats on and drove to a place across the street from the bank. It used to be a mercantile store, but like most things downtown, it had gone the way of the dodo bird. From where we were, we could see the bank and we could see the hotel across the way. Marvin and Donny were parked in the lot.

The little mercantile lot was now a free parking lot, and it was full of cars. Mostly people who worked for the bank. We didn't try to find a parking spot, we just drove to the rear of where all the cars were and pulled up there. As we sat, a police patrol car came by on the street between us and the bank. He didn't look our way. Which was good. I had the .22 bolt-action rifle in my lap; it held one shot at a time. In the backseat was a shotgun. We had pistols in the glove box. No land mines or golf clubs.

I opened the door quietly and got out of the car and looked over the roof, and over the roofs of the other cars in the lot. From there I had a clear shot.

I got back in the car.

I looked at my watch. One fifteen.

I took a deep breath. Leonard said, "It'll be all right."

"It'll be all right when it's all right," I said.

"We'll get them."

"He could have lied about the time," I said. "He could have done that."

"Yep," Leonard said, "but I think he feels safe. The coward's way is to be brave when he holds the cards. Not when he doesn't."

"I just hope I'm not the one to hurt her."

"Hell, Hap, when was the last time you missed a shot?"

I tried not to remember when that was, tried not to imagine I could miss.

"Listen, brother," Leonard said, "I can do the shooting for you. I'm not like you. You know, in Vietnam I killed a lot of men. The only ones I feel bad about are the ones I tried to kill, shot at, and missed. I remember them better than the dead ones 'cause all I can think about is they may have gone on to kill one of us. I'm not like you. I don't carry the burdens of popping off a bad guy. I can get closer somehow, and I can do it."

"No you can't. You're an all right shot, but when it comes to this business I'm the one to do it. And it needs to be done from as much distance as the shot will allow."

"You got me there."

I nodded. "Yeah. I do."

I never learned to love guns. Didn't sit around and talk about how big a hole they can put in something and from how far. I didn't need bigger, better, and more. I don't enjoy the smell of gun oil, don't even like cleaning them. I don't know all the brand names and all the calibers and such.

But I can shoot a long rifle better than damn near anybody outside of a trained sniper, and I'm okay with a handgun if it's not too extreme a shot. I just have a knack to aim at something and hit it. Put a long gun in my hands and I can normally put a shot up a gnat's ass, and that's without the gnat bending over and pointing to the target.

Right then, however, all I could think about was that I might miss. I had certainly missed before, but I didn't want this to be one of those times.

Leonard knew what I was thinking. He often does.

"You won't miss, Hap."

We didn't say another word. Just sat there and watched and listened to each other breathe. I paused once and looked in the mirror on the back of the sun visor. I should note I looked pretty cool in my hat, a brown fedora. Leonard didn't look so sharp in his. He loved hats, but like I keep telling him, he isn't a hat person. Every hat he wears looks like something left on a scarecrow.

One thirty came and they didn't. Had Smoke Stack given me a line of shit? I felt like I was going to burst out crying.

Five minutes later we saw a car with two of the guys that had been with Smoke Stack in the house that night. The skinny, potbellied guys.

The car was a replacement for the one they had originally stored in the shed Marvin told us about. A brown, speedy model. They parked it in a spot and sat for a moment. I got out of the car with the .22 and laid it over the roof. I was a good distance away, and I had a limited shot over the roofs of parked cars. My stomach fluttered.

Way I figured, those guys in the brown late model would hit the bank, rush out and into the getaway car as it arrived. Smoke Stack, Brett and Kelly, and Stumpy would be in that car. Brett would be at the wheel. When the robbery was done, the others would jump in the getaway car and go. Brett would have to drive them out of there. I hoped like hell she didn't try to get cute, wreck the car. She did, they'd kill her or the wreck might. With Brett, you never knew. She was a fighter.

Way they planned it, if things went wrong with the pickup, they had a spare car in the lot. But the best thing was to have a getaway driver waiting so the robbers wouldn't have to start up and back out. It wasn't elaborate. It was simple. Simple was what worked.

The two shitheads got out of the car, ready to go in the bank. They had on gloves and jackets under which I was sure there were guns.

I had the .22 beaded on the back of the head of one of them. A .22 isn't a heavy firing weapon, but it doesn't recoil much and in matters like this, it isn't firepower, it's aim. The .22 had another advantage. It wasn't particularly loud.

I took a deep breath, two more, then slowly let out all my air, steadied the rifle. My face was beaded with sweat and a drop ran into my eye. I wiped it away quickly with my arm. The sweat had spoiled my aim.

They paused, and the one I hadn't sighted talked on his cell phone. That would be the call for the getaway car, which would be nearby. And that would be the pause I needed to set my shot again.

They started walking toward the bank entrance. I sighted down the barrel, took three deep breaths again, let out all my air, and gently tugged the trigger. The sound of the shot was like someone snapping a whip. The guy I was aiming at folded his legs under him and sat down quickly like he was about to start meditation. I knew there would be a small hole in the back of his head, but the front would have one the size of a half-dollar. There would be a punch out of bone, an explosion of blood and brains on the concrete. As I watched, slowly, he leaned forward, his forehead hitting the cement.

The other man with him wheeled and pulled a gun and darted back toward his car. I shot and hit him in the side before he made it. He went down. I could hear him scream from there. He threw the pistol aside and got up on his knees and held both hands up in surrender; he was a professional quitter.

I could tell he hadn't seen me yet, had no idea where the shot had come from. He was rapidly turning his head from left to right, front to back, holding his hands up.

He yelled out to no one in particular, "I haven't got a gun. I give up. I quit."

All I could think about was Brett.

I timed the turn of his head and shot him between the eyes. He fell back. I tossed the .22 in the backseat and climbed back in the car. About that time, people came out of the bank. They gathered around the bodies.

We sat where we were. People were looking in all directions. I took deep breaths and let them out.

"Easy," Leonard said. "Two down."

Then we saw a black SUV pull into the lot.

Brett was at the wheel. Smoke Stack was beside her. One of the other shits was in the back, the one Smoke Stack called Stumpy. I didn't see Kelly.

I got out of the car again with the .22, keeping it held down low. But when Smoke Stack saw the situation at the bank, the crowd, his boys down in the lot, he had Brett drive on. Nothing speedy. She just eased out of the lot. So far, no one even knew the SUV was supposed to be part of what was going on.

I was sure neither Smoke Stack nor Stumpy had seen me. I got in the car, and we eased out of the lot with our hats pulled down low and followed the SUV.

It went slow as it turned down the street toward the square, and then it hit South Street and turned. Holding a ways back, but not too far.

My cell rang. I answered.

It was Marvin. "You on them?" he asked.

"On them," I said.

They went along for a few lights, driving casual, then they turned on Highway 7. We pulled down a little dirt road and got out and pulled off the pinstriping and threw it and our hats into the bushes. It was most likely wasted energy, but it was the only clever thing we had had time to plan, and frankly, it wasn't that damn clever.

We got back in the car and went after them, finally caught up and stayed behind them at a goodly distance. Another car passed and got between us. But that was all right. It was a kind of camouflage. We all three drove out Highway 7.

We went on for quite some time, and then the car between us turned off, and we fell back a little. There was road work ahead, and they fanned the SUV through, but stopped us. We sat there and waited. It was a cool day, but I was sweating. They were getting ahead of us.

"Should we run it?" I said.

"Stay cool," Leonard said.

That was like asking a polar bear to stay cool in Albuquerque in mid-July.

Finally they waved us through. Leonard put his foot to the floor. We didn't see them. We had lost them.

I called Marvin.

"Man, we lost them. We're gonna need you out here to help look. We got to do back roads. Shit, I don't know what we got to do."

"Take it easy," Marvin said.

"Easier said than done. Goddamn road work. It got us hung up."

"Where are you?"

"Out Highway 7."

"Highway 7. We're coming . . . wait. Donny. He wants to talk to you."

"Fuck him."

"It's about where they might be."

"Then put him on."

"Hap," Donny said, "I want to help."

"Then you better not be wasting my time with a chat."

"Smoke Stack, if he's out Highway 7, he's going to the Take Off. That's what he calls a pasture out there. I think his family might have owned it. It's about twenty acres, used to be a hayfield, has some aluminum buildings. He keeps an ultralight there. That's why he calls it the Take Off. He uses the pasture as a kind of airport. He could be going there. I was there with him once. Went out to help him get a car from one of the sheds. One we had stored for the getaway, before you found out about it. He could have stored the car back there."

"For a trade-off?"

"Maybe. But that's a place he could be. Maybe they're just hiding out there. I don't know. But it makes sense."

He gave me the directions. It was down a county road. We had passed it. Leonard wheeled the car and we drove back.

The place wasn't hard to find, not once we knew which road to take. Donny explained all that over the phone. There was a line of trees, and then a pasture. From the directions, we concluded we were at the right place.

We parked by a small bridge. I spoke into the cell. "We're here."

"Good luck," Donny said.

"Luck has got nothing to do with it," I said, and turned off the phone.

I took the .22 out and Leonard took the shotgun. We walked over the bridge and along the side of the road behind the trees for about a hundred feet. We stopped near the road and jumped over a ditch and looked through a gap in a patch of pines.

From there we could see a grown-up pasture and about a hundred yards out, a long low aluminum shed. It had two large double doors on it. One set of doors was wide open. I could see the ultralight Donny had mentioned. I had been up in one once, a two-seater. I was the passenger. It was like riding in a winged lawn mower.

The SUV was parked near the shed.

If Smoke Stack and Stumpy were going out of there in the ultralight, then there wouldn't be any room for Brett and Kelly. They'd either leave them, or pop them. I suspected the latter. But they hadn't done it yet because I could see Brett and Kelly by the shed. It looked as if they might be wearing handcuffs; their hands were tucked behind their backs and they were leaning against the building. The only way into the pasture, which was fenced with barbed wire, was over a cattle guard.

Smoke Stack and Stumpy were tugging the ultralight out of the shed.

"Looks like they aren't going to bother with a car," Leonard said.

"Go start the car," I said.

"You can shoot from here."

"I can. But I'm going through the trees and through the fence, and I'm going to walk straight toward them. I need to be closer and surer. You drive over that cattle guard like your ass is on fire, distract them. I'll take my shot then. It'll be Smoke Stack first. Then I reload and it's the other one."

"That's slow reloading with all that's going on, you and that single-shot squirrel rifle," Leonard said.

"I'm quick and it's a little late to upgrade."

Leonard walked back to the car and I started through the trees and through the wire. I heard the car engine start. It wasn't loud enough to startle anyone, far back as he was. And then I heard the car coming, like the proverbial bat out of hell.

I hurried across the pasture. Smoke Stack hadn't seen me yet. He was preoccupied with another part of his plan. He hadn't wanted to share the two-seater at all. And I knew why. All that money had to have a place to sit.

He had an automatic pistol drawn, and he turned and shot

his partner right through the head. I saw him heave something in a bag into the ultralight, then he started over toward Brett and Kelly, the automatic hanging from his hand. He was partially hidden by the ultralight. I could only get glimpses of him through the wings and the motor and the seating. He hadn't seen me yet. He was preoccupied.

I stopped and dropped to one knee and took my shot.

I saw his hair lift a little, my shot was so close.

But I missed. I NEVER FUCKING MISSED. And I had missed.

My heart sank.

Smoke Stack wheeled. And when he did, Brett jumped up, and, with her hands against her back, she leaped at him, hit him with a body slam, and knocked him spinning backwards, his gun flying from his hand. I dropped the .22 and started running toward him. Leonard was flying through the cattle guard then, bearing down on Smoke Stack.

Smoke Stack got up and out from under Brett, who struggled to her feet and tried to jump at him again. But Smoke Stack dodged her like a quarterback on the run and leapt into the ultralight. I heard the motor start up and a moment later the machine was bouncing over the field. I was running on a collision course with Leonard. He slammed on the brakes and I slid over the hood and jumped in on the other side.

"Go," I said.

The ultralight was gaining some speed. Its bounces were becoming higher. In a moment it would hop and then leap to the sky.

But the motor on that thing wasn't a match for a car. We were closing. As we passed Brett, who had struggled to her feet, she looked at me.

I waved.

The car bounced along until it was almost even with the ultralight. I hung myself out of the open window, eased out until

I was sitting on the edge of it with my legs dangling, my arms inside, keeping me lodged. And then I eased on arm out.

"Closer," I said.

Leonard did that. I cocked one foot up until it was on the window support, and I shoved off just as the ultralight was making its big jump.

I hit the wing of the ultralight, scrambling for a grip, and my weight nodded it toward the ground. The wing hit. The propeller gnawed at the pasture. There was a sudden whirl as the sky came down and then went up again, followed by a close look at, and a hard impact with, the ground.

I heard a noise like someone dragging a rake through gravel. It was the ultralight spinning in circles like a confused idiot. The money had come loose of the bag and some of it was spinning in the air and some had been caught in the propeller and chopped up. It looked like the last hurrah of a parade, the last bits of confetti thrown.

On my feet, I saw Smoke Stack coming toward me. He was so angry he was actually foaming at the mouth. His face was scratched up.

"Now you get your shot, buddy," I said.

"I'll fucking kill you."

He was like a locomotive. It wasn't like that night in his house. He was crazed with anger and maybe he had been on drugs, or most likely had just underestimated me. That happens a lot. But he was dead serious now.

I dodged his rush and kicked out. I was trying to hit him in the solar plexus, but he instinctively crunched his body and took the shot on his upraised forearms. The impact, the disorientation of the crash, had me off a bit, so the impact of hitting him like that knocked me down. He leaped on me like a big frog.

I heard Leonard slam the car door and start over. But me and Smoke Stack were into it. I spread my legs and got him between them. He tried to hit me. I put up my arms. I was deflecting most of the blows, but I was taking some of it. Finally I cupped one of his arms at the elbow and swung a leg to the side of his neck. I was trying to pull him into a triangle choke, but the angle wasn't right. He pushed my leg back so that it was being mashed across my face. It was damn uncomfortable. I used my other leg to kick at his hip, knocking him back a bit, loosening him. It allowed me to swing my leg free. I poked him in the eyes with my fingers, and when he went back and put a hand to his face, I rolled out from under him.

Now I was on my feet, where I preferred to be. I saw Leonard leaning against the car, the shotgun lying on the fender.

"You got him," Leonard said.

Smoke Stack came in swinging. I ducked him and came up with an uppercut that knocked him back. I kicked him in the nuts then, but he was too high on adrenaline for it to matter. He came swinging again. I glanced the blows off my forearms and got inside and grabbed his head and kneed him inside of the leg. Adrenaline wasn't enough to stop that pain.

His leg went out from under him. I swung a downward right cross, and back he went. He rolled onto his hands and knees and scuttled and finally got to his feet. He put a hand to his pocket, and when he brought it out, he had a knife.

He crouched, eased toward me. There was sound like a cannon going off and Smoke Stack's head disappeared in a blur of red and gray and flying white fragments. Within a blink of an eye, what was left of him was lying on the ground.

I looked at Leonard. He was lowering the shotgun.

"You proved your point, and you got your licks in," he said. "But that knife, that could have been a problem."

We found that Brett's and Kelly's hands were bound with plastic cuffs. We cut those off. I said to Brett, "You all right, baby?"

"Yeah," Brett said. "I'm fine. All they did was get an unauthorized look at my nubile body. A look like they got, I should have been paid money."

I grinned at her and we kissed.

I walked back and got the .22. The shell casing was still in it.

We packed up and drove out of there in Leonard's car, left the money and the bodies.

It was a few weeks later.

A tip had led the police to the bodies in the field. Way it looked was there had been a problem between thieves. Smoke Stack had shot his partner and tried to escape, but crashed. Someone had blown his head off. They took this to be another partner. They were glad to get most of the money back. I don't know about the shredded stuff. I envisioned some bank clerk gluing the pieces back together like an archaeologist reuniting shards of pottery. It was a silly thought, but it hung in my head.

The other partner, of course, wouldn't be found. Neither would the .22 that killed the two would-be robbers in the bank lot. The cops had an idea that one of the partners went rogue, first with a .22, then a shotgun. It was a silly theory, but thank goodness they liked that story and were sticking to it. They're not dumb, just arrogant.

It was a nice afternoon with a clear sky and a light wind. We were in the backyard grilling burgers, me and Brett and Leonard. The doorbell rang. That would be our guests.

I went through the house and let Marvin and Kelly and Donny in, walked them out back.

Leonard was flipping the burgers.

We greeted each other, talked.

Donny said, "I haven't said nothing, and I never will."

"I believe you," I said.

"I wouldn't want you mad at me," Donny said.

"That's good thinking," Leonard said.

"But I wouldn't say anyway. I . . . I can't thank you guys enough. You hadn't done what you did, I'd be dead."

"Absolutely," Leonard said.

"Thanks again for saving my little brother," Kelly said, "and thanks for passing on the payment I owed you guys. I can use the dough."

"Man," Leonard said. "You're the hero. You put yourself on the line. Changed your life, got your ass whipped by me, and thoroughly, I might add, and then you didn't even have any protection from those guys and still you went to work."

"You warned me," Kelly said. "You told me not to stay on the job."

"Yep," Leonard said. "We did."

"And, I sort of squealed when they put those cigarettes on me. I thought I could take it. I was sure I could. One burn and I was already starting to loosen my tongue."

"It hurts," Leonard said. "You're not a professional tough guy. We don't begrudge you trying to make the pain stop. Besides, in the long run it worked out."

"Well," Brett said, stretching out in a lawn chair, her long legs poking sweetly out of her shorts. "All's well that ends well and doesn't make mess on the rug."

"Here, here," Marvin said.

"You said it right, Brett," Donny said. "They were hyenas. And I don't want to be like that."

"Good thinking," Brett said.

"I find a woman I care about," Donny said, "I hope she's half the woman you are, Brett."

"Oh, honey," Brett said smiling. "That's so sweet. But too optimistic. You can't find anyone half as good as me. A quarter of my worth maybe, if you're having a good day. But half, don't be silly."

VEIL'S VISIT

with Andrew Vachss

1.

LEONARD EYED VEIL for a long, hard moment and said, "If you're a lawyer, then I can shit a perfectly round turd through a hoop at twenty paces. Blindfolded."

"I am a lawyer," Veil said. "But I'll let your accomplishments speak for themselves."

Veil was average height, dark hair touched with gray, one good eye. The other one roamed a little. He had a beard that could have been used as a Brillo pad, and he was dressed in an expensive suit and shiny shoes, a fancy wristwatch, and ring. He was the only guy I'd ever seen with the kind of presence Leonard has. Scary.

"You still don't look like any kind of lawyer to me," Leonard said.

"He means that as a compliment," I said to Veil. "Leonard doesn't think real highly of your brethren at the bar."

"Oh, you're a bigot?" Veil asked pleasantly, looking directly at Leonard with his one good eye. A very icy eye indeed—I remembered it well.

"The fuck you talking about? Lawyers are all right. They got their purpose. You never know when you might want one of them to weigh down a rock at the bottom of a lake." Leonard's tone had shifted from mildly inquisitive to that of a man who might like to perform a live dissection.

"You think all lawyers are alike, right? But if I said all blacks are alike, you'd think you know something about *me*, right?"

"I knew you were coming to that," Leonard said.

"Well," I said. "I think this is really going well. What about you boys?"

Veil and Leonard may not have bonded as well as I had hoped, but they certainly had some things in common. In a way, they were both assholes. I, of course, exist on a higher plane.

"You wearing an Armani suit, must have set you back a thousand dollars—" Leonard said.

"You know a joint where I can get suits like this for a lousy one grand, I'll stop there on my way back and pick up a couple dozen," Veil said.

"Yeah, fine," Leonard said. "Gold Rolex, diamond ring . . . how much all *that* set you back?"

"It was a gift," Veil said.

"Sure," Leonard said. "You know what you look like?"

"What's that?"

"You look like Central Casting for a mob movie."

"And you look like a candidate for a chain gang. Which is kind of why I'm here."

"You gonna defend me? How you gonna do that? I may not know exactly what you are, but I can bet the farm on this—you ain't no *Texas* lawyer. Hell, you ain't no Texan, period."

"No problem. I can just go *pro hac vice*."

"I hope that isn't some kind of sexual act," Leonard said. "Especially if it involves me and you."

"It just means I get admitted to the bar for one case. For the specific litigation. I'll need local counsel to handle the pleadings, of course. . . ."

"Do I look like a goddamned pleader to you? And you best not say yes."

"'Pleadings' just means the papers," Veil said, his voice a model of patience. "Motions, applications . . . stuff like that. You wanted to cop a plea to this, Hap wouldn't need me. I don't do that kind of thing. And by the way, I'm doing this for Hap, not you."

"What is it makes you so special to Hap?" Leonard asked, studying Veil's face carefully. "What is it that you *do* do?"

"Fight," Veil said.

"Yeah," I said. "He *can* do that."

"Yeah, so can you and me, but that and a rubber will get us a jack-off without mess." Leonard sighed. He said to Veil, "You know what my problem is?"

"Besides attitude, sure. Says so right on the indictment. You burned down a crack house. For at least the . . . what was it, fourth time? That's first-degree arson, malicious destruction of property, attempted murder—"

"I didn't—"

"What? Know anyone was home when you firebombed the dump? Doesn't matter—the charge is still valid."

"Yeah, well they can valid *this*," Leonard said, making a gesture appropriate to his speech.

"You're looking at a flat dime down in Huntsville," Veil told him. "That a good enough summary of your 'problem?'"

"No, it ain't close," Leonard said. "Here's my problem. You come in here wearing a few thousand bucks of fancy stuff, tell me you're a fighter, but your face looks like you lost a lot more fights than you won. You don't know jack about Texas law, but you're gonna work a local jury. And that's still not my big problem. You know what my big problem is?"

"I figure you're going to tell me sometime before visiting hours are over," Veil said.

"My problem is this: Why the hell should I trust you?"

"I trust him," I said.

"I know, brother. And I trust you. What I don't trust, on the other hand, is your judgment. The two ain't necessarily the same thing."

"Try this, then." Veil told him. "Homicide. A murder. And nobody's said a word about it. For almost twenty years."

"You telling me you and Hap—?"

"I'm telling you there was a homicide. No statute of limitations on that, right? It's still unsolved. And nobody's talking."

"I don't know. Me and Hap been tight a long time. He'd tell me something like that. I mean, he dropped the rock on someone, I'd know." Leonard turned to me. "Wouldn't I?"

I didn't say anything. Veil was doing the talking.

Veil leaned in close, dropping his voice. "It wasn't Hap who did it. But Hap knows all about it. And you, if keep your mouth shut long enough, you will too. Then you can decide who to trust. Deal?"

Leonard gave Veil a long, deep look. "Deal," he finally said, leaning back, waiting to hear the story.

Veil turned and looked at me, and I knew that was my cue to tell it.

2.

"It was back in my semi-hippie days," I said to Leonard. "Remember when I was all about peace and love?"

"The only 'piece' I ever knew you to be about was a piece of ass," Leonard said kindly. "I always thought you had that long hair so's it could help you get into fights."

"Just tell him the fucking story," Veil said. "Okay? I've got work to do, and I can't do it without Leonard. You two keep screwing around and the guard's going to roll on back here and—"

"It was in this house on the coast," I said. "In Oregon. I was living with some folks."

"Some of those folks being women, of course."

"Yeah. I was experimenting with different ways of life. I told you about it. Anyway, I hadn't been there long. This house, it wasn't like it was a commune or nothing, but people just . . . came and went, understand? So, one day, this guy comes strolling up. Nice-looking guy. Photographer, he said he was. All loaded down with equipment in his van. He was a traveling man, just working his way around the country. Taking pictures for this book he was doing. He fit in pretty good. You know, he looked the part. Long hair, but a little neater than the rest of us. Suave manner. Took pictures a lot. Nobody really cared. He did his share of the work, kicked in a few bucks for grub. No big deal. I was a little suspicious at first. We always got photographers wanting to 'document' us, you know? Mostly wanted pictures of the girls. Especially Sunflower—she had this thing about clothes being 'inhibiting' and all. In other words, she was quick to shuck drawers and throw the hair triangle around. But this guy was real peaceful, real calm. I remember one of the guys there said this one had a calm presence. Like the eye of a hurricane."

"This is motherfucking fascinating and all," Leonard said, "but considering my particular situation, I wonder if you couldn't, you know, get to the point?"

Seeing as how Leonard never read that part of the Good Book that talked about patience being a virtue, I sped it up a bit. "I was out in the backyard one night," I said. "Meditating."

"Masturbating, you mean," Leonard said.

"I was just getting to that stage with the martial arts and I didn't want any of the damn marijuana smoke getting in my eyes. I guess I was more conservative about that sort of thing than I realized. It made me nervous just being around it. So I needed some privacy. I wasn't doing the classic meditation thing. Just being alone with my thoughts, trying to find my center."

"Which you never have," Leonard said.

"I'm sitting there, thinking about whatever it was I was thinking about—"

"Pussy," Leonard said.

"And I open my eyes and there he is. Veil."

"That'd be some scary shit," Leonard said.

"Looked about the same he does now."

"Yeah? Was he wearing that Armani suit?"

"Matter a fact, he wasn't," I said. "He looked like everyone else did around there then. Only difference was the pistol."

"I can see how that got your attention," Leonard said.

"It was dark. And I'm no modern firearms expert. But it wasn't the stuff I grew up with, hunting rifles, shotguns, and revolvers. This was a seriously big-ass gun, I can tell you that. I couldn't tell if he was pointing it at me or not. Finally I decided he was just kind of . . . holding it. I asked him—politely, I might add—if there was anything I could do for him, short of volunteering to be shot, and he said, yeah, matter of fact, there was. What he wanted was some information about this photographer guy.

"Now hippie types weren't all that different from cons back then, at least when it came to giving out information to the cops. Cops had a way of thinking you had long hair, you had to be something from Mars out to destroy Mom, apple pie, and the American way."

"Does that mean Texas too?" Leonard asked.

"I believe it did, yes."

"Well, I can see their point. And the apple pie part."

"I could tell this guy was no cop. And he wasn't asking me for evidence-type stuff anyway. Just when the guy had showed up, stuff like that."

Leonard yawned. Sometimes he can be a very crude individual. Veil looked like he always does. Calm.

"Anyway, I started to say I didn't know the guy, then . . . I don't know. There was something about his manner that made me trust him."

"Thank you," Veil said. I wasn't sure if he was being sarcastic or not.

I nodded. "I told him the truth. It wasn't any big deal. Like I said, he wasn't asking anything weird, but I was a little worried. I mean, you know, the gun and all. Then I got stupid and—"

"Oh, *that's* when it happened?" Leonard asked. "That's like the moment it set in?"

I maintained patience—which is what Leonard is always complaining he has to do with *me*—and went on like he hadn't said a word: "—asked him how come he wanted to know all about this guy, and maybe I ought not to be saying anything, and how he ought to take his pistol and go on. I didn't want any trouble, and no one at the place did either.

"So Veil asks the big question: Where is the guy right now? I told him he was out somewhere. Or maybe gone, for all I knew. That's the way things were then. People came and went like cats and you didn't tend to get uptight about it. It was the times."

"Groovy," Leonard said.

"We talk for a while, but, truth was, I didn't *know* anything about the guy, so I really got nothing to say of importance. But, you know, I'm thinking it isn't every day you see a guy looks like Veil walking around with a gun almost the size of my dick."

"Jesus," Leonard said. "Can't ever get away from your dick."

"No, it tends to stay with me."

"How about staying with the story," Veil said, still calm but with an edge to his voice now.

"So I ask Veil, it's okay with him, I'm going back in the house and get some sleep, and like maybe could he put the gun up 'cause it's making me nervous. I know I mentioned that gun several times. I'm trying to kind of glide out of there because I figure a guy with a gun has more on his mind than just small talk. I thought he might even be a druggie, though he didn't look like one. Veil here, he says no problem. But I see he's not going anywhere, so I don't move. Somehow, the idea of getting my back to that gun doesn't appeal to me, and we're kind of close, and I'm thinking he gets a little closer, I got a small chance of taking the gun away from him. Anyway, we both stick. Studying each other, I think. Neither of us going anywhere."

"Neither the fuck am I," Leonard said. "Matter of fact, I think moss is starting to grow on the north side of my ass."

"All right, partner," I told him, "here's the finale. I decide to not go in the house, just sit out there with Veil. We talk a bit about this and that, anything but guns, and we're quiet a bit. Gets to be real late, I don't know, maybe four in the morning, and we both hear a motor. Something pulling into the driveway. Then we hear a car door close. Another minute or so, the front door to the house closes too. Veil, without a word to me, gets up and walks around to the drive. I follow him. Even then I think I'm some kind of mediator. That whatever's going on, maybe I can fix it. I was hell for fixing people's problems then."

"You're still hell for that," Leonard said.

"Sure enough, there's the guy's van. I'm starting to finally snap that Veil hasn't just showed up for an assassination. He's investigating, and, well, I don't know how, but I'm just sort of falling in with him. In spite of his sweet personality, there's something about me and him that clicked."

"I adore a love story," Leonard said.

"So anyway, I wasn't exactly shocked when Veil put the pistol away, stuck a little flashlight in his teeth, worked the locks on the guy's van like he had a key. We both climbed in, being real quiet. In the back, under a pile of equipment, we found the . . . pictures."

"Guy was a blackmailer?" Leonard asked, a little interested now.

"They were pictures of kids," I told him. Quiet, so's he'd know what kind of pictures I meant.

Leonard's face changed. I knew then he was thinking about what kind of pictures they were and not liking having to think about it.

"I'd never seen anything like that before and didn't know that sort of thing existed. Oh, I guess, in theory, but not in reality. And the times then, lot of folks were thinking free love and sex was okay for anyone, grown-ups, kids. People who didn't really know anything about life and what this sort of thing was all about, but one look at those pictures and I was educated, and it was an education I didn't want. I've never got over it.

"So he," I said, nodding my head over at Veil, "asks me, where does the guy with the van sleep? Where inside the house, I mean. I tried to explain to him what a crash pad was. I couldn't be sure where he was, or even who he might be with, you understand? Anyway, Veil just looks at me, says it would be a real mess if they found this guy in the house. A mess for us, you know? So he asks me, how about if I go inside, tell the guy it looks like someone tried to break into his van?

"I won't kid you. I hesitated. Not because I felt any sympathy for that sonofabitch, but because it's not my nature to walk someone off a plank. I was trying to sort of think my way out of it when Veil here told me to take a look at the pictures again. A good look."

"The guy's toast," Leonard said. "Fucker like that, he's toast. I know you, Hap. He's toast."

I nodded at Leonard. "Yeah," I said. "I went inside. Brought the guy out with me. He opens the door to the van, climbs in the front seat. And there's Veil, in the passenger seat. Veil and that pistol. I went back in the house, watched from the window. I heard the van start up, saw it pull out. I never saw the photographer again. And to tell you the truth, I've never lost a minute's sleep over it. I don't know what that says about me, but I haven't felt a moment of regret."

"It says you have good character," Veil said.

"What I want to know," Leonard said looking at Veil, "is what did you do with the body?"

Veil didn't say anything.

Leonard tried again. "You was a hit man? Is that what Hap here's trying to tell me?"

"It was a long time ago," Veil told him. "It doesn't matter, does it? What matters is: You want to talk to me now?"

3.

The judge looked like nothing so much as a turkey buzzard: tiny head on a long, wrinkled neck and cold, little eyes. Everybody stood up when he entered the courtroom. Lester Rommerly—the local lawyer I went and hired like Veil told me—he told the judge that Veil would be representing Leonard. The judge looked down at Veil.

"Where are you admitted to practice, sir?"

"In New York State, your honor. And in the Federal District Courts of New York, New Jersey, Rhode Island, Pennsylvania, Illinois, Michigan, California, and Massachusetts."

"Get around a bit, do you?"

"On occasion," Veil replied.

"Well sir, you can represent this defendant here. Nothing against the law about that, as you apparently know. I can't help wondering, I must say, how you managed to find yourself way down here."

Veil didn't say anything. And it was obvious after a minute that he wasn't going to. He and the judge just kind of watched each other.

Then the trial started.

The first few witnesses were all government. The fire department guy testified about "the presence of an accelerant" being the tip-off that this was arson, not some accidental fire. Veil got up slowly, started to walk over to the witness box, then stopped. His voice was low, but it carried right through the courtroom.

"Officer, you have any experience with alcoholics?"

"Objection!" the DA shouted.

"Sustained," the judge said, not even looking at Veil.

"Officer," Veil went on like nothing had happened, "you have any experience with dope fiends?"

"Objection!" The DA was on his feet, red-faced.

"Counsel, you are to desist from this line of questioning," the judge said. "The witness is a fireman, not a psychologist."

"Oh, excuse me, your honor," Veil said sweetly. "I misphrased my inquiry. Let me try again: Officer," he said, turning his attention back to the witness, "by 'accelerant,' you mean something like gasoline or kerosene, isn't that correct?"

"Yes," the witness said, cautious in spite of Veil's mild tone.

"Hmmm," Veil said. "Be pretty stupid to keep a can of gasoline right in the house, wouldn't it?"

"Your honor. . . ," the DA pleaded.

"Well, I believe he can answer that one," the judge said.

"Yeah, it would," the fire marshal said. "But some folks keep kerosene inside. You know, for heating and all."

"*Thank* you, officer," Veil said, like the witness had just given him this great gift. "And it'd be even stupider to smoke cigarettes in the same house where you kept gasoline . . . or kerosene, wouldn't it?"

"Well, *sure*. I mean, if—"

"Objection!" the DA yelled. "There is no evidence to show that anyone was smoking cigarettes in the house!"

"Ah, my apologies," Veil said, bowing slightly. "Please consider the question withdrawn. Officer: Be pretty stupid to smoke *crack* in a house with gasoline or kerosene in it, right?"

"Your honor!" the DA cut in. "This is nothing but trickery.

This man is trying to tell the jury there was gasoline in the house. And this officer has clearly testified that—"

"—That there *was* either gasoline or kerosene in the house at the time the fire started," Veil interrupted.

"Not in a damn *can*," the DA said again.

"Your honor," Veil said, his voice the soul of reasonableness, "the witness testified that he found a charred can of gasoline in the house. Now it was his expert *opinion* that someone had poured gasoline all over the floor and the walls and then dropped a match. I am merely inquiring if there couldn't be some *other* way the fire had started."

The judge, obviously irritated, said, "Then why don't you just ask him that?"

"Well, Judge, I kind of was doing that. I mean, if one of the crackheads living there had maybe fallen asleep after he got high, you know, nodded out the way they do . . . and the crack pipe fell to the ground, and there was a can of kerosene lying around and—"

"That is *enough*!" the judge cut in. "You are well aware, sir, that when the fire trucks arrived, the house was empty."

"But the trucks weren't there when the fire *started*, judge. Maybe the dope fiend felt the flames and ran for his life. I don't know. I wasn't there. And I thought the jury—"

"The jury will *disregard* your entire line of questioning, sir. And unless you have *another* line of questioning for this witness, he is excused."

Veil bowed.

4.

At the lunch break, I asked him, "What the hell are you doing? Leonard already *told* the police it was him who burned down the crack house."

"Sure. You just said the magic word: crack house. I want to make sure the jury hears that enough times, that's all."

"You think they're gonna let him off just because—?"

"We're just getting started," Veil told me.

5.

"Now officer, prior to placing the defendant under arrest, did you issue the appropriate Miranda warnings?" the DA asked the sheriff's deputy.

"Yes sir, I did."

"And did the defendant agree to speak with you?"

"Well . . . he didn't exactly 'agree.' I mean, this ain't the first time for old Leonard there. We knowed it was him, living right across the road and all. So when we went over there to arrest him, he was just sitting on the porch."

"But he *did* tell you that he was responsible for the arson, isn't that correct, officer?"

"Oh yeah. Leonard said he burned it down. Said he'd do it again if those—well, I don't want to use the language he used here—he'd just burn it down again."

"No further questions," the DA said, turning away in triumph.

"Did the defendant resist arrest?" Veil asked on cross-examination.

"Not at all," the deputy said. "Matter of fact, you could see he was waiting on us."

"But if he *wanted* to resist arrest, he could have, couldn't he?"

"I don't get your meaning," the deputy said.

"The man means I could kick your ass without breaking a sweat," Leonard volunteered from the defendant's table.

The judge pounded his gavel a few times. Leonard shrugged, like he'd just been trying to be helpful.

"Deputy, were you familiar with the location of the fire? You had been there before? In your professional capacity, I mean." Veil asked him.

"Sure enough," the deputy answered.

"Fair to say the place was a crack house?" Veil asked.

"No question about that. We probably made a couple of dozen arrests there during the past year alone."

"You made any *since* the house burned down?"

"You mean . . . at that same address? Of course not."

"Thank you, officer," Veil said.

6.

"Doctor, you were on duty on the night of the thirteenth, is that correct?"

"That is correct," the doctor said, eyeing Veil like a man waiting for the doctor to grease up and begin his proctology exam.

"And your specialty is Emergency Medicine, is that also correct?"

"It is."

"And when you say 'on duty,' you mean you're in the ER, right?"

"Yes sir."

"In fact, you're in *charge* of the ER, aren't you?"

"I am the physician in charge, if that is what you're asking me, sir. I have nothing to do with administration, so . . ."

"I understand," Veil said in a voice sweet as a preacher explaining scripture. "Now, doctor, have you ever treated patients with burns?"

"Of course," the doctor snapped at him.

"And those range, don't they? I mean, from first-degree to third-degree burns. Which are the worst?"

"Third degree."

"Hmmm . . . I wonder if that's where they got the term, 'Give him the third degree'. . . ?"

"Your Honor. . . ," the DA protested again.

"Mr. Veil, where are you going with this?" the judge asked.

"To the heart of the truth, your honor. And if you'll permit me . . ."

The judge waved a disgusted hand in Veil's direction. Veil kind of waved back. The big diamond glinted on his hand, catching the sun's rays through the high courthouse windows. "Doctor, you treat anybody with third-degree burns the night of the thirteenth?"

"I did not."

"Second-degree burns?"

"No."

"Even *first*-degree burns?"

"You know quite well I did not, sir. This isn't the first time you have asked me these questions."

"Sure, *I* know the answers. But you're telling the jury, doctor, not me. Now you've seen the photographs of the house that was burnt to the ground. Could anyone have been *inside* that house and *not* been burned?"

"I don't see how," the doctor snapped. "But that doesn't mean—"

"Let's let the jury decide what it means," Veil cut him off. "Am I right, Judge?"

The judge knew when he was being jerked off, but, having told Veil those exact same words a couple of dozen times during the trial already, he was smart enough to keep his lipless mouth shut.

"All right, doctor. Now we're coming to the heart of your testimony. See, the reason we have *expert* testimony is that experts, well, they know stuff the average person doesn't. And they get to explain it to us so we can understand things that happen."

"Your honor, he's making a speech!" the DA complained, for maybe the two-hundredth time.

But Veil rolled on like he hadn't heard a word. "Doctor, can you explain what causes the plague?"

One of the elderly ladies on the jury gasped when Veil said "the plague," but the doctor went right on: "Well, actually, it is caused by fleas, which are the primary carriers."

"Fleas? And here all along I thought it was carried by rats," Veil replied, turning to the jury as if embracing them all in his viewpoint.

"Yes, fleas," the doctor said. "They are, in fact, fleas especially common to rodents, but *wild* rodents—prairie dogs, chipmunks, and the like."

"Not squirrels?"

"Only *ground* squirrels," the doctor answered.

"So, in other words, you mean varmints, right, doctor?"

"I do."

"The kind of varmints folks go shooting just for sport?"

"Well, some do. But mostly it's farmers who kill them. And that's not for sport—that's to protect their crops," the doctor said, self-righteously, looking to the jury for support.

"Uh, isn't it true, doctor, that if you kill *enough* varmints, the fleas just jump over to rats?"

"Well, that's true. . . ."

"That's what happened a long time ago, wasn't it, doctor? The Black Death in Europe—that was bubonic plague, right? Caused by rats with these fleas you talked about? And it killed, what? Twenty-five *million* people?"

"Yes. That's true. But today, we have certain antibiotics that can—"

"Sure. But plague is still a danger, isn't it? I mean, if it got loose, it could still kill a whole bunch of innocent folks, right?"

"Yes, that is true."

"Doctor, just a couple of more questions and we'll be done.

Before there were these special antibiotics, how did folks deal with rat infestation? You know, to protect themselves against plague? What would they do if there was a bunch of these rats in a house?"

"Burn it down," the doctor said. "Fire is the only—"

"Objection! Relevancy!" the DA shouted.

"Approach the bench," the judge roared.

Veil didn't move. "Judge, is he saying that crack *isn't* a plague? Because it's my belief—and I know others share it—that the Lord is testing us with this new plague. It's killing our children, your honor. And it's sweeping across the—"

"That is *enough!*" the judge shrieked at Veil. "One more word from you, sir, and you will be joining your client in jail tonight."

"You want me to defend Leonard using sign language?" Veil asked.

A number of folks laughed.

The judge cracked his gavel a few times and, when he was done, they took Veil out in handcuffs.

7.

When I went to visit that night, I was able to talk to both of them. Someone had brought a chess board and pieces in and they were playing. "You're crazy," I told Veil.

"Like a fuckin' fox," Leonard said. "My man here is right on the money. I mean, he *gets* it. Check."

"You moved a piece off the board," Veil said.

"Did not."

"Yeah, you did."

"Damn," Leonard said, pulling the piece out from between his legs and returning it to the board. "For a man with one eye you see a lot. Still check though."

I shook my head. "Sure. Veil gets it. You, you're gonna get life by the time he's done," I said.

"Everything'll be fine," Veil said, studying the chess board. "We can always go to Plan B."

"And what's Plan B?" I asked him.

He and Leonard exchanged looks.

8.

"The defense of *what*?" the judge yelled at Veil the next morning.

"The defense of necessity, your honor. It's right here, in Texas law. In fact, the case of *Texas v. Whitehouse* is directly on point. A man was charged with stealing water from his neighbor by constructing a siphon system. And he did it, all right. But it was during a drought, and if he hadn't done it, his cattle would've starved. So he had to *pay* for the water he took, and that was fair, but he didn't have to go to prison."

"And it is your position that your client *had* to burn down the crack . . . I mean, the occupied dwelling across the street from his house to prevent the spread of disease?"

"Exactly, your honor. Like the bubonic plague."

"Well, you're not going to argue that nonsense in my court. Go ahead and take your appeal. By the time the court even hears it, your client'll have been locked down for a good seven-eight years. That'll hold him."

9.

Veil faced the jury, his face grim and set. He walked back and forth in front of them for a few minutes, as if getting the feel of the ground. Then he spun around and looked them in the eyes, one by one.

"You think the police can protect you from the plague? From the invasion? No, I'm not talking about aliens, or UFOs, or AIDS, now—I'm talking crack. And it's here, folks. Right here. You think it can't happen in your town? You think it's only Dallas and Houston where they grow those sort of folks? Take a look around. Even in this little town, you all lock your doors at night now, don't you? And you've had shootings right at the high school, haven't you? You see the churches as full as they used to be? No you don't. Because things are *changing*, people. The plague is coming, just like the Good Book says. Only it's not locusts, it's that crack cocaine. It's a plague, all right. And it's carried by rats, just like always. And, like we learned, there isn't but one way to turn that tide. Fire!

"Now I'm not saying my client set that fire. In fact, I'm asking you to find that he did *not* set that fire. I'm asking you to turn this good citizen, this man who cared about his community, loose. So he can be with you. That's where he belongs. He stood with you . . . now it's time for you to stand with him."

Veil sat down, exhausted like he'd just gone ten rounds with a rough opponent. But, the way they do trials, it's always the prosecutor who gets to throw the last punch.

And that chubby little bastard of a DA gave it his best shot, going on and on about how two wrongs don't make a right. But you could see him slip a few times. He'd make this snide reference to Leonard being black, or being gay, or just being . . . Leonard, I guess, and, of course that part is kind of understandable. But, exactly like Veil predicted, every time he did it, there was at least one member of the jury who didn't like it. Sure, it's easy to play on people's prejudices—and we got no shortage of *those* down this way, I know—but if there wasn't more good folks than bad, well, the Klan would've been running the state a long time ago.

The judge told the jury what the law was and told them to go out there and come back when they were done. Everybody got up to go to lunch, but Veil didn't move. He motioned me over.

"This is going to be over with real quick, Hap," he said. "One way or the other."

"What if it's the other?"

"Plan B," he said, his face flat as a piece of slate.

10.

The jury was out about an hour. The foreman stood up and said "Not Guilty" about two dozen times—once for every crime they had charged Leonard with.

I was hugging Leonard when Veil tapped me on the shoulder. "Leonard," he said, "you need to go over there and thank those jury people. One at a time. Sin*cere*, you understand?"

"What for?" Leonard asked.

"Because this is going to happen again," Veil said. "And maybe next time, one of the rats'll get burned."

Knowing Leonard, I couldn't argue with that. He walked over to the jury and I turned around to say something to Veil. But he was gone.

DEATH BY CHILI

"WELL, I CAN ALMOST SEE murdering someone for a good chili recipe," Charlie Blank said, "but not quite."

"What if it had been barbecue?" Leonard asked.

"Now, that's different."

"Ah, hah!" I said. "That's because you're prejudiced. You think barbecue is *The* Texas food, when any idiot knows it's chili."

"Only if you can't get barbecue," Charlie said.

"One thing is for sure," I said. "Goober Smith's recipe for chili isn't going to grace anyone's dinner table from here on out. Other than the person killed him for it, that is."

It was a cold, rainy afternoon, dark as night, and we were sitting around Leonard's dining room table drinking coffee and eating vanilla cookies, which Leonard thinks are some kind of food of the gods, but they're just these plain ole vanilla things that you can eat about twenty-three zillion of and not realize you've eaten anything till you get on the scale. Even if you don't like 'em much, you tend to eat 'em.

Anyway, we were sitting at the table and Charlie was telling us about Goober Smith. It was a story we'd all heard before, but not the details. Charlie, who's a lieutenant on the police force, got the story from someone at the cop shop, someone who had been around in 1978 when Goober got his head blown open and went face down in a bowl of chili.

"Whoever it was came up behind him and let the boom drop," Charlie said. "Killed him deader than the five-cent candy bar, then snuck off with his chili recipe. That recipe used to win all the chili cook-offs around these parts."

"What I wonder is what this person did with the recipe," I said. "If they were stealing it to win cook-offs, it never surfaced. Right?"

"Goober's chili was supposed to be as distinctive as a chicken with dentures. No one could use it if they stole it. Unless they were at home."

"Must have been some really fine chili," Leonard said.

"Jack Mays thought it was the best," Charlie said.

"That the cop told you about this?" I asked.

"Yep. He used to go around to cook-offs all over East Texas tryin' to see if he could get a taste and figure who killed Goober. Solving the murder was kind of an obsession with him. Everyone else had given up. Course, Jack's retired now."

"Now you're on it," I said.

"I tinker with it now and then," Charlie said.

"And how are you tinkering?"

"Not so good. I've looked at it from every angle possible. Why would someone come into Goober's place at night, catch him at the table, shoot him in the back of the head with a Luger, and steal his recipe?"

"What I'd like to know," Leonard said, dunking a cookie, "is how anyone knows his recipe was stolen. He could have had it in his head."

"Nope," Charlie said. "He was adamant about the fact he kept it under lock and key in his wall safe, and the safe was cracked open and money was still in it. Only thing seems to have been missing was the recipe. Least ways, no one ever found it."

"*Seemed* to be missing," Leonard said. "But you don't know for sure. Right?"

"I guess so," Charlie said. "Well, it's all chili through the intestines now, isn't it?"

"Wasn't the final official word it was suicide?" I asked.

Charlie nodded. "He was found sitting at the kitchen table, nude. The Luger was on the floor by the chair, and his brains were all over the place, and he was facedown in an empty bowl that had contained chili. There was a pot of it on the stove."

"What made Jack think it wasn't suicide?" I asked.

"Funny stuff. The bullet had gone out the top of Goober's head, hit the ceiling. The casing from the Luger was on the floor behind him, and there was powder residue on his hand. No note."

"Sounds like suicide to me," Leonard said.

"Problem was, a Luger ejects its shell forward. You put the barrel to your head, the shell casing would have been thrown forward onto the table or the floor. That wasn't the case."

"Could have rolled," I said.

"Floor behind Goober was raised, a living area. It couldn't have rolled uphill. And the lead in the ceiling. Had Goober put the gun to his head, even if he'd slanted it, doesn't seem likely it would have gone into the ceiling at that angle. It could have, I guess, but it doesn't seem likely. Someone else could hold it at that angle more comfortable. It's difficult to do it yourself and get those results. Add to it the safe was open and the money was there but there was no chili recipe, and you got a mystery."

"Did Goober have reason to commit suicide?" Leonard asked.

"He was sick," Charlie said. "Rumor was it was a bad disease of some kind, but what it looks like is someone came up behind him, shot him with the Luger, wrapped his hand around the gun, and let it fall so it would look like suicide. Then they stole the recipe."

"The safe blown open?" Leonard asked.

"No. But that doesn't mean it wasn't cracked by someone knew how. Or someone had the combination. An old girlfriend was one of the suspects, but nothing ever came of that. Actually, I still have my eye on her."

"The Luger belong to Goober?" Leonard asked.

"No one knows. Wasn't registered. A war souvenir. Goober's dad had been in World War II, so it's possible it had been passed down, but if it was, that doesn't mean Goober shot himself with it. Someone could have used it on him."

"My uncle had a Luger like that," Leonard said. "A World War II souvenir. I have it now."

"Hey, I got to go, boys."

Charlie put on his coat and I walked him to the door. It was very cold out there. Good chili weather. Charlie and I shook hands, and he drove off in the rain.

When I came back inside, Leonard was pouring us fresh cups of coffee.

"That recipe thing, that is kind of weird," he said. "A real-life mystery."

"For what it's worth," I said.

"I've heard about Goober Smith all my life," Leonard said. "And the stuff about his chili and his murder and the missing recipe, but I never thought there was anything to it until Charlie gave us the skinny."

"Want to watch a movie tonight? I see *She Creature* is coming on. We could pop some popcorn, get some Sharp's."

Leonard seemed distant, but he said, "Sure."

We popped popcorn and watched the movie, but Leonard didn't really seem into it. He had a kind of glassy stare through it all.

I was making out with this marvelous raven-haired beauty, and she was just about to expose her breasts when she grabbed me by the arm and shook me like I was in a paint shaker.

I came awake to Leonard standing by the couch where I slept.

"Hap," he said, shaking me, "I solved the mystery."

"What mystery?"

"Get up."

"You're kidding. I was dreaming of and just about to make love to a black-haired beauty."

"She'll wait."

I pushed the covers down and sat on the edge of the couch. I felt like I had been plowed into the ground for fertilizer. Outside the rain hammered the house like a drum solo.

Leonard turned on the light. He brought a chair to the front of the couch and sat down on it. He was holding a Luger.

"This is my uncle's Luger," Leonard said.

"That's nice. Right now I'd like to shoot you with it."

Leonard held it in front of him. "I'm going to eject a shell."

"How nice."

He did. It flew up and over my head. "That was great, Leonard. Now let's go back to bed."

"Forward, just like Charlie said." Leonard put the Luger in his lap. "But if this is the Luger." He made a gun with his thumb and finger. "And I put it to my head, it wouldn't fire in such a way as to shoot a bullet into the ceiling."

"Which is what Charlie said."

"Right. But, think about this. Goober was naked, as suicides often are. He knows he's dying, or is going to be terribly ill, so he decides to kill himself. You try and hold the Luger in the normal way, it isn't comfortable. I mean, you hold it just right it could fire through the head and ceiling, but like I said, it's not a comfortable way to hold it."

"I don't think comfort was on his mind."

"So he holds it this way, which is really more natural."

Leonard put his finger to his head, thumb down. "Think about it."

I did. I was starting to get interested.

"So, when he pulls the trigger, he gets powder burns on his hand, and upside down, it would eject the shell casing backwards, behind Goober."

"What about the way the bullet went into the ceiling?"

"Well, if it's flat against the head, it won't go into the ceiling at all. It could be slanted, held either way, but it's very comfortable holding it upside down, and easier to give it a slant, and therefore easier to fire through the skull and into the ceiling."

"As I said, I doubt Goober was all that worried about comfort right then."

"Okay. But the rest of it adds up pretty good, doesn't it?"

I thought about that for a moment. "That's all well and good," I said, "but that still doesn't explain the open safe, the missing recipe."

"I think it does," Leonard said. "Goober was secretive about his recipe to the point of phobia. So, when he decided to commit suicide it was the one thing he wanted to take with him."

"But it wasn't found."

"Because he ate it."

"You mean he put it in the chili?"

"That's what I think. He made up a last batch, tore up the recipe like seasoning, put it in the chili. Had himself a big bowl, then blew his brains out. That way, no one would ever have his recipe. That's why nothing else was taken from the safe. Simple really. Charlie and Jack are all wet. It wasn't murder. The first impression was correct. Goober really did kill himself."

"You know what, Leonard? I think you're right for a change."

"Good, now I can go to sleep."

"Course, it's all just guess work and will probably never be proven one way or another."

"I'm satisfied," Leonard said.

"You going to tell Charlie?"

"Sure. Tomorrow. I want him to know how smart I am."

Leonard turned off the light, went into the bedroom, and closed the door. I stretched out on the couch and pulled the covers over me. I looked at the ceiling a while.

Sonofagun, I thought. He probably did figure it out.

The rain hammered on the house. Lightning flashed through the curtains over the living room window.

I closed my eyes, hoping the raven-haired beauty would be back.

Lansdale Chili

First, you cook a lot of hamburger meat. I'm not sure how much is a lot, but, you know, a lot. Anyway, you brown it, drain off the grease, and put it in a pot. Now cut some steak into strips and brown it, cut this up in chunks, and put it in the pot. Add a couple cups of water and six to twelve ounces of tomato paste. Put in two teaspoons of sugar, four teaspoons of chili powder, and ten cut-up juicy jalapeño peppers. Stir and add more water, be your own judge, but don't make it too watery.

Now, a dash of cayenne pepper, a dash of Tabasco sauce, a teaspoon of garlic or some real chunks of garlic, add one tablespoon of olive oil—that's so it won't all clog up like a brick inside you.

Cut up two to three medium ripe tomatoes and toss this into the mix. Slice up a small onion and add it. Half a teaspoon of oregano. A tablespoon or two of black pepper and a half cup of ketchup.

Let this simmer for a damn long time, adding water when needed, but don't add too much. Keep it thick. If it looks a little watery, then add more ingredients. It's better at this point to add a cat or a parakeet than it is to add too much water.

After a few hours take a Pepcid and have chili.

If it doesn't taste quite right, you probably followed the recipe too closely or didn't take enough Pepcid. Throw it back into the pot, add some more of everything but water, and try again.

If your chili comes out of the pan in wads, then maybe you *do* need to add some water.

DEAD AIM

"Too many guns is not like too many guitars."
—Hap Collins

EACH TIME OUT, I assume that a job we're hired to do will be exactly what we think it's going to be, and frankly, some are. I don't talk about those much because they're boring. And for a long time I didn't think of myself as a freelance troubleshooter, but instead, a guy looking for work to tide me over until I got my career going, whatever that might be. Then Leonard explained to me that I was actually practicing my profession, and that I was good enough at it and it was really what I wanted to do. That all that stuff about finishing out a degree at my age and becoming a teacher, or some such thing, was just so much talk.

After a short nervous breakdown, and a period of finding my center, as they say in martial arts, I got back on the horse, and now I'm riding, in the dark. But I'm at least on the horse and not being dragged around by it. I realized that Leonard was right. I also realized that like it or not, at the bottom of it all, I was a sometime killer.

When Leonard and I accepted a simple protection job, or what seemed simple, I was hoping, as always, that we'd just get it done and go home and Marvin would give us a check that didn't bounce, and we'd be as happy as a stud horse in a corral full of fillies.

A guy named Jim Bob Luke recommended Marvin's agency for the job. It's not exactly a legit job, which is frequently the case. The problem was a lady who had known Jim Bob Luke asked him to help her out. She had an ex-husband who was stalking her, and had actually threatened her, but she couldn't prove it. It was her word against his. Jim Bob was going to be busy and couldn't drive to LaBorde to help out, so he put us onto it.

Me and Leonard drove over to see the lady. She was offering us good money to split between us and the agency. What she wanted us to do, as she put it, was meet up with her husband and have a discussion with him. The way she said it, it sounded like we were just going to set a date at a restaurant and have tea. Of course, that's not what she meant at all.

It was early afternoon in September and some of the hot had gone out of the day. Midday it could get pretty warm in East Texas, but not like a month or so earlier when you could fry an egg on the sidewalk, and going barefoot on cement was like walking across a pancake griddle. It was a pleasant change. Cooler weather was in the offing.

Me and Leonard were the kind of guys that never took anything at face value, or at least we liked to think of ourselves that way. So we thought we'd go over and talk to our client, Mrs. Devon, soon to be the ex-Mrs. Devon, and see if we thought her complaints were legit, or if she was just looking to have someone beat the shit out of her husband for vengeance and entertainment.

From the mouth of the street she lived on, across the way, we could see a new apartment complex, and not far from that was a long street full of fast food joints and doctor's offices and the like. Along the street where she lived, there were a few houses still clinging to the past, like ancient souls waiting silently for death, or hoping for a last visit from somebody before they were knocked down flat and carried out.

Next to those were marginally better houses, prefab style, the sort of thing where a shell of a house could be put up in the weekend, and two weeks later plumbing and water would be ready. All that was needed then was furniture, kids to yell at, and a dog to crap on the lawn, which at least for a few months would be a patch of bulldozed red clay.

Mrs. Devon's house was back from the street a bit. There were hedges on either side of her driveway, and they were well-trimmed but a little anemic. In the open garage there was a blue Cadillac that had aged well, and a closed-up barbecue grill pushed up against the wall with a sack of charcoal bricks stacked on top.

We parked behind the Cadillac and got out.

When the door was answered it was by a lady about six feet tall with black hair and a nice shape. She must have been about forty, and you could tell it if you looked real hard, but it was a nice forty, and the body seemed to belong to someone about twenty-five; she obviously had a gym membership, a trainer, and a special diet. She smiled and showed us that she had nice teeth. Her face was nice too. Her eyes were as green as Ireland. When she moved, something primal inside me moved.

After she confirmed we were who she was expecting, we came in and sat down on an elderly but comfortable couch. She asked us if we'd like a drink, and we ended up with ice tea.

"Jim Bob told me you could help me," she said.

"Probably," I said. "I mean, we have to check things out."

"In case I'm lying and just want you to beat up my husband?"

"That would be it," Leonard said.

"He hasn't been all that clever about it," she said. "I don't think he's trying to sneak, it's just that no one has really seen him do anything, or will admit to it. No one but me. I really don't want him arrested. I just want him to stop. The divorce is going to go through, and I don't think he cares about that. He doesn't love me, and I don't love him. He just doesn't like losing me. He wouldn't have minded dumping me. But I dumped him first. That sort of got his panties in a twist."

"When was the last time you saw him?" Leonard asked.

"A few days ago. I had a gentleman over."

"Someone you're dating?" I asked.

"Someone I had one date with. Henry showed up and beat up my date. Bad."

"So there's your proof," I said. "Have your date press charges."

She shook her head. "No. My date wasn't willing to turn him in, because Henry threatened to kill him if he did."

"You think he's capable of that?" I said.

"I don't know. I don't think so. But my date thought so."

"That happened here?" Leonard said.

"Yes. I had left the back door open. I didn't think he was that dangerous. Henry, I mean. But he's big and scary."

"How big is he?" I asked.

"Six-five, maybe three hundred. Not a fat man. Does that scare you?"

"Hell yeah," I said. "But it won't stop us if we believe you."

"All I got is my word, and no one else is talking. I thought I could give you his address and you could just check on him. Follow him around or something, see what you think. See if he shows up here. I've got so I lock all my doors and the windows too. I don't know that he's dangerous, but the beating he gave that man . . . it was quick and it was awful. I think he may have broken his ribs."

"So he comes by a lot?"

"He used to knock on the door. Now he mostly just drives by, or pulls up in the drive and sits there. By the time I call the cops, he's gone. They've talked to him, but he just says I'm lying, and

I can't prove it any other way. They can't post a man twenty-four seven just on my word. And won't. That's why I've come to you."

"Give us his address," I said. "We'll check on him. One of us can stay here with you if you like."

"I have an extra bedroom so one of you can be here all the time. Jim Bob recommended you two and your boss, Mr. Hanson, very highly."

"How do you know Jim Bob?" Leonard asked.

"We dated in high school. I lived in Houston then."

"Jim Bob went to high school," Leonard said. "I thought he came out of the womb the way he is, wearing that hat and driving that old Cadillac."

"That would have been painful for his mother, don't you think?" she said.

"It would," I said. "It certainly would."

"You lock up," I said, "and we'll go get a few things we might need, like an axe handle, and we'll be back."

"An axe handle?" she said.

"Call it insurance," Leonard said. "You want the protection, you got to allow us to protect. And discourage."

"You won't kill him, will you?"

"Of course not," I said.

"Look, I really don't want him hurt."

"Only if he tries to hurt us," I said.

"Why don't one of you stay now?" she said. "Start this minute."

"Because we have to decide if we believe you or not."

"Oh."

"In the meantime, lock this place up tighter than a nun's chastity, and we'll be right back."

We walked out and waited for her to lock the door behind us. When we heard the lock click, we walked to the car.

In the car, backing out, I said, "What do you think?"

"Sounds legit," Leonard said. "I think she's scared and wants to get on with her life and wants him to know he's not welcome."

"If we beat the dog shit out of him, you think he'll quit?"

"Hard to say, but I do know it works more often than you hear about. I had someone tell me, you know, you do that, they just come back. I've done it a few times, so have you—"

"And they didn't come back."

"Yep."

"But sometimes they do."

"Yep," Leonard said. "Sometimes they do."

"Henry sounds like he could be pretty hard-core."

"Worrying about him being big?" Leonard asked.

"Crossed my mind."

"What the axe handle's for, my boy."

"And if he turns us in for whipping his ass?"

"We were visiting a friend of a friend. That friend being Jim Bob, and she being the friend of that friend. Henry arrived. Violence broke out. Axe handles were lying about, and . . . well, you can figure from there."

"And we just happened to be there when he showed up? With axe handles?"

"Exactly," Leonard said. "It doesn't have to be a true story, it just has to be our story. . . . You know, you're getting cautious in your old age."

"I am. I like having a nice home and Brett and a comfortable place to lay my head and put my dick."

"Since I'm living at your house these days," Leonard said, "I like you got a nice home and a comfortable place for me to lay my head, though I'm still in search of a place to lay my dick."

"About that . . ."

"Yeah. I know," Leonard said. "Like Ben Franklin said, fish and friends smell after three days."

"No. I'm asking about you and John. The dick part, and the

deeper meanings that go with it. How are things developing between you two?"

"Nothing much. We talk by phone now and again. I'm almost done with that business. I think you can only brood so long, wait on someone so long, and then you got to move on. But, I'll move out soon enough."

"Not what I meant," I said. "Stay as long as you like."

"Hell, I know that. I was joking. You can't get rid of me."

Brett was off on rotation from work. She was sitting at the kitchen table wearing white shorts and a big, loose, red T-shirt. Her thick red hair was tied back in a bushy ponytail. She wasn't wearing any shoes. Her toenails were painted as red as her hair. She was drinking coffee. Leonard and I went over and poured ourselves a cup from the pot.

"Well?" Brett said.

"We think she's for real," I said.

"So, how are you going to play it?" Brett said.

"Leonard is going to stay there for awhile, and I'm going to be on phone service here at the house. Later, we can swap out."

"What's she look like?"

"She wouldn't hurt anyone's feelings at a glance," I said.

"How about if they concentrated?" she said.

"No one's feelings would be hurt that way either," I said.

"Then you best just let Leonard stay there."

"You're just saying that because I'm queer," Leonard said.

"Exactly," Brett said.

"You don't trust me?" I said.

"I trust you, but I don't know her, and Little Hap likes pussy almost as much as life."

"You know better than that," I said. "Well, you're right about the pussy part and life and all that. But you know what I mean. I'm trustworthy."

"Yeah, but I'm still a little jealous."

We had our coffee, then we got a few things together for Leonard. Toothbrush and toothpaste. Deodorant. Axe handle from the closet. A small handgun. That kind of stuff.

"Be sure and not shoot anyone," I said.

"Gotcha," Leonard said, got his keys, and drove his car away. I watched from the kitchen window until he was out of sight.

"He gone?" Brett asked.

"Yep."

"Great," she said. "Let's screw like mongooses."

We screwed like mongooses and one extra beaver and a water snake, and then lay in bed and watched TV. We watched *The Fugitive Kind* on some movie channel. I wanted a cool jacket like Marlon Brando wore in that movie. I knew I'd never have one. Besides, I didn't have anything against reptiles, and it was supposed to be made out of them.

When the movie wrapped, another came on, and we watched part of that, but it wasn't much, and we gave it up. I had a book to read and Brett had a biography. We stacked pillows behind us and lay there nude and read. It was one of our favorite things to do, following the whole mongoose thing, which got a number-one rating.

Three hours or so later, feeling lazy, I lay down and dozed. Brett woke me, freshly showered, dressed in blue jeans and a blue top, tennis shoes on her feet.

"Baby," she said, "you're taking me out. Get up and shower."

I got up and showered, dressed, and we drove into town to a Mexican restaurant that served a good steak, better than average tacos, tamales, and the usual rice and beans, and so far no stomach poisoning. When it comes to good eats, nothing beats Mexican food, though Japanese is close. Sometimes I eat meat, I think about the poor cows, and then I think since I ate them, I might as well wear leather too. No use letting a discarded cow suit go to waste. But I wished I could just eat lettuce and tomatoes and tofu. Doesn't work for me, though. I get sick. Hypoglycemia. I think about a lot of things on a full stomach. It's easier to think about not eating something anymore when you just ate it.

When we got back to the house, Brett pulled on the big loose shirt she had been wearing earlier in the day and, as a treat to me, left off the panties. I pulled on my pajama bottoms as a treat to her, and a loose T-shirt, and climbed in bed. This was my favorite kind of day. Lazy.

I said, "You said you were jealous earlier, of Sharon Devon. You weren't serious, were you?"

"A little," she said.

"I've never known you to be jealous."

"I didn't think I was. I guess it's because I want to see this arrangement as permanent."

"I already saw it that way."

"I did too, but you know, there were doubts in the back of my mind."

"Because we're not married?"

"That was there in an old-fashioned way," she said. "But I don't think that really matters. Not really."

"But it is a braver commitment, isn't it?"

"Maybe," she said.

"Look, honey," I said. "I want to be with you. I'll keep it like it is, or I'll marry you. Whatever, baby. It's you and me."

"You once said something to me about having kids."

"I was just in a mood."

"I think you meant it."

"I did mean it. But, you pointed out what should have been obvious to me: we're a little too old."

"I'm younger than you," she said.

"Everyone thinks you're twenty years younger," I said. "And you look it. Pretty soon they'll be thinking I'm your grandpa."

"That could happen," she said. "But, just in case. I looked into fertilization drugs, you know, to see. Case I might need them."

"I wouldn't want to have a kid just because you think I want one," I said.

"I know that."

"You are a mother, but I've never been a father. I figure I don't become one, that might even be best."

"You do know things would change," she said.

I nodded. "I know. And what worries me is—"

"You don't know if you can really change."

"I been trying so long now, that I'm starting to think the trying and not doing it is as much a part of who I am as what I actually end up doing. Which seems to be hitting people in the head, shooting people—"

"And being their rescuer. Hap Collins, have I ever told you that all your doubts about yourself are none of my doubts? That I worry about you using my toothbrush instead of yours, and you sometimes pee on the floor, but as far as your worth as a person, even if you have done some things you consider dark, they do not faze me or concern me at all. Except if we have kids. And it's not about what you're doing, but about what it could do to a child."

"I wouldn't want him or her to grow up like me," I said.

"I would want them to have your integrity," she said.

I started to say something, but it was like a fist was in my throat.

"Let's read," Brett said.

We read a long while, watched the late movie, and then we did the mongoose thing again before going to bed.

When I woke up the next morning, it was to a knock on the bedroom door. I sat up. Brett was gone. Off to the hospital to nurse someone. Since I was upstairs in our bed, I opened my drawer and took out my revolver and lay back against my pillows.

I said, "Who is it?"

"Marvin."

"Come in."

Marvin opened the door. He hobbled in on his cane and found a chair in the corner.

"How'd you get in?"

"You gave me an emergency key, remember?"

"Is this an emergency?"

"No. But I thought I'd take advantage of my key ownership and see if I could get some coffee. It's nine already."

I put the revolver in the nightstand drawer and pulled off the sheets and got out of bed, forgetting I hadn't replaced my pajamas after mine and Brett's mongoose moment last night.

Marvin said, "Oh, the humanity."

Downstairs, with my pajama bottoms on, as well as a top, I started the coffee pot. I said, "You don't have coffee at your house? The office?"

"Actually, I forgot to buy coffee for either place. Wife is mad at me."

"Coffee is like a goddamn staple," I said. "You don't forget that. That's just wrong."

"What my wife told me."

"So, what's up besides you being here drinking my coffee?" I said.

"Talked to some cop friends. They said Mrs. Devon reported her husband beating a boyfriend up, and the boyfriend, though he looked like he had been through a meat grinder, wouldn't press charges. Told them he got that way falling down. They didn't have proof otherwise. They think his masculine ego was harmed and he didn't want to harm it any more by admitting he got his ass beat like a bongo drum."

"So, do the cops believe her ex is bothering her?" I asked.

"They do, but they can't spend all their time waiting for him to show up."

"Course, if he shows up and kills her, they can put their time into that," I said.

"Well, they'll have a pretty good idea who did it. At least solving it will be easy enough."

"There's that," I said.

"Here's the thing, though. They told me if he bothers her, and you're there, don't mess him up too bad, 'cause then you'll be up a creek."

"They know we're watching?"

"Not officially, just my contact at the cop shop. He knows, and he's not telling. But, you mess this guy up too bad, they'll have to look around, and you two may come up in the investigation."

"What's the world coming to that you can't just give a good old-fashioned ass-whipping anymore?"

"He's doing what they think he's doing, they want you to whip his ass, just not so much he can make a good stink. If you can find him some place other than her place, that would be best."

"May not get to choose," I said.

About noon I drove over to Mrs. Devon's house, and parked in the back behind the garage, next to Leonard's car. We weren't being wide open about what we were doing, but we weren't being sneaky either. Sometimes a stalker isn't a full-blown nut, and just the presence of someone who might embarrass them, or put a stop to their actions, can end the matter.

Other times, however, it's worse than that, and what it takes is kicking their asses up under their hairline. Then, sometimes that's not enough. This situation was wide open.

I had been inside the house about five minutes, drinking a cup of coffee offered to me by Mrs. Devon.

I was sitting at the table with her and Leonard and the axe handle, which I had named Agnes.

She said, "Really. I don't want him hurt. I think you should just talk to him."

"That's the plan," I said. "This is just to dissuade six feet and three hundred pounds, if the need should arise."

"I really don't think it will come to that," she said.

I thought she was sounding a lot more confident today. Maybe it was just a good night's sleep.

The doorbell rang.

Mrs. Devon looked at me and Leonard, and we looked at each other. I got up and went to the door and looked through the little square of glass. There was a guy there. He wasn't big. He was carrying a briefcase. I didn't take him to be Mr. Devon.

I opened the door. The man looked at me in a kind of stunned manner. "Is Mrs. Devon in?" he asked.

"Who's asking?" I said.

"It's okay," Mrs. Devon said, came over, opened the door wider, unlatched the screen, and let the man in. "This is my lawyer, Frank Givens."

She gave him a quick kiss on the cheek and led him into the house and to the table, where he took a seat. I locked the screen back, and then the main door. I sat down in front of my coffee again. Givens was staring at Agnes lying on the table.

"I hope I'm not in the way, Sharon," Givens said.

"Of course not," she said. "This is Hap Collins and Leonard Pine. They are protecting me."

"Has Henry come back?" Givens asked.

"Not yet," she said. "And if he does, my friends here hope to encourage him to leave."

"Being a lawyer I don't know exactly what to say to that."

"We just want to talk to him some," Leonard said. "We can explain someone's position real good, we take a mind to."

"I bet you can," he said.

"They do look like gentlemen who can take care of themselves," Mrs. Devon said, "but then again, Henry is someone who can take care of himself as well."

"Yeah, but there's two of us," I said.

"And we have an axe handle," Leonard said.

"Its name is Agnes," I said.

"Have you seen him yet?" Givens asked.

"No," I said.

"Have you seen those old stills from the silent movie about the Golem?"

"Maybe," I said. "But if I haven't, I get the idea."

"Thing is, he really wants Sharon back," the lawyer said. "Not because he loves her, but because he wants her back. He thinks he owns her."

"Me and Henry were all right for awhile," she said. "I just made a big mistake."

"How long have you been married?" I asked.

"About . . . what is it, Frank?"

Frank looked as if the answer soured his stomach. "Almost four years."

She patted Frank, the lawyer, on the arm, said, "Me and Frank, we were married once."

"Oh," I said.

"It's all right," she said. "That was some years ago."

I looked at Frank. The look on his face made me feel that he might not think it had been that long ago.

"We were married young," Mrs. Devon said. "We got along fine, but the fire played out. And then I was on my own for awhile, a few years ago I met Henry. He was interesting. Worked in the oil business, and then the business played out, and so did we. I know that sounds terrible. Like it was the money. And maybe it was. We had a nice place, not like here. . . . Oh, I guess this is all right. But we had a nice place, and then the money was gone—"

"And the fire went out," I said.

"Are you being judgmental?" she asked.

"Quoting you," I said.

"You aren't paying us enough to be judgmental," Leonard said.

"Please be respectful," Givens said.

"I didn't mean anything by it," I said. "I'm just saying the fire went out for you, but not for him. I can see you're a woman that could have that effect on someone."

She smiled at me. "You think so?"

"I think so," I said.

She looked at Leonard and smiled. "What do you think?"

"I think heterosexual stuff is confusing to me. I like what men have in their pants, not women."

"Oh," she said. "Oh."

"That bother you?" Leonard said.

"No. No. Not at all. I just didn't know. I mean, you look so masculine . . . I didn't mean it that way."

"Yeah you did," Leonard said, "but it's all right. Look. The gay folk who fit your idea of gay folk are the ones that stand out. We come from both ends of the spectrum. Some of us even learn how to have sex with heterosexuals and fake a happy orgasm. Mostly those guys are preachers and politicians. Me, I'm a tough guy. Even us queers can make a fist. End of story."

"I assure you, I didn't mean anything by it," she said. "You come highly recommended. The both of you."

Looking at Mrs. Devon I had an idea then why Jim Bob wanted us to do this job. He probably still had the hots for her. She wasn't only good-looking, it was the way she talked, the voice, the way her eyes half-closed when she was serious. I even felt a little sorry for Henry then, and Frank Givens the lawyer. I felt like she was a woman that could tell you a sincere lie.

"I can see you're well protected by these gentlemen," Givens said. "That being the case, I'll get right down to business. I have the divorce papers with me. They're all set. He's contesting the divorce, but at this stage, there's nothing he can do to keep you from going through with it. All you need to do is sign."

"But he can be a pain in my ass," she said.

"That he can, Sharon," Givens said.

We left Givens and Mrs. Devon, who we had been told to call Sharon, sitting at the table discussing divorce plans. Me and Leonard went out in the backyard and stood around.

"How about that, Givens is her ex-husband," I said.

"And he still loves her," Leonard said. "And she doesn't even know it."

"Oh, she knows it all right," I said. "I think she's something of a manipulator."

"Starting to doubt her stories about hubby?"

"Not necessarily. I'm just saying she's manipulative. I think she's using Givens to get the kind of deal she wants for very little money. And she might be feeding him a little possibility, if you know what I mean."

"A chance to rekindle the fire."

"Yeah."

"Do we stick with it?" Leonard said.

"So far we don't know things are any different than what she says. But I do have the feeling I'm in a play. A bit actor."

"I know what you mean," Leonard said. "I feel a little played in some way, and I don't even know what it is. But we're getting paid."

"Yeah," I said. "There's that."

"Goes on too long we might have to ask for more money."

I nodded.

"But, if she doesn't offer us any more, and we haven't discouraged her hubby—"

"We'll stay anyway," I said.

"Yep," Leonard said. "It's our way. It's not a good way, but it's the honorable way."

"And it's just about all we got."

"Our honor?"

"No. Our way."

What we decided was Leonard would stay at the house, as originally planned, and I would try and locate the husband. If I could catch him leaving his place, lurking around Sharon's house, as soon as he acted like a threat, then I'd go after him. Probably after I called Leonard for reinforcements. We're tough, but we're not stupid. Double-teaming would be the best system. That way, we could possibly convince Henry the better part of being an asshole was staying at home and minding his own business, letting Sharon go her own path.

Sounded and seemed simple enough.

I had an address for him, and me and Agnes went over there and sat on a hill that looked down a wooded lane. I could see his driveway from there. I sat for a moment and got my shit together, then drove down and past his house and took a look.

The house was pretty nice, but it wasn't well attended. I could understand that. I hated yard work. The front yard was grown up and the trees needed trimming, and it stood out because the houses on either side of his were out of *House Beautiful*.

He had an open carport, and in the carport was a not too old Chevy truck. I drove to the end of the street, to the dead end there, turned around, and went back up and sat at the top of the hill. Up there the neighborhood changed, and was not so nice. I parked in the lot of an abandoned laundromat. There were other cars there. It had become a parking spot for the chicken-processing plant on the far side of the highway that broke Haven Street, the street Henry lived on.

I had a good view from my parking spot, and nothing was going on down below. I wondered if Henry had a job now that the oil had played out. I wondered if he had money. I wondered if he was as big as they said. I wondered why I was doing this.

I had a CD player with me, and I listened to a CD Leonard had given me, Iris DeMent. It was good stuff. A few years back I wouldn't have listened to it. When I was young I associated country with ignorance and backwoods. The music still carried some of that with it, but no more than what a lot of rap carried with it; when it was ignorant, it was urban ignorant. It always depended on who was doing it, and how it was done. I was thinking about that as seriously as if I were going to write a paper on it, when the house I was watching moved. Well, the door did. I saw a man big enough to eat the balls off a bear while it was alive and make it hold its paw against the wound walk out to the mailbox, open the lid, and yank out some mail. He was so big I was surprised he could get his hand in there. Frankly, I didn't know people could grow that big. He may have been six-five or six-six, but in that moment he looked seven-six. His shoulders were just a little wider than a beer truck and he was about as thick the other way as City Hall.

We had to deal with that motherfucker, we were going to need a bigger boat. Certainly a bigger axe handle. I think we had to graduate to a baseball bat. Maybe a cannon. He might take the axe handle away from us, swallow it, and pull it out of his ass as a sharpened stick with our names tattooed on it.

As I watched him walk back to the house, a little chill went up my back and crawled across my scalp. I pulled out my cell and called Leonard.

"Yeah," Leonard said.

"You know, this Henry guy. I just saw him. He's big."

"How big?"

"Do you remember that robot in *The Day the Earth Stood Still*?"

"Ouch."

"Exactly," I said.

"He still at home?"

"Yep."

"You gonna keep watching?"

"Ever vigilant," I said. "Just wanted you to know what we were up against. And for all we know, he's armed."

"You're exaggerating?"

"Nope, I'm being conservative. You know the remake of *The Day the Earth Stood Still*?"

"Yeah."

"The robot in that one. More that size."

"Bigger ouch," he said. "Watch yourself."

"If I want to see something way pretty, that's exactly what I do."

I closed up the phone and put on an old rockabilly CD and listened to that. This went on for hours, me sitting and listening to CDs. I went through everything I had twice and got so bored I was close to playing with my dick. Then I saw people coming from across the street toward the lot. A bunch of people.

I looked at my watch.

It was quitting time at the chicken plant. Or at least it was a shift change. Pretty soon I'd be the only car in the lot, and that wouldn't be as good. I was considering what to do next, if I needed a new parking spot or what, when I glanced down the street and saw Henry's Chevy pull out of the drive.

I followed him to a Burger King. He went through the drive-through and I pulled in after him. Looking at his head through the back window, it looked as big as a bowling ball, but with a close haircut.

He made his order, and then I ordered some fries and a big soda, and followed to the checkout window. He went through. I went through. He drove home. I parked again in the abandoned lot. It was just me up there with Agnes, my drink, and fries. And, of course, my precious thoughts.

Leonard called.

"You want to switch shifts?"

"Nope. I'm fine. I think I'll wait until after dark, then you can drive over and we'll swap out."

I told him exactly where I was parked, and hung up.

I rolled down my window. The air was cool. The mosquitoes, however, were busy. I was about to roll the window up again when I heard a shot.

I was positive it had come from Henry's house. I had seen a flash of light behind the window. And it was a gunshot. I was certain. I had heard quite a few of them. I thought about just going home or waiting for a neighbor to call, but all the houses were dark on either side of Henry's, and since it wasn't really late, I figured no one was home. If they were, they might not have even recognized what the sound was. Sometimes shots don't sound like much, especially when they come from a small-caliber gun.

I had a revolver in my glove box. I got it out. I picked Agnes off the seat and got out of the car. I put the gun under my shirt, in my waistband. I carried Agnes in my left hand and held her down by my side. The street was pretty dark for the neighborhood. There was no one moving about except a cat, and he didn't seem all that interested.

I went across the street slowly and came up in Henry's yard. I thought I should have called Leonard, but I hadn't. I had just reacted. In the stealth business they call that poor planning.

I took out my phone and turned it off and put it back. All I needed was for it to ring while I was putting on the sneak. I went to the front door and touched it, using my shirttail to tuck my hand into. No use leaving prints.

The door was locked.

Okay.

I eased around the edge of the house, and now I had my gun out. I was breathing a little heavy. Maybe Henry had fired the shot. Popping a rodent. Didn't like a TV show and was showing it what he thought of it. There could be all kinds of explanations. The one I figured most likely was that someone had shot someone.

Taking a deep breath, I eased my head around the edge of the house, stooping down low to do it. No one was there. The yard was open, with no fence at the back, but there were some thick trees and they went over the hill toward where the highway curved.

I eased around and took a better look. The back door was a sliding-glass door. It was open. I went over there on tippy-toes and looked inside. Dark in there. I moved away from the door and leaned against the wall and thought things over. The smart thing was to call Leonard. Or go away. Those were good choices and safe.

Me and my gun and Agnes went inside.

It was dark and I couldn't see, and I figured if anyone was still in the house, they'd have had time to adjust to the dark. They would be able to see fine. They'd be able to shoot fine.

I leaned against a wall and thought that any moment there would be a shot I wouldn't hear, and it would be all over.

Around the corner from where I leaned was a hallway. There was a break to the left. There was some light in there, but it was the outside light. It was darker in the house than outside.

I moved from my spot, inching carefully into the room beyond the hall. It was a kitchen. A nice kitchen with a nice table and chairs and a coffee pot I could see on the counter, and leaning over the sink, his elbows in it, his knees on the floor, was our big guy Henry.

I said, "Henry?"

Henry didn't call back.

I went over easy, and a little wide. There was a light switch on the wall next to the sink. I used the back of my wrist to flip it on. The top of Henry's head was up against the windowsill. He must have been looking out the window when it happened. Maybe at me and my car up there at the parking spot; he might have had my number early on, standing there in the dark seeing what I was doing while someone was coming in to see what he was doing. Someone with a gun. There were brains and blood on the wall and a little on the window, and a lot of it had run down into the sink; most of it had gone down the drain, but as the blood pumped slower, it had started to go thick. He was still big, but that didn't matter much now. You don't get too big for a bullet, if it's placed right.

I didn't shake him to see if he would come around.

I leaned Agnes against the wall, got out my phone and called Leonard.

"Yeah," Leonard said.

"You know that big guy?"

"Uh-huh," he said. "Henry."

"We are not going to have to fight him. We are not going to have to deal with him."

Leonard was silent for a moment. "That doesn't sound good."

"Not for him it isn't."

"You hurt him?"

"No."

"Killed him?"

"No. But someone did."

"Shit," Leonard said. "You sure he's dead?"

"Oh, yeah. The splattered brains gave him away."

Lights jumped around outside the window. I took a look. Cop cars.

"My turn to say shit," I said.

"What?" Leonard said.

"I think our donkey is in a ditch."

The chief of police said, "I see you so much, maybe we ought to have a chair put in, something with your name on it, like those movie directors have."

"That would be nice," I said. "Maybe with a built-in drink holder."

We had gotten off the subject, but we had sure been on it a lot for the last hour or so. My butt was tired and I had answered the same question so much it was starting to sound new when I heard it. I was starting to think maybe I should make up new answers. The truth wasn't working.

"Why don't you kind of run over things again," the chief said.

"So you can see if I slip up?"

"That's the idea, yeah."

"I might ought to call for a lawyer."

"You asking for that?" the chief said.

"No, I'm just thinking about it. But without a lawyer, I'm going to say it one more time. I didn't kill him."

"You had a gun on you."

"Weak ploy, Chief. Wrong caliber."

"You can't know that," the chief said.

"I've seen what a gun like mine can do. It would have made a bigger mess."

"Maybe you had another gun."

"Sure. Two-Gun Hap. What did I do with the other one, hide it up the big guy's ass?"

"We can take a look."

"Go right ahead. There's no one going to stop you. Least of all Henry. You can prowl around in there all day. Bring the kids."

"All right," the chief said. "I don't think you did it."

"That's nice of you," I said.

"Least not by yourself," he said. "I'm thinking there was you and your partner, Leonard, and he got away. Quick out the back door."

"That's a shitty theory," I said. "He was with Sharon Devon, being a bodyguard."

I had told him all of this, but he liked to pretend we had never discussed it. It's how we danced. I figured Leonard was in another room with someone else, being interrogated same as me.

"So, what's your theory?" he asked.

"My theory is I was there to make sure he didn't bother his soon to be ex-wife."

"And how were you to do this?"

Now we were getting into new territory. "Idea was to keep an eye on him."

"And if he went to see his wife with bad intent?"

"I was supposed to dissuade him."

"And how, pray tell, were you supposed to do that?" the chief asked.

"I was going to reason with him. Really, man. We been all over this so many times you could tell me my story."

"Reason with him, huh," he said. "I got to keep coming back to the part about you were in his house and he was dead and you had a gun and an axe handle."

"Sometimes reason requires visual aids," I said.

"Just wrap it up a little," he said, leaning back in his chair, placing his hands behind his head. "Tell me the good part, about how you went in the house and found him like that. Tell me why you went in again."

I sighed. "I was watching the house. I heard a shot. I went down there and went in the back way. The door was open. Henry was hanging on the sink. I think he knew I was following him. Not at that moment. He didn't know anything right then. But before that I think he knew. He made me."

"A clever boy like you?" the chief said.

"Even squirrels fall out of trees. But maybe he was looking up the hill at me in my car. Someone was in the house. They may have come in the back way. The door was open. They snuck up on him."

"That could be Leonard," the chief said.

"But it wasn't," I said.

"You might not have found the door open," he said. "You might have broke in to kill him. The lock had been worked. We could tell from the scratches. A lock kit. You could have come in using that."

"Did you find a lock kit on me?"

"Maybe you stashed it somewhere with the other gun, the one you used to shoot Henry."

"Yeah," I said. "I stuck them both down the commode along with my spare Range Rover and flushed them."

"Yeah, that doesn't seem so likely," he said. "I think all those things together might cause a clog. I mean, you know, after the Range Rover."

"What was I saying?"

"You heard a shot."

"So, someone slipped in and shot Henry. I heard the shot. I went down there. When I did, whoever killed him saw me. I figure they were in that patch of woods behind the house. They called the cops. It put you on me and off of them, whoever them is."

"The one with the lock-pick kit and the right-caliber gun?" he said.

"That would be him or her, yes."

"You want a candy bar?"

"What?" I said.

"Candy bar," he said. "I got a couple in the drawer."

"Really?"

He opened his desk drawer and took out two Paydays and put them on the desk. "Go ahead," he said.

I took one and peeled the wrapper off and put it on the desk. "It's a little warm, kind of melted," I said.

"It's free," he said.

"That's true," I said, and took a bite. When I finished chewing, I said, "You don't think I did this, do you? I mean, you said you didn't, but really, do you?"

"No, but you're the kind of guy who could do it," he said.

"Shoot him in the back of the head?"

"I think you'd do it any way you could get it done," he said. "I planned to shoot a guy big as Henry, I'd have shot him in the back of the head. You know, these are pretty good."

"Yeah," I said, and ate the rest of mine.

The chief eased out his breath. "No, I don't think you did it, but it's my job to ask, and I can't treat you any different from anyone else."

"And if you act like you're really on my side, give me a candy bar and all, I'll slip up and tell you something that will hang me."

"It's the sort of thing that's happened," he said.

"But not to me," I said.

"So it's not working?"

"Nope."

"You can go," he said. "But we might come back around to this again. Same questions. Maybe some new ones to go with it. Could be your answers will change."

"Just restock on candy bars," I said.

I got up and went out.

———————

Leonard came to the house about an hour later. When he came in I poured him a cup of coffee and put it on the table along with a bag of vanilla cookies.

"I had a candy bar," I said. "Did you?"

"No . . . they gave you a candy bar?" he said.

"Yep. It's my charm."

"What kind of shit is that?" he said. "They didn't offer me a candy bar. They didn't offer me a fucking stick of gum."

"Did you talk to the chief?"

Leonard shook his head. "I talked to a major asshole who was about five-four and wanted to be six-six and wished twelve inches of that would be dick. Tell you another thing, I saw Sharon there when I came in, and she looked at me like I had crapped a turd on the tile."

"Yeah?" I said.

"Yeah. And the guy grilling me, he said she rolled over on us."

"They lie like that to get you to give things up," I said.

"I know that, Hap. You think I don't know that?"

"I know you know that," I said. "I'm just saying."

"What I'm telling you though, I saw her there in the hall, and I got the vibes."

"Tell me about the vibes," I said.

"I think we been butt-fucked vibes, that's what they were."

"Define butt-fucked."

"She had you go over there to watch the guy, and then she had someone go over there and pop him, and guess who takes the rap?"

"They're going to have a hard time proving I shot him with the wrong gun and hit him with an axe handle when I didn't."

"They think she hired you and me to pop him," Leonard said. "That's how it looks, so to help herself out, to make them not think that, she's got to paint us like we went rogue on the

122 | HAP AND LEONARD

deal. Just decided it was easier to lay him down than to follow him around. She may have had it planned that way all along."

"It could be like that," I said. "Though you were at her house."

"But that doesn't do you any good, and she could still make me part of the plan. Say I wasn't there. I could get the rap as the actual shooter."

"She sure seems to be tossing us on the track in front of a train quick-like," I said. "Quick enough you got to wonder."

"Yep. . . . Where's Brett?"

"She picked up a shift for a friend. . . . So what do we do now?"

"I suggest," Leonard said, "we don't let ourselves get screwed any more than we already have. That's what I suggest."

"How do we do that?" I asked.

"I ask questions, as wise men do. I do not provide the answers."

"So, you think I'll come up with something?" I said.

"Probably not," he said. "Why I asked where Brett was."

At Marvin's office I sat in the chair in front of the desk and Leonard sat on a stool by the counter with the coffee. He had the bag of vanilla wafers with him. He had not offered me or Marvin any, and I was the one who bought them for him. He was sipping a cup of Marvin's bad coffee and eating the wafers. He would put one in his mouth and close his eyes and look as satisfied as a lion with a gazelle in its stomach. If he had had a Dr. Pepper, his favorite drink, he would have floated to the ceiling and farted vanilla.

"That doesn't sound good," Marvin said, after I explained it to him. "You know what's worse? She never paid her bill."

"That is the least of our worries," I said.

"It's high on my list," he said. "Hey, I didn't ask you guys to kill him. I just wanted you to do right, get me paid so I could dole out a few bucks to you two. That way, I would have enough for a house payment."

"Funny," I said. "Leonard, think you might want to get in on this? Considering we might go to prison or get a needle in the arm for something we didn't do?"

"I wasn't in the house," Leonard said. "I think I can turn on you and get a lighter sentence."

"And me," Marvin said, "I'm in pretty good shape. I just hired you guys to do a simple observation job. What the lady wanted. And the two of you went crazy. You went in there and shot him with an axe handle, Hap."

"Nice," I said.

"Look here," Marvin said. "Let's figure this thing. Jim Bob knows the lady, so maybe we start with him."

"Nobody knows where he is," I said. "I tried him on the phone before we came here. He's not answering for whatever reason. For now, he's out."

"Then we got to think about what it was we were asked to do. Lady comes in and says she has a recommendation, and it's from one of our best buddies, Jim Bob. She says she needs someone to protect her. To discourage someone. We take the job. You guys go over there and talk to her and hear her story and meet her lawyer. How am I doing so far?"

"Good," I said.

"She tells you her husband is big, and it turns out he is. She tells you he is scary and he beat up a boyfriend, a date, whatever. But the guy that got whipped won't press charges. Course, really, he doesn't need to. The cops can go after Henry anyway, if they want. But they think: All right, guy got a beating, wouldn't stand up for himself, so why should we bother? Kind of a Texas thing going there."

"Maybe," I said. "Shit, Leonard. Would you at least not smack?"

"Sorry," Leonard said.

"But whatever, they know he's going to be a shitty witness. Maybe he'll say he fell down a few times and got banged up because he wants to keep his Man Ticket. Won't admit he got a licking. By the way, this guy that took a beating. Who is he?"

I looked at Leonard.

Leonard said, "I don't know."

"Nor do I," I said.

"You know what?" Marvin said. "I think this guy, whoever he is, would be a nice place to start. I think anyone with detective skills would have already thought of that."

"We've been a little preoccupied," I said.

"And you have limited detective skills," Marvin said.

"Well, yeah, there's that," I said.

"Let me show you some detective work," Marvin said.

He called his friend on the force. The one that knew the guy's name. He wrote down the name and gave it to us.

Robert Unslerod.

Unslerod lived out in the country in a trailer. That was surprising. Not the kind of man Sharon Devon would date. Least I didn't think so. She struck me as someone who liked money, a man who wore a tie and took her to good dinners and when he dropped trousers he'd be wearing silk shorts. She was someone that at least wanted a man with a nice car to take her out. The car parked in front of the trailer looked like something the farm pigs drove when they went out for a spin. From the looks of things Unslerod seemed to belong in mine and Leonard's category. He seemed like the sort of guy Sharon Devon would wipe her ass on at best.

We knocked on the trailer door, but no one answered. Maybe Unslerod was actually taking a spin in his Porsche and this is just where he came to store his garbage. When he didn't answer,

I got a pad and pen out of my pocket and pressed it against the door to write a note.

The door swung open a little. A smell came out of there that was, to put it mildly, unpleasant.

"Not good, sir," Leonard said.

"Nope."

We went back to the car and stood by it.

"Call the cops?" I said.

"Might just be a dead raccoon under the trailer," Leonard said.

"That stink is from inside the trailer," I said.

"Might be a dead kitty cat inside," Leonard said. "Maybe he went off for the week and forgot to leave Fluffy his kitty food and water dispenser."

"And maybe that's not it at all," I said.

"Yeah, well, probably not," Leonard said, opened the car door and got my revolver out of the glove box and held it by his side. "You get the axe handle."

I got the axe handle. We went back to the trailer and I nudged the door with the toe of my old Tony Lama's. It slid back. I stuck my head around the corner. It was dark in there. The stink was terrible, worse when we got completely inside.

There was a pile in the hallway between the living room and the bedroom, near the open bathroom door. It didn't look like a lump in the rug. It was too big to be a cat.

"Shit," I said.

We went over and looked. It was a man, facedown. The floor under him was dark, like a hole had opened up there. He was only wearing dark boxer shorts; my guess was they were not silk. We couldn't tell too much about him there in the dark, but what we could tell was that he wasn't just having a little nap.

Leonard went past me, and, holding the revolver in front of him, he looked in the bathroom.

"No one," he said. He went along to the bedroom. The door was cracked. He looked in there. "And the hits just keep on coming."

I went over and looked. There was a nude woman on the bed. There was enough light through the curtains I could tell she wasn't napping either. It was hard to tell what she might have looked like. She was swollen up and her head was bloated. All I could tell was it was a female.

I used my elbow to turn on the light. She didn't look any more identifiable. She looked worse. She was lying on her back with a hole in her forehead. It reminded me of the hole in the back of Henry's head. The sheet under her head was dark and caked with blood. The sheet pulled over her went up to her waist. I was tempted to pull it over her head, but I resisted.

Back in the hall I used the axe handle to turn on the light so we could get a look at the man. He was facedown and was stuck to the floor by dried blood.

"Did you touch anything?" Leonard asked.

"The door with the toe of my boot and I used my elbow on the light. Wait a minute, I put the note paper against the door . . . I didn't touch anything but the paper though."

"Okay, let's keep it that way."

We went outside and breathed in clean air.

"They been dead awhile," Leonard said.

"No shit, Sherlock."

"And me without my deerstalker."

We got in the car. Leonard put my revolver back in the glove box. I put the axe handle on the backseat.

I said, "I hope no one saw us drive in."

"Probably not," Leonard said. "No houses much. We didn't pass any cars."

It was a good guess. There was only a little dirt road leading to the trailer, and the property was a pasture with high grass and some trees at the back. Still, someone could have watched us turn in. Nothing for it but to hope no one had seen us arrive.

I pulled onto the road and eased along. Driving fast would just draw attention to us.

"This whole business is starting to stink worse than that trailer," Leonard said.

"Yeah," I said. "I'm beginning to feel like you and me have been puppets all along, and that Sharon Devon is our puppeteer."

"Time we cut the strings," Leonard said.

We went to my place and Brett was home. She was cute in some old overalls worn over a paint-splattered shirt; it had got that way when we repaired a door and painted it. She had the cuffs of the overalls rolled up and she was barefoot. Her toenails were painted bright red. It went with her hair, which was tied back with a yellow tie. I made some coffee and we told Brett everything we knew. I always told Brett everything I knew. The only people I would tell that sort of thing were her and Leonard, maybe Marvin. Under certain circumstances, Jim Bob. In fact, when I got through telling Brett all we knew, she said, "Seems like you got to start with who put you in her camp.

"Jim Bob," she said.

"Makes sense," I said, "and maybe we can do that, but I got to say, if we were fooled, Jim Bob was fooled. And on top of that, I have tried him, without luck. He's not answering his phone. I figure he's turned it off on purpose. He may be in the middle of a job, and the kind of work he does often means the cell is off."

"I wasn't saying he had anything to do with it," she said. "Just that he might give you some insight."

"Yeah, he and Devon used to date," Leonard said.

"Way back," I said. "What I figure is she may have always been selfish, and over time, she became more of that. A whole lot of that. Enough so that it might lead to something that had to do with murder. Jim Bob, if he hadn't seen her in awhile, he wouldn't know that. Wouldn't suspect it. He'd remember her as the woman he dated."

"Problem with that," Leonard said, "is I was with her when Henry was killed. And somehow I can't see her breaking into that trailer and popping Unslerod and his girlfriend."

"Yeah," I said. "I figure whoever picked Henry's lock picked the trailer lock, caught Unslerod heading for the bathroom, shot him, and was in the bedroom before the woman knew what happened. They were probably both dead in less than fifteen seconds. If it took that long. Wouldn't have to be a professional killer, but someone who knew locks and was sneaky as an alley cat."

"Or professional," Leonard said. "I'm voting professional, but I'll settle it could be either way."

"Maybe you guys ought to forget all this," Brett said. "You're off the job. Not your problem, really. Maybe you stay out of it, she won't try to pin it on you."

"I don't want to feel like I let her set me up and she got away with it," I said. "Or that I somehow helped any plan she had all along to kill Henry. I don't know how I helped, but I have this horrible feeling I did. We only got how bad Henry was from her. Unslerod, what did he do? What did his woman do? I don't like it."

"You know what?" Leonard said. "Actually, we didn't just hear how bad Henry was from her. We heard it from the lawyer."

"And he's still in love with her," I said.

"Bingo," Leonard said. "You got any more cookies?"

Brett got up.

I said, "Don't show him the stash."

She laughed and opened a drawer next to the sink. It had two bags of vanilla cookies in it.

"And you know what, hon," she said to Leonard, "I got you some Dr. Peppers."

"Oh, hell," Leonard said. "I swear, darling, I am going to quit being queer and go straight so I can take you away from Hap and you can keep me supplied in cookies and Dr. Peppers."

Leonard was taking a nap on the couch, and Brett was upstairs in bed reading. I turned on the computer in Leonard's bedroom we had built onto the house for him and did some checking on Frank the lawyer. What I got was Frank's firm had been around a while. He owned it and employed other lawyers; in other words, he ran a large aquarium for sharks. I looked to find out about his cases, discovered his firm was pretty good. They had nice odds on their winnings. Not too many losses. They did everything from divorce to murder trials, but they didn't seem to be ambulance chasers. As far as I could tell, they didn't advertise on TV. They had been around long enough they didn't have to. I called Marvin, told him what I found, asked if he might be able to find out more from some of his contacts. "After all," I said, "as you have pointed out, you are the detective."

"An attempt at flattery?"

"How's it working?"

"I see it coming as clearly as an elephant trying to walk a high wire, so not so well."

"But, then again, aren't you the true detective?"

"Damn you, Hap Collins," he said. "It is working. You have found my weak spot."

I went upstairs and locked the door and took off my clothes and slid under the sheets with Brett. She was sitting up in bed with pillows at her back. She had the sheet pulled up over her. She had her reading glasses on, pushed down on her nose. She put the book in her lap.

"I hope you don't think you're going to get any," she said.

"Any what?" I said.

"Don't act coy with me," she said.

"I just got naked," I said. "It has nothing to do with you. I'm comfortable naked. Some of us are quite comfortable with our bodies, our nudity."

"Oh," she said.

"Yep."

"I'm reading, you know."

"How's the book?"

"Sucks."

"So, want to do the nasty?"

"That is far from romantic," she said. "But lucky for you I think a lot of that stuff is nonsense. The romantic stuff. I'm not as girly as I look. And then again, the book sucks, so that makes your suggestion a little more interesting."

"Dear, believe me," I said. "You are as girly as you need to be."

She laid the book on the bed beside her. She dropped the sheet. She was naked too.

"Surprise," she said.

The phone call woke me up. Brett stirred in my arms.

"You get that," she said.

I slipped loose of her and put my feet on the floor and picked up the phone. It was Marvin.

"You busy?" he asked.

"Not right now," I said.

"This Henry guy," he said. "He seems to have been a pretty straight dude. Made a lot of money in oil. He was a land speculator for the companies. His job was to get people to give up beautiful land so it could have trees cleared, the soil torn up by a bulldozer, concrete and oil drills put down. He made a lot of money. And then he didn't."

"It comes and goes," I said.

"People were drilling everywhere because of the oil shortage talk, and then when they drilled in some places and didn't find as much as they hoped, they quit drilling so much."

"And he quit making money," I said.

"But here's some things," Marvin said. "He has a daughter. Her name is Nora. My cop friends say she has been arrested. A lot. Mostly stupid stuff. Small amounts of drugs. Being at the wrong place at the wrong time with the wrong people. Not exactly a Bonnie Parker, more just troublesome. Lindsay Lohan without the fame and without that much money. Daddy had enough money to help her out of deep doo-doo, though, until he didn't."

"So what has she got to do with this?" I said.

"I'm not sure," Marvin said. "Maybe nothing. But she didn't get mentioned by Sharon Devon, did she?"

"Nope. The girl didn't come up in conversation," I said.

"My friend at the cop shop said Sharon and Henry always came down together to bail her out and such, and that it was pretty clear to them that the girl was close to Sharon. Like a mother. Her actual mother was dead. Car accident. Got an engine block through the chest."

"So, you're saying why didn't the dog bark in the night-time?" I said.

"That's right. If they had a daughter and were divorcing, and the daughter was close to them both, why didn't she come up in your conversation with Mrs. Devon? And where is she? She was supposed to be living with Henry. The cops have been looking for her too, and nothing. No one knows what happened to her."

"Connected?"

"Maybe," Marvin said. "Cops have tried to find her every which way, but it's like she fell off the face of the earth. I'm not sure what that means or what we should do, but something about it bothers me."

"The lawyer," I said.

"What do you mean?"

"I mean I figure he knows something more than we know and we ought to know it."

"Lawyers have client privilege," Marvin said.

"Sometimes that wavers if they think you're going to beat the hell out of them," I said. "Not saying we would, but maybe he could think we mean to, even if we don't say we plan to. Just sort of insinuate."

"Maybe we ought to just drop it," Marvin said. "A reason we ought to, and I have been holding this back for dramatic effect, is Sharon Devon went down to the station and said she didn't think you had anything to do with Henry's death, and that she sent you there, and you were only doing what she asked."

"That's kind of different than before," I said.

"I guess she thought about it," Marvin said.

"Or decided she didn't need that dodge anymore."

"Well, there's a little bit more," Marvin said. "She's got a big insurance policy. Henry left everything to her and he's got this policy that's worth about seven hundred and fifty thousand dollars. They weren't divorced, and he hadn't changed his will or his policy, so it all goes to her."

"So she didn't have any reason to make too much of a stink about us being involved," I said.

"It clears the palate some," Marvin said. "It gets attention away from her, and it's just another unsolved murder. And there's all that money. Maybe not as much as he would have had a few years back, but it's more than starter change."

"You think she had him hit?" I said.

"It happens," he said, "but if so, why hire us in the first place?"

"It made Henry look like a bad man and it made us look like someone who might have put him down, and it confused the situation. It doesn't seem to take much confusion to mess a jury up these days. If she could plant in people's mind that he was dangerous, any sympathy there might be for him could be negated."

"You sound like you're holding something back, Hap,"

Marvin said. "It's not what you're saying, but I know your tone well enough to know there's something missing here."

"Not really," I said. "I was going to get around to telling you. Maybe, like you, I was holding it back for dramatic effect. I meant to tell you earlier, but I wanted to think about things first. Unslerod, you remember him?"

"The guy that got beat up by Henry," Marvin said.

"He's dead, and a woman who was with him is dead too."

"Shit."

"I haven't called about it. I figured they weren't going to get any deader. Maybe stinkier, but not deader."

I gave Marvin the location of the trailer. That way he could contact his friend at the department, maybe keep me and Leonard out of it. Marvin too.

"This is getting more complicated," Marvin said.

"Still think we should let it go?" I asked.

"I think we ought to," Marvin said. "And I want to."

"But we won't, will we?"

"Of course not," Marvin said.

I had no sooner got off the phone than there was a knock on the bedroom door.

Leonard called out, "I woke up and I was all alone and I didn't know where you were."

"Go fuck yourself," I said.

"Get up and let him in," Brett said.

I got up and pulled on my pajama pants and T-shirt, unlocked the door, and let Leonard in.

"The cookies are missing," Leonard said.

"I put them up," I said. "You eat all of them if I don't hide them. You'll have a tummy ache."

"You hid Leonard's cookies?" Brett said. She was sitting up in bed with the sheet pulled around her. Her red hair fell against the white sheets and her fine skin and made her look like a goddess.

"They're not his cookies," I said.

"Are too," Leonard said.

"Yeah," Brett said. "They are. You go down there and give the baby his cookies."

I said, "You're spoiling him, you know."

When the lawyer, Givens, came out of the restaurant, we were waiting in the parking lot. We had followed him from his work and parked as near to his car as possible. We had been waiting all morning for him to leave his office, not even sure he would, but hoping eventually he'd come out. If he went to lunch we could maybe pull off talking to him easier than trying to set a time at his work and him not wanting to talk to us; we tried it that way, he could avoid us for ages. So, when he left we were watching from across the street and we followed him, and now, here we were, waiting.

While he was in the restaurant enjoying a good meal, Leonard and I were eating hot dogs from Sonic, which frankly, wasn't half bad.

We ate and waited, and after about an hour he came out. As he got close to my car we got out and started walking like we were going into the restaurant. He looked up from fumbling with his car keys and saw us.

"Hello," he said, and gave us one of those smiles you would expect from someone who had just discovered his zipper was down.

"Hey," I said, like it was a big surprise to see him. "How are you?"

"Okay. Just grabbing a little lunch."

"Yeah, well, good," I said. "We thought we'd have a little lunch ourselves."

"That's nice," he said. He couldn't have been more awkward than if he were standing on a mile-long razor blade over a gorge.

"You know, things really didn't work out for us on that gig with Mrs. Devon," Leonard said.

"Yes, of course," he said. "I know. Sorry about that."

He tried to dart for his car.

I said, "Thing is, we think a lot of what happened stinks. We think maybe we got played for fools."

"I'm sure you're mistaken," he said.

"Then you wouldn't mind talking to us?" I said.

"Did you follow me here?" he asked.

"Happy coincidence," Leonard said.

"Well, I don't know I have anything to say," he said. "Mrs. Devon is my client, and—"

"Oh, come on," I said. "It's just us guys talking here."

"She's more than a client. She's also a friend," he said.

"Ah," Leonard said, "I bet you feel more than that for her. I mean, hell, you were married to her for awhile, and to think that big jock Henry was riding her around the bedroom like she was a pony had to get your goat."

"That is inappropriate," Givens said.

"So is framing our ass," Leonard said.

"Mrs. Devon has made it clear you had nothing to do with what happened," Givens said. "It was just an unfortunate coincidence."

"Coincidence, huh?" Leonard said. "You know what I'm thinking, and I'm just thinking here—"

"And for him to do that, he has to really be serious," I said, "because it hurts his head."

"There you have it," Leonard said. "But I'm thinking since you knew Hap was watching Henry's house, you sneaked over there and picked the lock and shot Henry. Hap hears the shot, like maybe you thought he would, and he comes in and looks bad for it."

"I already told you Mrs. Devon says it was a coincidence, and the police believe her."

"That's good," I said. "Really, but we still got to wonder if that was part of the original plan, to have our dicks mashed between two bricks."

"I didn't shoot anyone. I don't even own a gun, and I don't know how to pick locks, and if I were going to frame someone, I'd find a better way to do it than that. Hoping you heard a shot and came in and got framed. That's not a very good plan."

"It wouldn't have mattered if I came in," I said. "All that mattered was I was there, and the cops could fill in the rest of the blanks."

"Wouldn't you have to have the same kind of gun that killed him?" Givens said. "Wouldn't you have to have a gun that had been fired?"

"Okay," I said, "you're starting to sound more convincing. Listen, let me put it another way. We really don't know you had anything to do with it. We're just fishing. But we don't like being played for idiots. Some might think that happens daily, but they would be wrong. Leonard just looks foolish, he's not."

"Thanks," Leonard said. "That was mighty white of you."

Givens said, "Good day," and made like a bullet for his car.

I trailed after him. When he got to the car, unlocked it and was opening the door, I said, "Thing is, if you two have something going on that's got nothing to do with us, maybe we can help. Maybe you ought to talk to us."

Givens looked back at me, paused. I thought for a minute he was going to say something, but instead he got in his car and drove away.

"He hesitated," Leonard said. "I think that help line got to him."

"I was just throwing it out there, seeing if it had a hook on it."

"I think it did," Leonard said. "And some bait, and he almost went for it. That makes me think maybe he's telling the truth. Or part of the truth. That they didn't set us up. But it's also got

Hap Collins (James Purefoy) and
Leonard Pine (Michael K. Williams)

"Not nearly as many miles as either of those but they were
made up of plenty of great forest and deep water,
and they were beautiful, dark and mysterious—a wonder
in one eye, a terror in the other."
—*Savage Season*

"Leonard put on his equipment, shuffled his feet, put up his hands and made his way toward me."
—*Savage Season*

"Well, what say we go up to the house and
meet the rest of the gang?"
—*Savage Season*

me thinking he knows more about what happened than he's letting on."

"I keep telling myself if we're out of it, we ought to let it go," I said.

"I know," Leonard said. "But you know, that would be a first, and I'm not sure I want to start down that road. Next thing, I'll break down and buy my own cookies. And you know that ain't right."

We had just pulled away from the restaurant when my cell rang.

It was Marvin. He said, "I got a call from Givens."

I had it on speaker, so Leonard heard it. "That was quick."

"So, does this mean we're in trouble?" I said.

"No," Marvin said. "I think something you did may have worked out. He wants to see you at his office, downtown in an hour. It's a pleasant request. He even said please and that he's thought over what you said and he wants to talk straight."

"Interesting," I said.

"Find out how interesting."

We stopped by Starbucks and sat at a table and had coffee in mugs. Since I found out you can have it in a ceramic mug if you don't plan on carrying it off, I had it that way every chance I got. It tastes better.

We drank our coffee, and then went over to the law office and rode the elevator up to the third floor. When we got there the office door was open. Frank Givens and Sharon Devon were both there. Sharon was in a chair near the desk. She looked as if she had just seen her own ghost.

Givens was standing up behind his desk. As we came in, he said, "Shut the door."

I shut it.

"I started to say something in the restaurant lot," Givens said, "but you see, part of the problem was who I had lunch with today. I wanted to get out of there as swiftly as possible. Before he came out. I didn't have your number, so I called your boss."

"Sometime boss," Leonard said. "Actually, he can't do without us."

"So you weren't there to eat?" I said.

"I lied," Givens said. "I went in and I sat in a back booth in a conference room and got talked to by a person who is part of the problem. Him and his bodyguard."

I looked at Leonard, said, "Is any of this making any sense?"

"Not to me," he said. "But I'm still trying to figure out the ending to *The Sopranos*."

"I'm sorry," Givens said. "Please sit down."

There were two very comfortable leather chairs, and we sat in them.

Sharon Devon had not spoken a word. She looked as if she had been crying. Her eyes were red as sunrise and she looked more her age today, as if she had finally lost the war against it. I felt sorry for her. I feel sorry for just about everybody.

"We led you along some," she said.

"Figured that," Leonard said.

"Me and Henry," Sharon said, "we weren't really having trouble."

"Okay," I said.

"We were just pretending," she said.

I glanced at Givens. He didn't look too happy. I couldn't tell if it was about Henry and her not actually having trouble, or about something worse. I decided a little of column A and a little of column B. I had a suspicion there might even be a column C.

"So we were just sort of window dressing?" Leonard said.

She nodded. "Yes. You see, we have a daughter, Nora."

We knew that, of course, but we didn't say so.

"She is by Henry's previous marriage. I was never able to have children. But, I love her quite a bit. Nora was precious to me. She wasn't quite a teenager when we first met, but I took to her right away, and she to me. After that came the teenage years and Nora was pretty wild. Not that uncommon. I was pretty unruly myself. Nora started seeing boys we didn't want her to see, and she started experimenting with drinking and drugs. It made what happened later easy." She paused. Givens got up, went to a cabinet and pulled out a bottle of water, got a glass and a coaster and brought it over to her. He placed the glass on the coaster and unscrewed the cap on the water bottle and poured about half a glass.

Patiently, she waited while he did all this, as if a pause like this was the most natural thing in the world. For the two of them, maybe it was. When he was finished she sipped her water, delicately, placed the glass back on the coaster.

"You see, Henry really was in oil," she said. "And he really did have a loss of money. But part of the reason wasn't just a shift in natural fortune. There was a dismantling of fortune, and Henry was the cause. He liked to gamble. He liked to gamble a lot. Then the business went bad and he got into debt with the wrong people. He bet on some football games, some horses. He bet on just about anything. He would have bet on the number of freckles on my ass if I'd have been willing to let someone count.

"I loved him, but he was a gambling addict, and no matter how bad the people were he got into debt with, he kept letting the debt get deeper. Then they put interest on what he owed. Lots of interest. About double. They wanted him to get in deep, because they assumed he was a big shot, and that whatever problem he was having paying would go away, because they had had a few ups and downs with him before, and in the end, he had paid it off, and with interest. Lots of interest."

"But the downs didn't stop," I said.

She shook her head. "No. They didn't. He went to them and told them there was no way he could pay all that back if they kept compounding the interest, which they were doing. They didn't listen. He was late, so they added on a late fee, and added interest on that. He told them if they stopped compounding it, maybe he could pay it back, in time. He probably couldn't have paid it back if they had let him go back in time to the beginnings of the earth and work it off up until now. The business, it wasn't coming back. Not the way they thought it might. Fact was, he had lost the business, but they didn't know that."

Sharon paused and drank some more of her water.

"He let them think he was still making money. Maybe that was the right thing, to let them think that, because if they didn't think he could pay, they didn't have any reason to let him live. They even threatened me. We had some money. But it was just eating money, gas, enough to pay a few bills. We didn't have enough to pay them so that it would mean anything to them. That's when we came up with a plan. Idea was we'd divorce and sell the house."

"I don't see why you would have to divorce," I said. "Don't see the plan in that."

"Turns out it wasn't too good a plan," she said. "We tried to get clever because we thought we were smarter than a bunch of thugs."

"You probably are smarter," I said, "but not as clever. They're two different things."

"Or as ruthless," Leonard said. "That's something makes them real different."

"Why didn't you just go to the cops?" I said.

"For the same reason I said," Sharon said. "We thought we were smarter. We didn't want people to know about Henry's gambling debts. We thought we could work things out and no one would know, and we could make some kind of life together again."

"So what was the plan?" Leonard said.

Sharon drank more of the water and looked as if she might break out crying. She didn't. She said, "Thing was, Henry thought if we were divorced, at least they'd leave me alone. They didn't. And the man that I said I dated, that got beat up—"

"Let me guess," I said. "He isn't really your type."

"No," she said. "He was a messenger for the people Henry owed."

"And Henry beat him up, causing more problems," Leonard said.

"Yes," she said, "but there was already a problem. You see, the messenger came to my house because he said he wanted us to know that if we didn't pay he had our daughter. She had been seeing someone that was part of the problem. Jackie Cox. She was in with the wolves already."

"Ah, I got it," I said. "The Dixie Mafia Cox family."

"You know them?" she said.

I shook my head. "I know who they are. They took the place of someone who used to run this area's business. Those people we did know. They came to kind of a sad end."

"Rumor is," said the lawyer, "you were involved."

"Rumors are all over the place," I said.

"Jimson and his crew," the lawyer said, "they got killed in a filling station in No Enterprise, and the rumor is from cops I know, you and Leonard might have had something to do with that."

"We had our problems with Jimson," I said. "But no. That wasn't us."

And it wasn't. It was a young and lethal lady named Vanilla Ride who had put them down, but that's a different story.

I said, "I don't want you to be too disappointed about that, though. Me and Leonard, we've had our moments, and I figure you wouldn't have asked us here if you didn't know that, and didn't want us to have a moment again."

"Jackie was seeing our daughter," Sharon said. "She met him

because of my husband and his gambling dealings. He didn't intentionally introduce her to Jackie, but he used to have these tough guys coming around, and Jackie, he's the son of one of them."

"Richard Cox," I said.

She nodded her head. "They got tight quick. Maybe because he was a bad boy, and Nora liked bad boys. But then Henry owed them the money, things went bad, and then they sent this Unslerod around."

"He was kind of a tough guy they used," Givens said.

I didn't mention that he wasn't that tough anymore, and unless Marvin got in touch with his cop friend, Unslerod and his girlfriend were still collecting flies in a trailer out in the boonies.

"He said they had our daughter," Sharon said, "and if Henry didn't find some way to pay half, soon, and the other half almost as soon, they would harm her. Henry was already living apart from me, trying to set the divorce up to maybe make me safer, and then this guy came around. He was looking to talk to Henry. He thought he was tough."

"But Henry was tougher," I said.

"Much more so," she said. "He gave him a beating and they didn't get any money. It was a foolish thing to do, them having our daughter. I don't think Henry believed them at first. Then they sent this."

She opened her purse and took out a plastic bag and dug in the bag. When she got through with that she pulled out another plastic bag and unwrapped that. There was a pair of red thong underwear inside.

"These are hers," she said. "I bought them for her and her father didn't like that I did. All the girls were wearing them, she said, and I thought it was harmless. Anyway, they're hers. I know they are. It proves to me they have her."

"What we would like," Givens said, "is that you go and get

her back. That you make these men stop bothering Sharon. They killed her husband and took her daughter, and now they're pressuring her to pay. She can't pay. They have come through me with all this. They said Sharon goes to the cops, or doesn't pay something on what she owes, and by something they mean a substantial amount, they will send the part of her daughter that fits in the underwear to her in a cardboard box with a bow on it."

"How much time did they give you?" Leonard asked.

"Three days," Givens said, without waiting for her to answer.

At Marvin's office, he said, "So, how do you read it?"

"I think Henry got his dick in a crack," I said, "and he was too arrogant to take care of matters when he could, so he just kept it there and the crack got tighter. He didn't pay, so they took his daughter. They sent around a guy they thought was tough to collect and tell Henry how things were, that being Unslerod, and maybe he thought he'd play tough on Henry. Henry was tougher. Maybe Unslerod pissed Cox off with his failure, or maybe it was some other reason, but it seems more than likely Cox had him taken care of. His girlfriend was probably just in the wrong place at the wrong time. Later on it was Henry's turn. I figure Unslerod and the woman were dead some days before Henry, considering how their bodies looked. Way I understand it, Cox doesn't like failure, and he gives it a very short shelf life."

"Question comes to me," Marvin said, "guy owes you, why whack him if you want the money that bad?"

"That's the question me and Hap got to thinking on coming over here," Leonard said. "We got to thinking on it hard enough that I cell phoned Sharon. I asked her how they expected her to pay what was owed, and she said—"

"Insurance money," Marvin said, and snapped his fingers at the same time.

"Yep," Leonard said. "You are a wizard. She has a shit-full policy. Seven hundred and fifty thousand. Henry managed to keep that up, as protection for Sharon. That isn't even all Henry owes, but it's a good part of it. She told me that, I cleverly asked, doesn't it take time for the policy to pay out? And she said it did, and you know what?"

"The lawyer is helping her out," Marvin said, leaned back in his desk chair and placed his hands behind his head. "He's going to put the money up for her in return for the insurance money."

"Yep," Leonard said. "He's not only an ex-husband carrying a torch, he's a fucking saint."

"Sure he is," Marvin said. "Sure he is."

We drove over in my car and met the lawyer. We were going to go with him to the Dixie Mafia guy and they were going to give us the girl in exchange for the lawyer's money. When the insurance paid off, Givens was going to get his money back from Sharon. He was carrying a briefcase when he came outside his office and met us at the curb.

It was a nice day, and I wondered, as I often wondered, if it might be my last day on earth, if this might be the day I set out to do something simple and it turned bad and I'd end up in a ditch with crows pecking at my eyes.

Givens climbed in the backseat with his briefcase. He said, "We got to drive to Tyler."

"All right," I said, and I slipped away from the curb. "We meeting in the city?"

"That's the plan," he said. "It should go easy enough."

"They explained it to you?" Leonard said. "You got all the particulars down?"

"They just want the money," Givens said.

"What about the boyfriend?" I said. "Cox's son?"

"He was just the bait," Givens said. "He was the one that got her to trust him."

"And that's kind of what we are, aren't we?" I said.

Givens was quiet for a long moment. "I don't think I follow you."

"I might have to throw a few words in, but I figure you'll put it together pretty quick. I'm talking about you getting us to trust you, same as you say Jackie did with Nora."

Givens didn't say anything. I looked at his face in the rear-view mirror. He was doing a fair job of looking puzzled.

"Let me see the briefcase," Leonard said.

"Why?" Givens said. He put a hand on top of it where it rested on the seat.

"Because if you don't," Leonard said, "I'm going to have Hap pull over by the side of the road and I'm going to kick your ass so hard you'll be peeking out of your asshole."

"What in the hell is wrong with you guys?" he said.

"Let's just say we don't like your story," I said. "We look in the suitcase, see the money there, we might believe you better."

"It's there," he said.

"Show it to us," Leonard said. "And right now. I'm feeling edgy."

"He wanted vanilla cookies," I said, "but he got up too late, and I had eaten all of them with my coffee. You don't want to make him mad when he hasn't had his cookies."

Givens had no idea what his life had to do with vanilla cookies, and frankly, neither did I, but it was on my mind. Cookies are not cheap, I'll have you know. Not when your brother eats them by the bagful. What really made me mad was Leonard didn't gain a pound. I looked at cookies too long and I could feel myself gaining weight.

Leonard leaned over the seat and held out his hand, said, "And that gun you got under your coat. I saw it when you got in the car. Reach for it and I'll be over this seat pronto and stick it up your nose."

"I just brought it for safety," he said.

"But you told us they said not to bring guns," I said. "They making like a special deal just for you?"

"Hand me the case," Leonard said. "While you're at it, hand me the gun. Never mind."

Leonard went over the seat and was on top of Givens so fast Givens probably thought Leonard had a warp drive up his ass. I glanced in the mirror. Leonard was practically sitting in Givens' lap. He reached the gun from under Givens' suit coat and threw it in the front passenger's seat. Then he slapped Givens across the face, twice, fast as the beat of hummingbird's wings, then got off Givens' lap and picked up the briefcase. Givens held his hand to his mouth as blood dribbled between his fingers.

"You didn't have to do that," Givens said.

"I thought I did," Leonard said. "Soon as I saw that bulge in your coat, I knew you'd lied to us, that you were putting our lives in danger by bringing your gun, or that there was more to things than you wanted us to know."

"Another thing," I said, "just for the record, we brought guns ourselves. Because, you know what? We didn't believe you. First, you're a lawyer, and that's a mark against you, and second, you still got a thing for Sharon, and third, you putting up that kind of jack for your former wife seems unlikely, love her or not. You may be a lying scumbag lawyer who makes a lot of jack, but it's hard to think even you got seven hundred and fifty thousand just lying around? Possible, not likely. So, that means you got something else going on here. Something that might even make you look like a bit of a hero, and we would be there to witness you turning the money over and taking the girl back. That could ingratiate you to Sharon, couldn't it?"

"We don't do this right," Givens said, "it'll turn out bad. Real bad."

Leonard opened the briefcase. "Well, now, ain't this some shit," he said.

Leonard turned the case toward me. It only had a pile of empty manila folders inside.

"That won't pass for money," I said.

"No," Leonard said. "It won't."

I pulled over to the side of the road and put the car in park and looked back over the seat at Givens.

"Lay it out," I said. "No stalling. No stories within stories. Lay it out."

"No one was meant to get hurt," Givens said.

"Yeah," I said, "it's all fun and games till someone loses an eye."

"Henry owed the money, and well, I know the people involved. You might say I handle their affairs."

"You're their lawyer," I said. "The Cox family."

"That, among other things."

"That's goddamn typical," Leonard said.

"I do odds and ends for them here and there. Henry owed them and they wanted their money, and they knew I knew Sharon and that I had been married to her."

"Favor time," I said.

"Yeah," he said. "They wanted me to put the screws on her to make Henry give up the money. I thought if we had someone threaten Henry he'd give it up. I was sure he had money in some hidden account somewhere. They sent Unslerod around and he didn't work out so well."

"Henry turned out to be tougher than they thought," I said.

"He did," Givens said. "Then Unslerod decided he'd blackmail me by threatening to let Sharon know I worked for the organization."

"The organization," Leonard said. "I like that. The Dixie Mafia and Cox you mean."

Givens nodded.

"That meant you had to get rid of Unslerod," Leonard said. "And when you did, the woman just happened to be there."

"Something like that," Givens said, and I saw in his eyes then something that made me shiver a little. He may have been a frightened weasel, but I knew in that moment I had to keep my eye on him. Because nothing is more dangerous than a frightened weasel. They have no loyalties but themselves.

"That was cold," Leonard said.

"He was a deadly man," Givens said.

"But not so deadly you couldn't sneak up on him and shoot him," I said. "And then the woman."

"It just worked out that way," Givens said. "I used a credit card on the door and I surprised him. Well, he surprised me too. I shot him, and then I went in the bedroom and she was there and I didn't have any choice. I shot her too."

"No choice, huh?" I said.

"I didn't think so," Givens said.

"So what happened next?" I said. "Better yet, let's go back in time to Nora."

"I didn't want to do that, but I set it up so Jackie could meet Nora. He got her interested in him, and then she moved in with him."

"She wasn't kidnapped?" Leonard said.

"No," Givens said, sighing so loud it was like a windstorm blew into the car. "What I thought was it could look like a kidnapping. Cox said that would be good, and his boy Jackie was for it. And so was Nora."

"Nora was in on it?" I said.

"Yeah," he said. "She was. Big time. Way we arranged it was we'd hold her for ransom and Henry would come through. Like I said, we all thought he had money and was holding back, and that if he thought Nora was in danger he'd give it up."

"Only problem was he didn't really have any money," I said.

"Correct," Givens said. "No money. Or at least I don't think so now. He loved Nora. I think he would have come through if he had any."

"So you revised the plan, and the revised plan included bad things for Henry," Leonard said.

"I didn't so much revise it because I wanted to, but because I had to. Cox had one of his men do in Henry. A black guy named Speed. He's big as Henry, but more dangerous."

"Let me guess the rest," I said. "You told them they had to do Henry because you knew about the insurance policy. You never planned to give Cox your money until you got the policy money. You'd just pretend to take Sharon off the hook. Me and Leonard would be there as witnesses, and you'd hand them the briefcase full of folders, and they would give you Nora, and you would bring her home like she was let go, and when the money came through, you'd give it to Cox because he liked the plan and didn't mind temporary ownership of folders and a briefcase. When you paid them the insurance money, minus you and Nora taking a little off the top for your troubles, no one would be the wiser."

"It wasn't all that Henry owed," Givens said. "But it was enough for them to be satisfied, and it would take Sharon out of the mix."

"And you'd look real good in her eyes," I said.

He nodded. "I suppose that's true."

"You and Nora are some pair," I said. "Nora cheating her grieving stepmother for some dollars and for this Jackie Cox, and then you cheating Sharon. Not to mention committing murder."

"That's pretty much it," Givens said.

"You know," I said. "One revision on what I said earlier. I don't think you brought us along so we could say what a hero you were. I think you brought us along because Sharon insisted. She said she wanted us along to make sure things went well. She wanted us to protect you and Nora. How am I doing?"

"All right, I guess," Givens said.

"You know what, Givens?" Leonard said. "I didn't check you out so good. I see you are trying slowly to ease your hand down to your sock, where I suspect just under your pants leg is a holstered handgun that you hope to pull and shoot me and Hap with."

Leonard poked the gun he had gotten off the front seat against the side of the lawyer's well-combed hair, just over his temple. "What you want to do is tug up your pants leg, pinch the gun out by the grip with thumb and forefinger, and hand it to me easy as if it might blow up."

Givens did as he was told. Leonard took the gun. He tossed it over the seat into the passenger seat and hit Givens across the head with his own gun, right over the ear. It knocked Givens sideways. He reached up and held his head. When he moved his hand there was blood on his fingers.

"You sonofabitch," Givens said.

"And don't you forget it," Leonard said.

I had some tissues in the car and I gave some to Givens and had him wipe the blood off his head and hand.

"What we're going to do," I said, "is we're going to go through with this plan. Almost. We're going to have you waltz in there with the briefcase. We're going to have you be a really nice guy and not let on we know dick about what you're doing, 'cause if you do, we will kill you deader than a tree stump.

"When we get the girl, both of you get a drive to the police station. We'll call Marvin and have him grease the path for us with the cops. We'll turn you and her over to them, let you figure out how to explain extortion, illegal gambling profits, murder, and fraud, or whatever the fuck crimes we got here. Thing is, we play this right, we get you two and they get the briefcase, thinking they're going to get insurance money later, and you get to leave without a hole in your head. How's that plan?"

"Cox won't forget," Givens said.

"We'll see how that turns out," I said. "We got long memories ourselves."

Givens didn't say anything. I figured he didn't like the plan.

The meeting place was on the first floor of a two-floor parking garage in Tyler. Just before we got there we pulled over, and Leonard made Givens get up front in the passenger seat, and he sat directly behind him. He had both of Givens' guns and one of his own he had brought, and I had mine from the glove box tucked in a holster at the small of my back, with my shirt pulled down over it.

When we drove inside the garage we went to spot 15, as Givens said for us to do. A big black car—of course it was black—was waiting. We pulled up behind it and a man got out. He was an exceptionally large black man that moved like a cat; frankly, he moved the way Leonard and I do. I'm just telling it like it is. One bad man can spot another, even if that bad man is me and I'm feeling a lot less bad these days. I figured he was the aforementioned Speed. He was dressed in an expensive black shirt, coat, pants, shoes, and a very glossy black dress jacket that couldn't have been off the rack, not and fit those shoulders. His head was shaved and it looked to have been waxed. It was shiny enough you could have used it as a mirror to comb your hair.

"You go on and get out," Leonard said to Givens. "I'd be real cool, I was you."

Leonard got out, and Givens got out.

Speed looked at me behind the wheel. He was expression-less, which was expression enough. Guy like that, not showing much in his features, you had to watch him. Wasn't the kind of fella that would give you many signals before he shot or punched you or drove a car over your ass.

I had my window rolled down. I said, "Hey, how's it hanging?"

152 | HAP AND LEONARD

Speed ignored me. He looked at Leonard and Givens. They had come around to the front of the car.

"Givens," the big man said.

"Speed," Givens said.

"Hey," Leonard said. "How about this weather?"

"Which bozo is this?" Speed asked.

"Leonard," Givens said. "Guy behind the wheel is Hap."

"How's it hanging?" I said again.

Still no evaluation of the general hanging condition of his meat was offered by Speed.

"Here's the thing," Speed said. "You got no guns, right?"

"Not exactly," Leonard said. "I actually got some guns."

Speed turned his attention to Givens. "You were told no guns."

"They go their own way," Givens said.

"That's right," Leonard said. "Way I see it, since we're all pals we won't be shooting anybody, right? You came with a gun, because I see it under your well-cut coat."

"You don't leave the guns," Speed said, "we don't go."

"How about we get where we're going, we all put our guns in a pile," I said. "Till then we keep them. You see, the lawyer here told us your rules, but we're here to make sure he don't get shot and we don't either. To make sure it works out that way, we got to have rules of our own. One of which is we hang onto our guns until it looks like it's okay to let go of them."

I knew that since this was a scam, there was no real threat in saying we wouldn't give them the briefcase. Cox wanted the meeting to happen, to set it up so Givens could give him the insurance money eventually.

It was a big joke, but a joke only works if you play it right. Thing was, they didn't know we were in on the joke. We had a few laughs of our own planned.

Speed let what I said move around in his thoughts for awhile. His expression didn't change.

"You follow me out," he said.

He got back in his car and we backed out from behind him. He pulled from his parking place and drove off. We followed. I saw that he was on his cell already.

When Bad Guys start directing you outside of town it's always a crapshoot. But that's where we were going, outside of town. We passed what used to be Owen Town. It was really nothing more than an asphalt path and a couple of storage buildings. It had never been a town since I was alive, but it used to be a place where aluminum chairs were made. I worked there when I was young.

We went along until we came to the cutoff for Starrville, a little burg so small most of the inhabitants could have lived in one house, and maybe a shed out back. We didn't go all the way there. Instead, we stopped in the Starrville Cemetery. There was another black car like the one Speed was driving already parked there. The windows were dark. A man got out from behind the wheel. He was a big white guy with a crew cut. He was almost as big as Speed. His jacket, an ugly plaid thing, fit him the way a designer dress fits a hippopotamus.

Speed got out of his car. We got out of ours. After a moment, the back door of the other car opened and a man slid out, leaving the door open. It was Cox. I had never met him, but had seen a couple photos of him on the Internet, usually something to do with law-breaking. He always claimed to be innocent, and always got out of whatever problem he was in. He was a tall, lean man with gray, well-cut hair, and a look about him that said he liked things his way. He was dressed in a nice gray suit to go with the hair. My dad always told me not to trust anyone who ran around in the middle of the day with a suit on. If they wore one because they were on their way to preach, he told me to watch them even closer.

"So," said Cox, "we're here to deal."

"If you got something to deal with," I said.

"They got guns," Speed said.

Cox glanced at Speed. "What did I tell you?"

"No guns," Speed said, but he didn't look worried about the situation. My guess is it was mostly show. My bet is when I saw Speed was on his cell phone, he was calling ahead to tell Cox we had guns.

"We just want to play even," I said. "Your man here has a gun. And I'm going to guess the guy in the plaid coat has one too. Wouldn't surprise me you had one. All I'm saying is we all keep our guns and stay friends. Having us put ours up and you keeping yours, that wouldn't be playing fair. And me, I'm all about fair play."

"You said we would put them all in a pile," Speed said.

"I lied," I said.

"All right," Cox said. "We'll play your way." He looked at Givens. "Got the money?"

Givens held up the briefcase they both knew was empty.

"Good," Cox said.

"You got the girl?" Leonard said.

"I do," Cox said.

He looked back at the car. A young man who looked a lot like Cox, but with black hair, got out. He poked his hand back inside the car, when he pulled on it, a girl came out with it. She was dressed in jeans and a T-shirt. She wasn't wearing a bra. This wasn't a negative. She had unreal red hair and a pretty face, but there was something about it that made you want to throw a pie at it.

Givens said, "These men, they know what the real deal is."

I looked at Leonard. He looked at me. The cat had just jumped from the bag.

Givens walked over to Cox's car carrying the briefcase. He stood by Cox.

"They know," he said. "They know and they're trying to work me to get the girl back. They know she's in on it."

"Yeah," Cox said, "and how do they know that? You tell them?"

"They figured it," Givens said.

"That's right," Leonard said, "we're pretty smart for old country boys. We can even tie a square knot in the dark."

I let my hand drift to the edge of my shirt. Speed eased his coat back. I think the guy in plaid was still trying to figure out what everyone had said. Cox didn't look any different at all. Oh, maybe a bit irritated, but nothing more. The girl looked at the young man, who I figured was Jackie, then looked at Cox. She seemed to be waiting for someone to tell her something.

"All right, so they know," Cox said.

"They plan on taking me and her to the police," Givens said.

"They do, do they?" Cox said.

"That's exactly the plan," Leonard said.

No one said anything for a while. A plane flew over. I wished they were parachuting in reinforcements.

"I think there's more of us than there are of you two," Cox said.

"What a mathematician," Leonard said.

"Me and Leonard get to shooting though, your numbers may decrease," I said.

"Speed here," Cox said, "he's fast on the draw, and he hits what he aims at."

"I'm not that fast on the draw," Leonard said, "and I'm not that good of a shot, but I still might hit something. But him, Hap, he can shoot. That motherfucker is a natural. He don't really know from guns, but he knows shooting. It's like a god-damn inborn knack."

"This is true," I said. "I'm like a fucking prodigy."

I didn't add that my expertise was really with long guns, though I did all right with a handgun. And Leonard was right.

I didn't know that much about the workings of guns, really. Not the way gun nuts do, the guys talking about them the way you ought to talk about a woman, but I could hit stuff. As for fast on the draw, I had no idea. I never thought of slapping leather with anyone. I usually had my gun out and ready.

"We got quite the conundrum then, don't we?" Cox said, and grinned a little.

"Pretty conundrummy," Leonard said.

Speed was a little to my left rear, but I could see him well enough. Across the way was Crew Cut, and not far from him were Cox and the girl, Jackie, and Givens. Leonard was off to my right.

"You know what?" Leonard said. "I'm going to step a little wide, in case my man here decides to shoot. He's got dead aim, but I don't want to be in the line of fire. He might let a lot of bullets go."

"You really good?" Speed asked me.

"There's all manner of opinions floating around," I said.

"He will blow your head off, Speed," Leonard said, without looking back at me, keeping his eyes on the others. "It will happen so fast you'll never know you have a hole in you."

I thought: Don't build it up so much, Leonard. This Speed guy, he looks like someone who would like to try me out, and I'd rather not. But I didn't let on I was worried. I smiled a lot. I was one confident and happy-looking sonofabitch.

"I'm thinking I might like to try you, fast man," Speed said.

Shit. I knew it.

"We don't have to, you know," I said.

"You sound a little scared," Speed said.

"It's just I don't like having to clean my gun," I said. "All that smoke in the barrel. The cost of a bullet."

"You know what I think," Speed said, pushing his coat back so the butt of his holstered gun could be seen. "I don't think you're that—"

I drew and wheeled and shot him, right in the center of the chest. I wheeled again, toward Crew Cut. He was struggling his gun out of the holster beneath his coat. I shot him in the arm. The gun he'd grabbed went flipping away and he fell back against the car, grabbed his arm, said, "Shit."

Leonard had his gun out now. It was about time.

"Damn, Hap," Leonard said. "That was some good shooting."

"Wasn't bad," I said. "Disarm the dick cheese."

Leonard pointed his gun at them. He said, "You, Nora, you get their guns from them, bring them over here and toss them on the ground behind the car. You get feisty, I'll put a hole in you. I got a rule, anyone tries to hurt me gets hurt, male, female, wild animal. And if they got hide-out guns, those better come out slow and easy too, not be hanging around for later. Something like that would make me irritable, and like the Hulk, you wouldn't like me when I'm mad."

Nora did as she was told. It was quite a pile of guns she dumped behind the car. When she was finished, Leonard said to her, "You come over here and get in our car. Sit in the backseat, put your hands in your lap, and look prim."

Nora got in the backseat of the car the way a child in trouble will do.

I went over to Speed. I had been watching him carefully ever since he hit the ground, except for when I shot the Crew Cut fellow. He was bleeding badly and his eyes were blinking very fast. He wasn't even trying to reach for his gun. I knelt down beside him.

"Damn, my man," Speed said, coughing a little. "I never even cleared leather."

"That's because I'm faster than you," I said.

Speed made a barking laugh that tossed blood onto his lips. "You're the real deal," he said.

"Frankly," I said, "I didn't know that until just now."

I pulled his gun from its holster, just in case he might be

stronger than he looked, though the way he lay there he gave the impression that lifting his fingers would be a serious workout. I lifted his head up so he wouldn't choke on his blood. I turned my head, said to the young man: "Your name is Jackie, right?"

He nodded.

"You have the sports coat man there give you his coat."

"My arm hurts," Crew Cut said. "And I like this coat."

"Give him the coat anyway," I said, "or you won't have to worry about hurting."

Jackie went over and Crew Cut worked his way out of the coat. Jackie brought the coat to me. He said, "Don't hurt Nora. This wasn't any of her idea."

"I don't believe that," I said, "but she isn't going to get hurt as long as she doesn't get cute. Now, sit down there on the ground in front of my car."

Jackie went over and did just that. I rolled the coat up and put it under Speed's head.

"Bullet didn't have much impact," Speed said, still gurgling blood.

"It was enough," I said.

"I mean I didn't feel it so much," he said. "But I can hardly move."

"That's because you haven't had time to feel it," I said. "Now shut up. You're spitting blood."

Speed lay quietly on the sports coat.

I got out my cell phone and made a call.

Next day we were at Marvin's office, in our usual spots. Marvin behind his desk, me in the chair in front of it, Leonard sitting by the coffee machine, munching on vanilla wafers. At least he had bought those with his own money.

Marvin said, "I called you here to tell you the cops believe your story, about how you thought you were just getting the girl back and they tried to kill you, so you shot them. They're not too happy about you going out there without calling them, not telling them what the deal was, but I think they're in a forgiving mood. They been wanting Cox on something that would stick, and you two talking at a trial, and Givens talking to save his own bacon, that'll nail him. And way I figure it is you'll be all right 'cause they'll be shit-blind happy you helped nail Cox."

"What about Speed?" I said.

"They think he's going to make it and get to go to prison," Marvin said. "He appears to be as tough as boot leather."

"But he's not near as fast as he thought he was," Leonard said. "My man here is like fucking Wild Bill Hickock."

"I got lucky," I said. "And I shot him while he was talking."

"Well," Marvin said, "I think his future career is woodshop in prison."

"What about Nora?" I asked.

"The kid, Jackie, he's saying she didn't know anything about it, and so's the old man. She's gone back to her stepmother. I think the cops will let that stand. Givens will get some time too. He's backing Jackie's story about the girl having nothing to do with it. Guess he wanted to have the same story Cox had. He's helping put Cox in prison, but maybe he didn't want to go the whole hog, thinks he might get a brownie point or two."

"Think he will?" I asked.

"Nope," Marvin said. "They will most likely have him shanked in prison. They do, no tears here."

Leonard said, "Me either."

I have to admit, I didn't see myself shedding tears for that lying, conniving weasel.

"I believe Nora thought she found true love," I said, "and would get some money out of her father, and she'd have some teenage revenge on her stepmother. For what, I'm not sure, but it seems that's how she was thinking. She was close to her, but maybe she got unclose when she started to grow up and thought Daddy was putting more attention into Sharon than her. No idea really."

"Frankly," Leonard said, "my take is she's just stupid. Probably glad it's over, probably glad to be home. Probably forget Jackie in a year's time. You can bet the way she'll tell it to Sharon is she was forced. I think that little shit's a born liar. One of those entitled turds who think they have the best of everything coming just because they are who they think they are, not necessarily who they are."

"That's some serious psychoanalyst shit going on there," I said.

"Naw," Leonard said. "I just sort of made that up."

"Actually, that's what I really thought," I said.

"I think that's what Sharon wants her to do—just pretend things are fine between them until they are," Leonard said. "In the long run, I think she figures what really happened won't matter, and she's probably right. And maybe Nora really did find true love, because Jackie didn't tell it different, and Cox didn't say his son was lying, so you got to give the old man points for going with what his son said. I think the cops want to let Nora go. They got the fish they wanted to fry and could care less about the minnows."

"Cox family values," I said. "Kind of touching. Go figure."

Brett and I were lying in bed. I said, "I love you."

Brett turned and put her arm across my chest. "I love you too."

"I asked you to marry me, would you? Right now, if I asked?"

"Are you asking?"

"I'm running a test," I said.

"A test, huh," Brett said.

"Yeah."

"I don't know, baby. Really, I don't. I want to, but you know, I got married once before and it ended with me setting my husband's head on fire."

"So, you get married, you have to go for gasoline and a match?"

She laughed.

"No, I'm just saying what happened before, my first attempt at wedded bliss. What I'd say about us is this. Let's give it some thought. Let's see if it's something that really matters, and if it does, we'll get past talking about it. Maybe we'll decide things are just fine the way they are and we don't need a piece of paper."

"It's not the paper, it's the commitment."

"I know. I'm just saying let's think about how much it matters to us. Give it some thought, some time."

"All right," I said.

"Do you want to play doctor?"

"No," I said. "I'd just like to hold you."

"Really?" she said.

"Really."

"That works too," Brett said, and so I held her.

THE BOY WHO BECAME INVISIBLE

THE PLACE WHERE I GREW UP was a little town called Marvel Creek. Not much happened there that is well remembered by anyone outside of the town. But things went on, and what I'm aware of now is how much things really don't change. We just know more than we used to because there are more of us, and we have easier ways to communicate excitement and misery than in the old days.

Marvel Creek was nestled along the edge of the Sabine River, which is not a wide river, and as rivers go, not that deep, except in rare spots, but it is a long river, and it winds all through East Texas. Back then there were more trees than now, and where wild animals ran, concrete and houses shine bright in the sunlight.

Our little school wasn't much, and I hated going. I liked staying home and reading books I wanted to read, and running the then-considerable woods and fishing the creeks for crawdads. Summers and afternoons and weekends I did that with my friend Jesse. I knew Jesse's parents lived differently than we did, and though we didn't have money, and would probably have been called poor by the standards of the early sixties, Jesse's family still lived out on a farm where they used an outhouse and plowed with mules, raised most of the food they ate, drew water from a well, but, curiously, had electricity and a big tall TV antenna that sprouted beside their house and could be adjusted for better reception by reaching through the living room window and turning it with a twist of the hands. Jesse's dad was quick to use the razor strop on Jesse's butt and back for things my parents would have thought unimportant, or at worst an offense that required words, not blows.

Jesse and I liked to play Tarzan, and we took turns at it until we finally both decided to be Tarzan, and ended up being Tarzan twins. It was a great mythology we created and we ran the woods and climbed trees, and on Saturday we watched *Jungle Theater* at my house, which showed, if we were lucky, Tarzan or Jungle Jim movies, and if not so lucky, Bomba movies.

About fifth grade there was a shift in dynamics. Jesse's poverty began to be an issue for some of the kids at school. He brought his lunch in a sack, since he couldn't afford the cafeteria, and all his clothes came from the Salvation Army. He arrived at history class one morning wearing socks with big S's on them, which stood for nothing related to him, and he immediately became the target of James Willeford and Ronnie Kenn. They made a remark about how the S stood for Sardines, which would account for how Jesse smelled, and sadly, I remember thinking at that age that was a pretty funny crack until I looked at Jesse's slack, white face and saw him tremble beneath that patched Salvation Army shirt.

Our teacher came in then, Mr. Waters, and he caught part of the conversation. He said, "Those are nice socks you got there, Jesse. Not many people can have monogrammed socks. It's a sign of sophistication, something a few around here lack."

It was a nice try, but I think it only made Jesse feel all the more miserable, and he put his head down on his desk and didn't lift it the entire class, and Mr. Waters didn't say a word to him. When class was over, Jesse was up and out, and as I was leaving, Mr. Waters caught me by the arm. "I saw you laughing when I came in. You been that boy's friend since the two of you were knee-high to a legless grasshopper."

"I didn't mean to," I said. "I didn't think."

"Yeah, well, you ought to."

That hit me pretty hard, but I'm ashamed to say not hard enough.

I don't know when it happened, but it got so when Jesse came over I found things to do. Homework, or some chore around the house, which was silly, because unlike Jesse, I didn't really have any chores. In time he quit stopping by, and I would see him in the halls at school, and we'd nod at each other, but seldom speak.

The relentless picking and nagging from James and Ronnie continued, and as they became interested in girls, it increased. And Marilyn Townsend didn't help either. She was a lovely young thing and as cruel as they were.

One day, Jesse surprised us by coming to the cafeteria with his sack lunch. He usually ate outside on one of the stoops, but he came in this day and sat at a table by himself, and when Marilyn went by he watched her, and when she came back with her tray, he stood up and smiled, politely asked if she would like to sit with him.

She laughed. I remember that laugh to this day. It was as cold as a knife blade in the back and easily as sharp. I saw Jesse's face drain until it was white, and she went on by laughing, not even saying a word, just laughing, and pretty soon everyone in the place was laughing, and Marilyn came by me, and she looked at me, and heaven help me, I saw those eyes of hers and those lips, and whatever made all the other boys jump did the same to me . . . and I laughed.

Jesse gathered up his sack and went out.

It was at this point that James and Ronnie came up with a new approach. They decided to treat Jesse as if he were a ghost, as if he were invisible. We were expected to do the same. So as not to be mean to Jesse, but being careful not to burn my bridges with the in-crowd, I avoided him altogether. But there were times, here and there, when I would see him walking down the hall, and on the rare occasions when he spoke, students pretended not to hear him, or James would respond with some remark like, "Do you hear a duck quacking?"

When Jesse spoke to me, if no one was looking, I would nod.

This went on into the ninth grade, and it became such a habit, it was as if Jesse didn't exist, as if he really were invisible. I almost forgot about him, though I did note in math class one day there were stripes of blood across his back, seeping through his old, worn shirt. His father and the razor strop. Jesse had nowhere to turn.

One afternoon I was in the cafeteria, just about to get in line, when Jesse came in carrying his sack. It was the first time he'd been there since the incident with Marilyn some years before. I saw him come in, his head slightly down, walking as if on a mission. As he came near me, for the first time in a long time, for no reason I can explain, I said, "Hi, Jesse."

He looked up at me surprised, and nodded, the way I did to him in the hall, and kept walking.

There was a table in the center of the cafeteria, and that was the table James and Ronnie and Marilyn had claimed, and as Jesse came closer, for the first time in a long time, they really saw him. Maybe it was because they were surprised to see him and his paper sack in a place he hadn't been in ages. Or maybe they sensed something. Jesse pulled a small revolver from his sack and before anyone knew what was happening, he fired three times, knocking all three of them to the floor. The place went nuts, people running in all directions. Me, I froze.

Then, like a soldier, he wheeled and marched back my way. As he passed me, he turned his head, smiled, said, "Hey, Hap," then he was out the door. I wasn't thinking clearly, because I turned and went out in the hall behind him, and the history teacher, Mr. Waters, saw him with the gun, said something, and the gun snapped again, and Waters went down. Jesse walked all the way to the double front door, which was flung wide open at that time of day, stepped out into the light, and lifted the revolver. I heard it pop and saw his head jump and he went down. My knees went out from under me and I sat down right there in the hall, unable to move.

When they went out to tell his parents what had happened to him, that Marilyn was disfigured, Ronnie wounded, and James and Mr. Waters were dead, they discovered them in bed where Jesse had shot them in their sleep.

The razor strop lay across them like a dead snake.

NOT OUR KIND

WHEN I GOT OUT OF SCHOOL that day, I drove over to the Dairy Queen to get a hamburger before I had to go to work at the aluminum chair plant. I had a work permit, so I got off early, and I usually grabbed a burger, and then I drove out to the plant and worked until midnight. A lot of us from high school worked there, making fifty-six dollars and fourteen cents a week, which wasn't even good for 1968.

I was sitting at the back of the Dairy Queen, eating quickly, and was about halfway through the burger when four boys from school came in. I knew one of them pretty well, and the others a little. We all knew each other's names, anyway. I can't say any of them were friends of mine. We ran in different circles.

They saw me and came over. Two of them sat down in my booth, across from me, and the other two sat out to the side at a table and leaned on their elbows and looked at me. I didn't like their attitude.

"What's going on?" I said.

"You're seeing it," the one I knew best said. His name was David. Last time I saw him was at the Swinging Bridge, and there had been a fight there for money. My new friend Leonard was there. He won the fight. It was a friend of David's he fought, and he beat the guy's ass like a tambourine and made some money.

Actually, that fight, lit by a huge tire fire, was the first time I met Leonard, and we hit it off, and we saw each other again in Marvel Creek, running into one another accidentally at first, and then finally on purpose. He lived over in LaBorde with his uncle, but they came to the general store in Marvel Creek to shop, which I didn't understand. Everyone in Marvel Creek goes to the larger city of LaBorde to shop, but his uncle had a store in Marvel Creek he liked, place where he had been buying shoes for a long time. He liked it, Leonard said, because the owner never told him to come around back, even before laws were passed that said he didn't have to.

David said, "We were talking about you the other day."

"Were you?" I said.

"Yeah. Some. We been seeing you around with that nigger."

"Leonard?"

"One name is as good as another for a nigger. 'Boy' will work. We'll call him 'Boy.'"

"I won't. And if I was you, I wouldn't call him that. You might find yourself turned inside out and made into a change purse."

"You think he's tough, don't you?"

"Don't you? You seen him whip some ass at the Swinging Bridge, same as me."

"We seen you whip some too," another of the boys said, "but that don't scare us none, about you or the nigger."

The big guy's real name was Colbert, but everyone called him Dinosaur on account of he was big and not that smart. He was a football player and he thought he was as cool as an igloo. He was said to be the toughest guy in school. That might have been true. He hadn't been at the bridge that night. I didn't know if he'd seen me and Leonard together or not, but he was riled about it, thanks to David.

I didn't like where this was going. I kept eating, but I didn't taste the rest of the burger.

"Way we see it," David said, and bobbed his head a little so as to indicate the others, "you aren't doing yourself any good."

"Oh, how's that?"

"Ought not have to spell it out for you, Hap. Hell, you know. Hanging with a nigger."

"You mean Leonard."

"Yeah. Okay. Leonard the nigger."

I nodded. I didn't realize until that moment that I really liked Leonard, and these guys I had known all my life, if only a little, I didn't care for that much at all.

"Word's getting around you're a nigger-lover," Dinosaur said.

"Is it?"

"Yeah. You don't want that," David said.

"I don't?"

"Are you trying to be a smartass?" Dinosaur said.

"I don't think so," I said. I put one foot out of the booth so I could move if I had to, could get a position to fight or run.

"There's talk, and it could reflect on you," David said.

"In what way?"

"You think girls want to date a nigger-lover? And way we hear it, this guy's queer as a three-dollar bill, and proud of it. A nigger queer, come on, man. You got to be kidding me."

"But he has such a nice personality," I said.

"You aren't going to listen, are you?" David said. "Girls don't want to date no nigger-lover."

"You said that."

"Because it's true."

"So, you have come here to spare me being viewed in a bad way, and to make sure I don't lose my pussy quota? That's what's up?"

"You're making light of something you shouldn't," David said. "We got a way of doing things, and you know it."

"We got to keep it protected," Dinosaur said.

"We?" I said.

"White people," David said. "Now that niggers can vote and eat with us, they think they can act like us."

I nodded, glanced at the two that hadn't spoken. "You guys, you thinking the same?"

They all nodded.

"Civil rights may change how the Yankees live," David said, "but it won't change us."

"That's why I don't like you guys."

This landed on their heads like a rock.

"You don't have to like us, but we can't have one of our own hanging about with niggers. He's not our kind. He's not one of us."

"You know, it's really been nice, but I have to go to work now, so I'll see you."

I got up and eased past Dinosaur, keeping an eye on him, but trying to look like I wasn't concerned.

They all stood up. I was about halfway to the door when they came up behind me. David grabbed at my arm. I popped it free.

"You better take in what we're saying," David said.

"I could throw you through that window glass right now," Dinosaur said.

"You might need yourself a nap and a sack lunch before you're able to throw me through that glass, or anywhere else for that matter," I said.

I was bluffing. I was a badass, and I knew it. But four guys, badass or not, are four guys. And one of them was a fucking freak of nature. I was reminded of how freakish he was with him standing almost as close to me as a coat of paint. He was looking down at me with a head like a bowling ball, shoulders wide enough to set a refrigerator on one side, a stove on the other.

About that time, the manager, Bob, came out from behind the counter. An older guy, red-haired, slightly gone to fat, not as big as Dinosaur, but I'd seen him throw out a couple of oil workers once for throwing ketchup-soaked fries against the Dairy Queen glass to see who could make theirs stick and not slide off. They didn't get very far in that game.

What I remember best was one of those guys, after Bob had tossed them out like they were dirty laundry, pulled a knife and held it on Bob when he came outside to make sure they were leaving.

Bob laughed, said to that guy, "Should have brought yourself a peppermint stick, you oil-field trash. They're a hell of a lot easier to eat."

This with the tip of the knife pressed to his stomach. The guy with the knife and his buddy believed Bob. Believed him sincerely. They were out of there so fast they practically left a vapor trail. It seemed they were standing there outside the Dairy Queen one moment, and the next their car's taillights were shining red in the distant night.

Bob said to David and the others, "All right, boys. Take it outside."

I thought, shit. Outside isn't going to be all that better for me.

We all started outside. Even Dinosaur didn't want a piece of Bob.

As we were going, Bob put his hand on my shoulder.

"You stay with me."

The others turned and looked at Bob.

"Unless I've developed a stutter, you know what I said."

They hesitated about as long as it takes to blink, and went out.

Bob waited until they were outside and looking through the glass. He made a shooing movement with his hand, and they went away. After a moment I saw their car drive by the window and on out to the highway.

"They'll be watching for you, son."

"I know."

"Hanging with niggers is frowned on. I got some nigger friends, but you got to know how to keep them at a distance. I go fishing with a couple of them, but I don't have them around at my house, sitting in my chairs and eating at my table."

"Thanks," I said. "I'll remember that."

"Still, no cause to pick on someone. You or the nigger. They don't get to choose to be niggers. And you can get along with most anyone, and learn from most anyone, even a nigger. I learned how to catch catfish good from one."

Well, Bob was better than the other four.

I bought a bag of chips and a Coca-Cola on ice to go, went out to my car, and drove to work. I was about halfway to the aluminum chair plant when Dinosaur, driving a Ford Mustang, pulled up behind me. The other three guys were in the car with him. They followed me to work. I parked close to the door and got out with my chips and Coca-Cola. I slurped at the Coca-Cola through a straw as I walked. I was saving the chips for dinner break. It was a light dinner, but I'd been trying to drop a few pounds. I was always prone to picking up weight, and I had to watch it.

I turned at the door into the plant and looked at them.

Dinosaur shot me the finger.

I shot him the finger back.

We had really showed each other. Funny how that can make people so mad. It's their finger in the air, and that's it. It has about as much actual effect as a leaf falling from a cherry tree in Japan.

They drove way, screeching tires as they left, and I went to work.

Next few days in school I'd see them in the hall, and I never once avoided them or tried to get out of the way. They were not always together, though sometimes they were, and Dinosaur bumped me a couple of times as he went by. I kept my cool. Once David said to me as he passed, "We'll get you, nigger-lover."

This went on for awhile, and now and then they'd follow me to work, but they never did anything. I had a ball bat in my car, and they knew that, because I let them see it by holding it up once while driving, knowing they could see it from their Mustang, as they were so close on my ass. What I feared is they'd hold up a gun or guns in response, but that didn't happen. Everyone wasn't shooting everybody back then.

This went on through the semester, and then the spring came, and one day I went downtown to buy some blue jeans and a union shirt. The old white union shirts had become popular. Everyone was dying them, or tie-dying them, and I guess I didn't want to be left out. What we had there in Marvel Creek was a kind of general store named Jack Woolens, and that's where I went to buy the shirt, couple pairs of jeans, and maybe what we called desert boots, which were tan, low-cut, comfortable shoes. I thought I had enough to afford it all. I was thinking on that, figuring I could skip one pair of pants if I had to, and I'd have enough for sure that way to get the shirt, shoes, and one pair of Lee Riders.

My hair had grown longer, and I had to comb it behind my ears at school and push it up off my forehead into a pompadour so I didn't get sent home. A bunch of us were wearing our hair longer, and there was even talk of a sit-in to protest how we were hassled by the principal, but I was the only one that showed up for the event. I ended up wandering around in the hall for a few minutes and went back to the lunchroom and had some Jell-O before going to math class. I had it washed and combed out this day, and it was bouncing loosely as I walked. I thought I was as cool as a razor edge in winter time.

I parked my junker and was walking along the sidewalk, almost to Jack Woolens. I could see the wooden barrels setting out front—one had walking canes in it and brooms, the other had axe and hoe handles.

As I came along the sidewalk, I saw Leonard coming toward me. He saw me and smiled. We hadn't seen each other in a while, but when I saw him I knew I had missed him. He was like a stray dog that wandered in and out of my life, and I felt like when we were together that something missing was fulfilled. It was an odd combo, him being a homo and me being straight, him being black and me being white, and him being more redneck than I was. He didn't like my long hair and had told me, and I didn't like that he thought we needed a conservative president. He was a stray dog I liked, and I decided right then and there I wanted to keep him, even if he might bite. He probably thought I was the stray dog. I doubt he worried about my bite, however. He came down the sidewalk with one hand in his pants pocket, the other swinging by his side.

That's when David and Dinosaur, and the other two thugs, got out of the Mustang parked across the street, having spotted me and caught me without my ball bat. They came across the street, almost skipping.

They got to me before Leonard.

They came up on the curb and managed their way around me in a half circle. The door to Jack Woolens was at my back. It was open. It was a cool day and air-conditioning wasn't as common then, so it was left that way to let in the breeze as well as too many flies.

"Gotcha now," David said.

"Gotcha what?" Leonard said, as he came up the sidewalk, both hands swinging by his sides now.

"You're the other one we want to see," said Dinosaur. "You and the girl, here."

"Wow," I said. "That bites. You see, Leonard, they're calling me a girl because my hair is long."

"It is too long," Leonard said.

"They are really pushing the wit, calling me a girl, noticing I have long hair. These guys, they ought to be on Johnny Carson."

"Fuck you," Dinosaur said.

"You're looking for us, well, you done found us," Leonard said.

"That's right," I said. "You have."

"We don't like what we see," David said.

"That's because you are a blind motherfucker and don't know a couple pretty fellas when you see them," Leonard said. "I could be on a fucking magazine, I'm so pretty. Shit. You could hang my goddamn dick in the museum of fucking modern art. Damn, Big Pile, you know you want to kiss my black ass, right where the tunnel goes down into the sweet dark depths."

"You gag me," David said.

"Fuck you," Dinosaur said.

"The big man is consistent with those two words," I said.

I didn't know what it was about Leonard, but he brought out the double smartass in me. I figured if I was going to die, I might as well go out with a few good remarks. And with Leonard there, well, I felt I had a chance. That we had a chance.

Leonard looked at me. "Yeah. He repeats himself because it's wishful thinking that slips out. Some of that Freudian stuff. Big white boy wants a piece of my fine, shiny, black ass I tell you, but his little ole dick dropped down there would be like tossing a noodle into a volcano."

"Now I'm starting to get gagged," I said.

"Ah, you'll get over it, Hap," Leonard said.

David said to Leonard, "You're a goddamn dick-sucking nigger and he's a nigger-lover."

"Nah," Leonard said. "I mean, yeah. I'm a dick-sucker, but me and Hap, we ain't fucking, just hanging. Oh, I should also add, I don't like being called a nigger, you cracker motherfucker."

"You got some sand," David said.

"I'm a whole goddamn beach," Leonard said.

"What we're thinking," David said, "is we're going to knock you two around until your shit mixes, until you get it through your head how things are supposed to be."

"That a fact?" I said.

"Oh yeah," Dinosaur said, "we're gonna do that."

Leonard grinned, said, "I guess you boys ought to get started. It's already midday."

"But the sun stays up for quite awhile," I said.

"Yeah, there's that," Leonard said. "We got plenty of time to whip their asses."

"Smartass nigger," David said, and glanced at Dinosaur, who moved forward.

That's when an older black man stepped out of Jack Woolens and reached in one of the barrels and pulled out an axe handle.

"I hear you peckerwoods calling my nephew a nigger?" the man said.

David bowed up a little. "We ain't got a thing against hitting an old nigger, or a lady nigger, or kicking around a dead nigger, which is what you're gonna be, you ancient watermelon fart."

That's when the old man swung the axe handle and clipped David across the jaw and made him stagger. I almost felt sorry for David. Even more so when the handle whistled again and caught him behind the neck and laid him out flat on his face on the cement.

The other three thugs froze, then seemed to come unstuck and started toward the three of us. Me and Leonard took fighting stances. That's when Jack Woolens came out behind us, a slightly paunchy old man with thinning dark hair.

"Stop it, goddamn it," Jack said.

They stopped, but when Dinosaur saw who it was, he said, "You old Jew bastard."

"Old Jew bastard fought Nazis, so he isn't afraid of your

kind. You aren't a pimple on a Nazi's ass, but you're made of the same kind of pus."

This stopped them. I don't know why, but they hesitated.

The old Jew bastard pulled an axe handle from the barrel and stepped up beside the black man. "Way I see it," he said, "is we have axe handles, and for now, you have teeth. You see it that way, Chester?"

Chester said, "Yeah. They got some teeth right now."

Dinosaur looked a little nervous. "We ain't even eighteen, and that nigger hit David with an axe handle."

"Hard as he could," Leonard said.

"That's against the law," Dinosaur said. "We're underage. Minors."

"Sometimes, you have extenuating circumstances," Jack Woolens said. "I once strangled a Nazi when I was in the O.S.S. Look it up, you never heard of it. It wasn't a social group. I strangled him and went back to the farmhouse where I was hiding in Austria, and slept tight. I knocked me off a piece the next day. Young German girl who thought I was German. I can speak it. I had the chance, I'd have strangled another fucking Nazi."

"No shit?" Chester said. "You speak German?"

It was like they forgot the thugs were there.

"Yeah, I was born in Germany."

"No shit?"

"Yeah. I did get a little scratch when I was strangling that Nazi by the way. I don't want to sound like I come out clean. That would be lying."

Jack Woolens put the axe handle back in the barrel, and showed Chester a cut across his elbow by nodding at it. It was a long white line.

"Knife," Jack said. "I had to wear a bandage for a few days."

"That ain't shit," Chester said. "Cracker tried to castrate me once. I got a scar on my thigh I can show you makes that look like hen scratch. I had twenty-five stitches and had to stand when I fucked for awhile and reach under and hold my balls up so it didn't slap my stitches. Want to see?"

"You win," Jack said. "Keep your pants on."

"I was moving when the cracker did that, cut me I mean," Chester said. "Cracker didn't turn out so well. They found his lily-white ass in the river, and there wasn't no way of knowing how he got there. Some kind of accident like being beat to death and thrown in the river is my guess. You know, said the wrong thing to someone, tried to cut their balls off, something like that. I ain't saying I know that to be a fact, him being dead in the Sabine River, but I'm going to start a real hard rumor about it right now."

Jack turned back to the barrel and retrieved the axe handle, casual as if he were picking out a toothpick.

The thugs continued to stand there. As if just remembering they were there, Chester thumped Dinosaur's chest with the axe handle. "Pick up this sack of dog shit, and carry him off. Do it now, 'cause you don't, it'll be hard to do with broke legs. You boys carry him now, you won't have to scoot and pull him away with your teeth, ones you got left. Gumming him might be difficult. One way or another, though, it ain't gonna turn out spiffy for you fellows."

Dinosaur looked at me, then Leonard, then the older men. He looked at his friends. Nobody bowed up. No smart remarks were made. Dinosaur seemed small right then. They picked up David like he was a dropped puppet, tried to get him to stand, but they might as well have been trying to teach a fish how to ride a tricycle. They had to drag him across the street and into their car.

When they got David inside, the others got in, and Dinosaur went around to the driver's side. He shot us the finger. He said, "This ain't over."

"Better be," Jack Woolens said.

Dinosaur drove his friends out of there.

"We could have handled it," Leonard said.

"Maybe," I said.

"Shit," Leonard said. "We could."

"Now they're tough guys," Jack said to Chester. "It's all over, and now they're tough."

"We were tough enough," Leonard said, "and we could have got tougher."

"Leonard," Chester said, pulling car keys out of his pocket. "Bring the car around, and don't squeal the goddamn tires."

"Like he can't walk a few feet," Jack said. "Like he's got a lot to carry. A pair of shoes on lay-a-way he bought. He can walk."

I looked at Leonard and he grinned at me. I loved that grin.

Chester said. "I got the lumbago."

"Lumbago," Jack said. "Now the lumbago he gets."

Chester grunted, said to Leonard, "Get the car, kid."

Leonard looked at me, smiled, and went away to get it.

BENT TWIG

WHEN I GOT IN FROM WORK that night, Brett, my redhead, was sitting at the kitchen table. She didn't have a shift that week at the hospital, so I was surprised to see her up and about. It was two a.m. I had finished up being a night watchman at the dog food plant, hoping soon my buddy Leonard would be back from Michigan, where he had gone after someone in some case he had been hired out to do for our friend Marvin and the detective agency Marvin owned. We did freelance work like that from time to time.

There was no job for me in this one, and since Leonard was without a job at all and needed the money more than I did, he hired on. I had a temporary job at the dog food plant. It was okay, but mostly boring. The most exciting thing I had done was chase some rats I had caught in the feed storage room, nibbling on some bags of dog food, stealing chow out of some hound's mouth, so to speak. Those rats knew not to mess with me.

I kept hoping Marvin would have something for me so I could quit, but so far, nothing. I did have that week's paycheck from the dog food plant in my wallet, though.

"What are you doing up?" I asked.

"Worrying," she said.

I sat down at the table with her.

"We have enough money, right?"

"We got plenty for a change. It's Tillie."

"Oh, shit," I said.

"It's not like before," Brett said. What she meant was a little of column A, a little of column B.

Column A was where she got in with a biker club as the local poke, and got hauled off to be a prostitute, partly on purpose, as it was her profession, and partly against her will because they didn't plan to pay her. We had rescued her from that, me, Brett, and Leonard. She had then gone off and got into a series of domestic problems over in Tyler, but those were the sort of things Brett got her out of, or at least managed to avert catastrophe for awhile. Every time Brett mentioned Tillie, it meant she would be packing a bag, putting her job on hold, and going off for a few days to straighten some stupid thing out that never should have happened in the first place. Since she was Brett's daughter I tried to care about her. But she didn't like me and I didn't like her. But I did love Brett, so I tried to be supportive as possible, but Brett knew how I felt.

"You have to go for a few days?" I asked.

"Maybe more to it."

"How's that?"

"She's missing."

"Wouldn't be the first time she took a powder for awhile. You know how she is. Goes off without a word, comes back without one, unless she needs money or a tornado got the double-wide."

"It's not all her fault."

"Brett, baby. Don't give me the stuff about how you weren't a good mother."

"I wasn't."

"You were young yourself, and I don't think you did all that bad. You had some circumstances, and you did what you could for her. She's mostly a mess of her choosing."

"Maybe."

"But you're not convinced."

"It doesn't matter. She's my daughter."

"You got me there," I said.

"I got a call from a friend of hers. You don't know her. Her name is Monica, and she's all right. I think she's got a better head on her shoulders than Tillie. I met her when I was there last. I think she's been a pretty good guide for my girl. Fact is, I sort of thought Tillie was getting it together, and I've been keeping in touch with Monica about it. She called to say they were supposed to go to a movie, a girls' night out. Only Tillie didn't show. Didn't call. And now it's three days later. Monica said when she got over being mad, she got into being worried. Says the guy Tillie lives with, that he could be the problem. He used to run whores, and Tillie could easily fall back into that life. I mean . . . well, there's a bit of a drug problem with the guy, and Tillie, sometimes. He could have gotten tough with Tillie. He might be trying to make some money off of her, or he might have got into something bad and Tillie got dragged with him."

"Monica think he's holding her at home?"

"Maybe worse."

"I thought he was supposed to be all right."

"Me too," she said. "But lately, not so much. At first, he was a kind of Prince Charming, an ex-druggie who was doing good, then all of a sudden he didn't want her out of the house, didn't want her contacting anyone. Didn't want her seeing Monica. But Monica thinks it's because he was choosing who he wanted Tillie to see."

"Prostitution," I said.

Brett nodded. "Yeah, it's how those kind of guys play. Like they care about you, or they got some of the same problems they're kicking, and the next thing Tillie knows she's on the nose candy again and is selling her ass, and then pretty soon she's not getting any money from the sell. He gets it all."

"The pimp gets it all, keeps her drugged, and keeps the money flowing in."

"Yeah," Brett said. "Exactly. It's happened to her before, and you know that, so—"

"You're thinking it could happen again."

"Yeah," she said. "I am."

"Course it doesn't matter, and it may not have been planned. He may have just fallen off the wagon and grabbed her as he fell. After he got the prize he wanted, he didn't want to share it or show it around."

"He liked showing her around at first, all right," Brett said. "He liked her to dress sexy, and then if anyone looked, he was mad. She was for him, and yet he wanted to parade her and not have anyone look at the parade. Later on, he wanted to bring people to the parade. Maybe when his drug habit got bad. I don't know. I don't care. I just want to know she's safe."

"And you want me to check it out?"

"I want us to check it out."

"Let me drive back to the dog food plant and quit with prejudice first."

"Short notice," Brett said.

"I know," I said. "But then so was this."

It felt odd going off to see about something like this without Leonard. I liked having him around in these kind of circumstances. He helped strengthen my backbone. I liked to think I was already pretty firm in that area, but it never hurt to have your brother from another mother there to keep you feeling confident.

Tillie lived just outside of Tyler, between there and Bullock, a little burg outside of the city. Tyler wasn't up there with Dallas and Houston, but it was a big town, or small city, depending on how you liked your labels. A hundred thousand or so, with lots of traffic, illegal immigrants, and college students. The immigrants they liked to hire to get work done cheap, then use them for every scapegoat situation possible, forgetting they wouldn't even be there to blame for what they did and for what they didn't do if they weren't offered the jobs in the first place.

When we got to Tillie's house we found two cars in the carport. Brett said, "That's Tillie's and Robert's cars. Both cars are here."

I went over and knocked on the front door, but no one answered. It's hard to explain, but sometimes you knock, you know someone's inside, and other times it has a hollow feel, like you're tapping on a sun-bleached skull, thinking a brain that isn't inside of it anymore is going to wake up. And sometimes you're just full of shit and whoever is inside is hiding. I remember my mother doing that from time to time when a bill collector came around. I always wondered if they knew we were inside, hiding out on paying the rent we hadn't earned yet, but would pay, hiding out from paying a car payment, hoping they wouldn't haul the car away.

I went around back and knocked, but got the same lack of response. I walked around the house with Brett and we looked in windows when there was a window to look in. Most were covered with blinds or curtains, but the kitchen window at the back had the curtains pulled back, and we could see inside by cupping our hands around our faces and pressing them against the glass. There was nothing to see, though.

Finally we went back out to my car. We leaned on the hood.

I said, "You want me to get inside?"

"I don't know," she said. "I called the police yesterday, well, it was the sheriff's department, but they wouldn't do anything."

"Not twenty-four hours?" I said.

"Actually, it has been. Over. But the thing is, they've dealt with her before." I didn't know all the details on that, but I figured as much. Tillie tended to get in trouble, run off from time to time, so they weren't quick on using man power to chase a sometime prostitute and drug user, and full-time pain in the ass.

"Okay," I said. "Going to make an executive decision. I'm going to break in."

There were houses around, but no activity, and I didn't see anyone parting the curtains for a peek, so I got a lock-picking kit out of the glove box that I use with the agency from time to time, went around back, and got to it. I'm not that good a lockpick, and to tell the truth, it's seldom like on TV, least for me. It always takes awhile. This door was easy though, so it only took me about five minutes, and then me and Brett were inside.

Brett called out. "Tillie. Robert. It's Mom."

No one answered. Her words bounced off the wall.

"Hang by the door," I said.

I went through the house, looked in all the rooms. There was no one handy, but in the living room a chair and a coffee table were turned over, some drink of some kind spilled on the floor and gone sticky, a broken glass nearby. I went back and told Brett what I had seen.

"Maybe now we can get the law interested," I said.

Outside, out back, I saw there was a thin trail of blood drops. I hadn't noticed it before, but now, coming out of the house and with the sun just right, I could see it. It looked like someone had dropped rubies of assorted size in the grass. I said, "Brett, honey. Go out to the car and sit behind the wheel. Here are the keys in case you need to leave. And if you do, leave. Don't worry about me."

"Bullshit," she said. "We'll get the gun out of the glove box."

I have a concealed carry permit, but I seldom carry the gun. Fact is, I don't like the idea of one, but in my line of work, and I don't just mean watchman at the dog food plant, the other stuff sometimes requires one.

We went and got the pistol out of the glove box, an old-style revolver, and walked after the blood drops.

It trailed into the woods, and then we didn't see much of it anymore. We went along the trail a bit more, and I saw where something had been pulled into the bushes, mashing them down. We went up in there and found a body lying on the ground. It was lying facedown. I shouldn't have moved the body, but I nudged it with my foot so as to turn it over. The face looking up at me was that of a young man and it had eyes full of ants and the victim's nose was flattened and scraped where it had been dragged along the ground. There was a bullet hole in the chest, or so I assumed. I had seen a few of them, and it had been delivered right through the shirt pocket. I could see there was another one in his right side. I figured one shot had wounded him, he had made a break for it, and whoever shot him caught up with him and shot him again, then dragged him in the bushes. I also noted the man had tattoos up and down both arms, and not very good ones. They looked as if they had been put there by a drunk trying to write in Sanskrit and hieroglyphics. Either that or a cellmate.

Brett was standing right there with me. She said, "That's him."

"Meaning Robert, Tillie's boyfriend."

"Yeah," she said, and started looking around. Me too. I sort of expected to find her daughter's body, but we didn't. We even went back to the house and walked through it without handling anything but the doorknob, just in case we had missed Tillie on first pass, stuffed under a bed, in a closet, or in a freezer. They didn't have a freezer and she wasn't under the bed or in a closet.

I put my pistol back in the glove box of the car and called 911.

What they sent out was a young guy wearing an oversized pair of pants and a badge as shiny as a child's Christmas dreams. He had a gun on his hip that was large enough to think he might have been expecting elephants to give him trouble. He had on a cowboy hat that seemed too tall, the brim too wide. He looked like someone playing shoot 'em up. He told me he was a deputy.

There was another guy with him, older, sitting on the passenger side of the car. The young guy got out and the old guy didn't. He just opened the door and sat there. He looked like a man waiting for retirement and not sure he'd make it. He might have been forty, but there was something in his face that made him seem older. He had a smaller gun on his hip. I could see that clearly, and he had a cowboy hat on his knee.

The younger man listened to us make our statement. He looked interested, and wrote some stuff down on a notepad. I told him I had a gun in my glove box and I had a permit, just so things wouldn't get dicey in case they found it later. After a time, the older man got out of the car and came over. He said, "You get it all down, Olford?"

"Yes, sir," said the deputy.

I saw then that the guy in front of us had a badge that said SHERIFF on it. It looked very much like those kind of badges we used to buy as kids, ones came with a cap gun and no caps. You had to buy those separate.

He asked us some of the same questions, just to see if we'd trip up, I figure. He didn't look at me much when I answered. He studied Brett constantly. I didn't blame him. She looked fine, as always. Long red hair tumbling over her shoulders, great body kept firm through exercise, and the kind of face that would make Wonder Woman beat herself in the head with a hammer.

"Walk me," said the sheriff to me.

"I'm coming too," Brett said. "I'm no shrinking violet."

"I bet you aren't," said the sheriff. "Olford, you go sit in the car and get your notes straight."

"They're straight, Sheriff," Olford said.

"Go sit in the car anyway," he said.

We walked along a ways. The sheriff, who we learned was named Nathan Hews, said, "Olford is the mayor's boy. Whatcha gonna do?"

"Did he get his uniform from Goodwill?" I asked.

"Don't be disrespectful," the sheriff said. "He stole that off a wash line."

We came to the body. I said, "I turned him over."

"Not supposed to do that," Sheriff Hews said.

"I know. But I checked to see if he was alive."

"When they look like this, facedown or faceup, you got to know they're dead."

"Maybe," I said.

"You know something," the sheriff said. "You called things in, said who you two were, I made some calls, checked some things out. The chief over in LaBorde, he said you're a real pain in the ass. That you usually run with a black guy named Leonard."

"Yep, that's me," I said. "I mean, I run with a black guy named Leonard. I don't know about the pain in the ass part."

"I think you do," he said. "Chief told me some things."

"Blabbermouth," I said.

When we finished looking at the body, we walked back to the car. The sheriff had Olford get a camera out of their car and go out and take some pictures.

"We don't have a real team," he said. "There's me, Olford, one other deputy, and a dispatcher. Sometimes we get free doughnuts though."

"That's keeping in form," I said.

"You betcha," he said. He looked at Brett. "You seem to be holding up well, considering your daughter is missing and a man is dead."

He was still playing us, trying to see we had anything to do with the business that had gone down.

"Trust me," Brett said. "I'm worried sick."

We had to stay at a motel for a couple of hours before the sheriff showed up with a lack of information. "We didn't find your daughter," he said to Brett. "That could be good news."

"Could be," Brett said. What the sheriff had missed in his absence was Brett breaking down and crying, but he probably noticed the red in her eyes. She listened to what he had to say and went into the bathroom and closed the door.

He said to me, "Listen, I'm going to square with you. Going to tell you what you probably have already figured. I'm a one-horse sheriff in a one-horse town with two deputies that are working their first murder case. They're more suited to chasing down renegade cats and dogs and figuring out who stole whose graham crackers at the nursery school. If we had one. I'm not telling you to go off on your own, and there's bigger law can be brought into this. But I was you, from what I know about you, I'd tell you on the sly, which is what I'm doing now, just in case you don't get it, to do some looking on your own."

I nodded, said, "You got any idea where I should start?"

"I said I was a one-horse sheriff, but I once upon a time did some city work. I came here so I'd see fewer bodies. So far, I've seen fewer. This is the first murder that isn't a suicide I've seen in five years. The dead man is Robert Austin, he was for some shit. The girl, your woman's daughter, word was she did some business, if you know what I mean."

"That word is probably good," I said.

"This guy, Robert, sold drugs and sold her. Town like this, people who used her services . . . well, everyone knows. Everyone here knows the size of their neighbor's turds and can tell one's stink from the other. Thing is, Robert, he was most likely selling drugs for Buster Smith. Buster runs a Gospel Opry show over in Marvel Creek."

"I was born there," I said.

"Then you know the place. Used to be tough as a doorstop and sharp as a razor. All that booze out there on Hell's half mile. Now it's a town known for antiques and all the tonks are gone. The Gospel Opry, well, they say that's a cover for old Buster. Marvel Creek sees him as a pious businessman. Me, I see him as a man gives real Christians like me a bad name."

"All right," I said.

"He's about fifty with slicked-back hair and a very cool manner. Wears awful plaid sports jackets all the time. I've met him a time or two, when I was over that way. I even went to the Opry once. Good entertainment. But the word kept drifting back about him, and though it's rumor, I've come to believe it. He's an operator living a simple life on the surface, putting himself in a squeaky clean front while he does the bad stuff out the back door. He's got everyone that matters over there in his pocket.

"Another thing, there's a guy named Kevin Crisper hangs out at the Go-Mart here, sits on a bench out front. It's his bench. He works his drug deals there, and rumor is, though we can't prove it, he works for Buster. I keep a watch on him, but so far I haven't caught him doing what he shouldn't be doing. He has a guy or two to help him out. They all got a few snags on their arrest sheet, but nothing that keeps them anywhere behind bars. I mean, I know what they're doing, and I can't prove it. I can't do to them what needs to be done. Thing is, though, Kevin Crisper does sales of drugs and gets a percentage. Buster gets the lion's share because he provides the goods. At least the dope. Tillie, and I want to say this before your girlfriend comes back, she was a self-operator, but word was she was getting pretty deep in the drugs, and that maybe she didn't know if she was about to shit or go blind. She was down in the dead zone with one brain cell or two for a life preserver, and that was it. Robert, he might have been farming her out through this Kevin. Probably was. And Tillie, like I said, she might as well have been a blow-up sex doll, way her mind was messed up."

"And you know all this and couldn't do nothing?" I said.

"That's right," he said. "Isn't that nice? Listen here, chief in LaBorde said you were smarter than you looked, so I'm thinking what I said before. There's stuff you can do I can't. Law and all. But, you get caught doing it, I didn't tell you to do it, and you say I did, I'll call you a big fat liar. I'll even arrest you. How's that for modern law enforcement?"

"I can live with it," I said.

It took some doing, but I finally talked Brett into letting me take her home. I called Leonard on my cell, but he didn't answer his. I left him a message. I drove over to downtown Bullock, which was a cross street, and went over to the Go-Mart and found Kevin Crisper. He was a man in his forties trying to look thirty. He had similar tattoos to Robert. Kevin looked like a man who had been soaked down wet and overheated in a microwave. Skin like that was last seen on Tutankhamun's mummy. That said, he had muscular arms, the kind of muscles some people are born with, long and stringy and deceptively strong.

I walked over to him, said, "I hear you can sell me some things."

"Some things?" he said. "What kind of things? I look like I got something to sell? Pots and pans? Maybe gloves or shoes?"

"I was told you had some entertainments. Guy named Robert told me. You are Kevin, right?"

"Yeah, that's me." Kevin lifted his head, said, "When did Robert tell you that?"

I backdated the time, just in case Kevin had some idea when Robert bit the big one. I added, "He said there's a girl that could do me some favors, you know. For some money."

"You heard all that, huh?"

"I did."

"He didn't offer just to take care of you himself?"

"He said he worked for you, and that I should talk to you."

"That's funny he should say that," he said.

"Look, you got the goods or you don't. I got money. I want some services. I'd like to party with a girl and I'd like to make myself right. You know where I'm coming from."

He nodded. "Say I know how to get this girl, the stuff you want to get right, you think I'd have it on me? Think I got that girl's pussy in my back pocket along with a sack of blow?"

"That would be handy, if you did."

"Listen here, tell you what. I like Robert, and since he sent you, I got a place where you can come for the stuff, and the girl. We don't use a motel. There ain't but one and everyone knows everyone."

"So where is this place?"

"You going to be around tonight?"

"Could be."

"You want some leg and some head-twister, then you got to be around."

"Head-twister?"

"Stuff I'm selling. It's a mixture. You take this stuff your dick gets hard, your head gets high, and you'll have so much fun you'll drive over and slap your mama."

"That right?"

"Way I hear. Course, I don't sample that shit myself."

"That's not much of a selling point," I said.

"Oh, it's not that. I sample the girl, of course, but the rest of it, that's product man. You dip into your own product, especially with it being available, you can get in Dutch pretty quick."

He gave me a time and an address. I thanked him and tried to look excited. I drove over to the one café and parked out front and sat behind the wheel and called Leonard again. I had some idea that the Michigan thing was near wrapped up, that he ought to be driving back down and in Texas by now, but it appeared it had taken more time than expected because I got the same thing. No answer. I left him a detailed message, even told him where I was supposed to be and at what time. I gave him the same directions Kevin had given me. I went in the café and had some coffee and a sandwich. I figured I might want to be fortified. I bought a sack lunch and an axe handle at the feed store and put it in the car, and then I drove out to where I was supposed to meet Kevin. Only thing was, I was four hours early.

I tried Leonard a few more times, leaving the same directions, but whatever he was up to, it didn't involve having his phone on. The location Kevin gave me was not deep in the woods, but it was out of town, which would of course suit his kind of services. But since I didn't think Tillie, possibly the only lady working the grid, so to speak, was truly available, and since I knew Robert was dead as a pair of post-hole diggers, and had a suspicion Kevin knew it as well, I thought I wouldn't rely on his hospitality to bring Tillie straight to me. Me and Brett and Leonard had rescued her once before, a few years back, from something stupid she had gotten herself into that sounded a lot like this, and frankly, there was a part of me that wanted to leave her to it. I couldn't do that because she was Brett's daughter. That was the big part. The other part was I was me. I seem to be one of those guys that would help a rabid dog across the street if I thought it were confused on directions.

I thought over the directions I had been given, and then varied from them. I found a little road to go down, a hunting trail, and then a little path off of it. I parked there and hoped no one found my car and decided they'd like to hot-wire it and drive it off, or, for that matter, just vandalize it. I got my pistol out of the glove box and stuck it in the pants at the base of my spine, and pulled my shirt over it. I got the food I had bought extra, a hamburger and fries and a canned Diet Coke, tucked the axe handle under my arm, and walked to where I understood the meeting place to be.

When I could see the house, which seemed pretty rickety and set off partly in the woods, I was pretty sure my suspicions were confirmed. Anyone coming here expecting pussy and drugs was a dumbass. I wasn't actually expecting either, but I was a dumbass, because here I was. I went to the house and checked the door. It was locked. I went around back. The door there was locked too, but it was thin. I thought that would be my surprise entrance, kicking the door down. I could do it now, and wait on him, but if he came around back, or that was his preferred way of entering, the joke could be on me.

I walked off in the woods to the left of the place and found a tumbled-down tree to sit on. I had my supper, which was alright if you had no taste buds and your stomach was made of cast iron. I only ate a few of the french fries, being as how they were greasy enough to give a garden statue the shits. I drank the Diet Coke and ate the burger. The meat seemed suspicious, but I was already hungry. I always got hungry when I thought I might kill someone or get killed myself.

As it grew dark, mosquitoes came out and buzzed around, and a few bit me. I wondered if they were carrying the West Nile virus, or maybe something worse. I slapped at them. I caught a chigger on its way up my pants leg, heading for my balls; I felt proud to have rescued them.

After a while I saw Kevin drive up and park and go inside

the house. I saw a light go on. He didn't have Tillie with him. He didn't seem to have anything with him. He was early too. I thought I would wait a few minutes, then surprise him. I looked at my watch. I'd give him a few minutes to feel secure, then I'd surprise him. Course, if he had a gun, which he would have, the surprise would be on me. Course, I had one too, but when guns come into play, anything can happen.

I thought about this, and I thought about that, and then I thought I felt something cold at the base of my skull, and since this was the dead of summer, even if it was just now dark, I knew it wasn't a cold breeze.

It was a gun barrel.

I can't explain how much like a dick I felt. Here I was putting the sneak on them, and they had put the sneak on me. I turned around slowly. A short fat man with a face that looked like it had been used for missile targeting, it had so many pocks, was smiling about fifteen thousand dollars of much-needed dental work at me.

"I could shoot you, you know," he said.

"Yep," I said.

"What we're gonna do is we're gonna walk up there and see Kevin. Stand up first."

I stood up, leaving the axe handle on the log. He patted me down with one hand and found my pistol and stuck it in one of his baggy pants pockets. He picked up the axe handle with his free hand and tapped my shoulder with it.

"Walk on up to the house," he said.

I was getting old, I figured. Any other time I would have been prepared. Or so I told myself. I had thought I was being smart getting there early, but they had put the sneak on me, putting moon-crater face in the woods to wait, and Kevin to come up like a staked goat.

"There's a road behind the woods here, dickhead," said Moon Crater. "I come up on that, then through the woods. I hid out and waited. I thought I might have to do some serious sneaking, but you picked a spot not that far from me. It was easy, man. Kevin said he thought you thought you were a smart guy, but you're not really so smart, are you?"

"I have to agree with that," I said.

In the house Kevin was waiting. He said, "No snatch or juice for you, huh? Course, that isn't what you were coming for, were you? I didn't like your looks from the start."

"You ain't got no mirrors at your house?"

Moon Crater whacked me across the back of the legs with the axe handle hard enough I went to my knees.

"I got a suspicion you got some other reason to see me. I got a suspicion you might be looking for Tillie, or Robert. I got to tell you, I think you know Robert's dead."

"You got me," I said. "I know he's dead. What about Tillie?"

"She's all right, but she won't be long," Kevin said. "Mr. Smith likes to get all the juice out of a product before he lets it go. He gets her hot-wired enough on something or another, he can sell her out until there's nothing to sell, you know. She then gets a hot shot, looks like an accident. They find her in a ditch somewhere with toadstools growing out of her ass."

"Robert didn't look like an accident."

"He proved more of a problem. Things got out of hand. You see, he was dipping, him and the cunt. We don't like dippers, unless maybe it's with chips and dip."

Kevin and Moon Crater liked that. Both of them laughed. I figured they didn't get out much.

"Get him in the chair," Kevin said.

They were ready for me. The chair was arranged in the middle of the floor. I did have a nice view through a window when Kevin moved out from in front of it, which he did from time to time. I could tell he lied about sampling his product. He had some of it in him right then, and it was giving him a nervous twitch. They put me in the chair and Moon Crater tied my legs and arms to it with rope while Kevin held Moon Crater's gun on me. When I was good and tied, Kevin said, "Now you got to tell me what you're up to."

"You can take a running leap up a donkey's ass," I said.

"Oh, that's not nice," Kevin said. "Jubil, hold this gun."

Jubil, aka Moon Crater, took the pistol. Kevin picked up my axe handle. I knew I was going to regret having bought that. He swung it hard against my shins. The pain jumped from my leg to my spine to the base of my brain. For a moment I thought I was going to be sick to my stomach and black out.

"That's got to hurt," Kevin said.

"You think?" I said. It wasn't much, and it wasn't good, but it was something, even if it sounded as if it were coming from a very small man under a pillow in the corner.

Kevin went over and put the axe handle by the front door. He reached in his pocket and took out a long pocketknife. He flipped it open.

"This house was left to me by old Grandma. It's not much, but I come here now and then for things. And I got a sentimental spot for it, even if it is starting to go bad. That being the case, what I want to say is, I don't want to bloody it up, I don't have to. So, for your sake, and mine, you should talk."

"I talk, you're just going to let me go?" I said.

"Sure," Kevin said.

"Bullshit," I said.

"Okay, you're right. I'm gonna kill you. But I can make it quick, a cut throat. Nasty to think about, but it gets over quick. Bleeds out good. Robert, I ended up having to shoot him a couple of times. Not so good. He was in pain right up until that last bullet. You, I can make you last a long time with this here knife."

"So my choice is I talk and you cut my throat, or I don't talk and you cut on me awhile till I do?"

"That's it," he said.

Right then, by the window, I saw Leonard's head go by. I stalled. I said, "So what would you like to know? I might have some answers, long as it doesn't involve math problems."

"Okay. First, who the fuck are you?"

I said, "I'm a census collector."

"That's going to get you cut," Kevin said. "I'm going to have to take an ear."

"Before you do," I said, "I really need to tell you something."

"What would that be?" Kevin said.

"Hell is coming," I said.

At that moment the door burst open, propelled forward by Leonard's foot. Leonard spied the axe handle, and he had it in his free hand before you could say, "My, is that an axe handle?"

Leonard said, striding forward, "Queer, roughhouse nigger, coming through."

He stepped forward quick and caught Moon Crater in the teeth with a left-handed swing of the handle. It knocked Moon Crater to the floor, sending the gun spinning away from him.

The light caught the black gleam of Leonard's close-shaved head, and it danced in his eyes, it danced along the length of the brand-new axe handle. The axe handle cut through the air like a hot knife through butter. When Kevin met the wood there was a sound like someone slapping a belt on a leather couch, and then there were teeth and there was enough blood flying out of Kevin's mouth I was sure Grandma's house was ruined. It splattered on the wall and on the window, teeth clattered on the floor.

Kevin hit the floor on his belly, dropped the knife. He tried to crawl for it, but Leonard stomped his hand and the axe handle came down again. This time it was a sound more like someone chopping the neck off a turkey with a meat cleaver.

Kevin didn't move after that lick, but just for good measure,

Leonard hit him again. He went over then to Moon Crater, who was trying to get up, and kicked him in the mouth. That dental work Moon Crater already needed was going to cost a lot more now.

When Kevin came awake, he was strapped to the chair where I had been. Leonard was nearby, leaning on the axe handle, I was squatted down in front of Kevin. Moon Crater was still stretched out on the floor. If he wasn't dead or in a coma, he probably down deep in some part of his being wished he was.

"Howdy," I said.

"Fuck you," Kevin said, but it was hard to be sure if that was actually what he said. He was spitting up blood.

"If you leave here," I said, "and it's possible, you might want to pick up your teeth, not confusing them with the gems that were in Jubil's mouth. You might want to put them in a glass of water and freeze them. I hear they can do wonders with knocked-out teeth now."

"Who are you?" he asked.

"My name is Hap, and this is my brother, Leonard. But you two have already met."

"Glad to make your fucking acquaintance," he said.

I stood up, turned to Leonard. "I didn't think you were coming."

"I was on my way home when you called. Started driving back two days ago, but I was in a blind spot for the phone. Bottom land. I got your message a little late."

"Not too late, though."

I turned back to Kevin. "Kevin," I said, "you and me, we got to talk, and I got to get some answers, and if I like them, I'm not even going to cut your throat."

They told us Tillie had been taken by the Gospel Opry guy, Buster Smith, and that Kevin and Moon Crater had helped him take her. She was in an old theater. I knew the theater. I was from Marvel Creek, and when I was growing up I went to many movies there. They had a stage at that theater, a movie screen behind it. They had kid shows and they brought out clowns and jugglers and special entertainment. It was awful and I was always glad when they got off the stage and turned off the light, leaving me with the roaches and a movie.

Leonard didn't want to leave them with their car and he decided he didn't want to fuck it up. He wanted to fuck them up. I don't like that sort of thing, but, hey, what you gonna do? They started it.

Leonard put them in the trunk of his car and I followed in mine after he dropped me off. We took them into the river bottoms. Leonard let them out of the trunk. They got out, though neither felt well. Leonard had really laid that axe handle on them. He said, "Thing I'm going to do is break both your legs. One a piece."

"No need in that, Leonard," I said.

"I know. I just want to do it."

"Look now," said Kevin. "Listen to your friend. We just work for that dickhead. We're out of it. We hope you get the girl back."

"Oh, we'll get her back if she's to be gotten back," Leonard said. "But here's the thing. You were going to kill my friend. Had I not showed up, you would have. So, which leg?"

Kevin and Moon Crater looked at me.

"He's sort of got his mind made up," I said. "And you were going to kill me."

"But we'll die out here if our legs are broke," Moon Crater said.

"Don't be so goddamn dramatic," Leonard said. "You'll still be able to crawl, maybe find a stick to support yourself or something. Really, it's not our problem.

"Which leg?" Leonard said. "Or I choose."

"Left," Kevin said. Moon Crater didn't choose. "But—"

Before Kevin could protest again, Leonard swung that axe handle. It whistled, caught the man on the side of the knee, which is where it's the weakest. I heard a sound like someone breaking a rack of pool balls. Kevin screamed and went down holding his knee.

"One," Leonard said.

Moon Crater made a break for it. I owed Leonard one, so I chased Moon Crater down and grabbed him by the shoulder and spun him around and threw a right cross into his face, and his face took it. He fell down. Before he could get up Leonard was there with the axe handle. I think it took about three whacks for Leonard to catch him good, I don't really remember. I looked away. But, I think it was the right leg.

We drove Leonard's car to a church lot, which struck us as ironic, and I drove us in mine over to Marvel Creek. I said, "What if those guys get out of the woods and call? Warn Buster."

"It's miles to their car," Leonard said. "It's miles to Bullock. They got broke legs. Besides, it was you didn't want me to kill them. Up to me, they'd be in the Sabine River somewhere with fish nibbling on them."

"You are cold, man," I said.

"Absolutely," Leonard said.

We thought we'd stake out the Gospel Opry, but when we drove by, there was action there. A big crowd. Leonard said, "They're loading them inside. What is it? Nine? Ten o'clock? I didn't know Jesus stayed up this late."

"True. He's usually early to bed and early to rise."

I got my gun and put it under my shirt in the small of my back. We left the axe handle in the backseat with its memories. As we walked up, we saw the crowd was growing.

I said to an old man on a cane, "What's up?"

"The Gospel Opry usually. Talent show tonight, though. Y'all don't know about it?"

"No," I said. "We don't."

"It's more fun than a barrel of monkeys. There's people who sing and dance and do comedy. Good clean fun." He looked at Leonard. "You'll be able to get in, son. I remember when your color couldn't."

"My, how times have changed," Leonard said.

I glanced around and saw a line going through another door, off to the side. I said to the old man, "Who are they?"

"The talent. They signed up to perform."

Leonard said, "Come on, Hap."

We got in line at the talent door.

"More fun than a barrel of monkeys," I said, "and they let your kind in, Leonard."

"Well, suh, I sho' is beholding to some peckerwoods for that. Sho' is."

Inside there was a little man at a desk. He wore a bad wig. He asked us our name. We gave him our first names. Leonard said we were a singing act.

The little man couldn't find us on the roster, of course.

"We were set," I said. "We called ahead and everything. They think we're the bee's knees over in Overton."

"Overton is so small you can throw a rock across it," the man said.

"Yep, but we're still big there," I said.

He thought about it a moment, said, "Look here. There's a couple of guys who play bagpipes that canceled. Laundry lost their kilts or some such something. I'll give you their spot. You didn't get registered, but it'll work out. So you sing?"

"Like fucking birds," Leonard said.

The man looked at him, grinned slowly. Jesus didn't seem to always be at his house. He waved us inside, and we went.

"A singing group?" I said.

"The bee's knees," Leonard said.

Way it worked is we were guided backstage. There were a lot of acts there. One old man had on what looked like a sergeant's uniform. He was potbellied, bald, and looked as if he should have been on oxygen. He had a ventriloquist dummy with him. It was dressed up like a private, with a field cap and everything. I got to tell you, I seriously hate me some ventriloquist dummies. When I was a kid, late at night, I caught an old movie titled *Dead of Night*, an anthology film. One of the sections was about a man and a ventriloquist dummy that takes over his life. It scared the living dogshit out of me. I see a block of wood that might be carved into a ventriloquist dummy, I get nervous. And this dummy looked as if the rats and someone with an ice pick had been at him.

"How long you been doing this?" I said.

He wheezed a moment before answering. "I used to make real money at it. No one will have me now, except these talent shows, some kids' parties. I don't do as well as I once did. They got the goddamn Internet now. Oh, you boys won't tell on me, will you? They like us to watch our language."

"We won't say a fucking word," Leonard said.

The old man laughed. He leaned in close. "Neither of you boys got a drink, do you?"

We admitted that we didn't.

"That's all right, then. Just wondering." He shook the doll a little, causing dust to stir up. "Private Johnson is getting worn out. My wife took a knife to him once, and used him to beat me over the head. It did some damage to him and me. I fart, it blacks me out and I wake up wearing a tutu."

He barked then at his joke, and then he carried on. "I haven't had the money to get him fixed. I act like the one eyelid he's got that droops is just part of the act. It adds character."

"Sure it does," I said. "You'll knock them dead."

I hoped he didn't knock himself dead. He was red-faced and breathing heavy and looked as if he might blow a major hose at any moment. Maybe his talk about farting and blacking out wasn't just a joke.

We all stood there in line, looking out at the stage. There were some dance acts going on out there. The band sounded like cows dying. The dancers moved like they had wooden legs. Next a young, beak-nosed man who played a fiddle so bad it sounded like he was sawing on a log did his act. It was the kind of noise that made your asshole pucker.

"The sisters will win this thing," said the old man. "I ain't seen them yet, but they'll probably show soon. Those dried-up-cunt bitches. They enter every week and win the five hundred dollars. It's those damn hymns. It gets the Jesus going in folks, and they feel like they got to vote for them. Shit, I'm up."

The old man waddled out with that horrible doll, picked up a stool on the way out. His act was so painful I thought I might use a curtain rope to hang myself, but at the same time I admired the old bastard. He wasn't a quitter. He wheezed and tried to throw his voice, but by the end of his act the dummy looked healthier than he did.

He came back with his doll and stool. He sat on the stool. "I tried to hit a high note there, when Private sang 'Boogie Woogie Bugle Boy,' and I damn near shit on myself. I think one of my rib bones moved."

"You did fine," I said.

"I did fine about fifty years ago and it was a spring morning and I had just knocked off a piece of ass. I did fine then. Least that's how I like to remember it. Might have been a hot afternoon in the dead of summer and it might have been a stump broke cow."

"Just sit there and rest," I said.

"You're all right," he said to me. "Sure you haven't a drink?"

"Sure," I said.

There was another dance troupe on stage, and a guy with some bowling pins he was going to juggle was next in line. Leonard and I glanced around, trying to take in the place. It didn't look like a joint where a prostitute would be kept, or in this case made to go for free until she was used up. It didn't look like a place where someone sold drugs. It looked like a place full of bad entertainment. That's what made it a good hideout, of course, but I wasn't convinced.

I noticed that the acts that finished were ushered along a certain path, and that there were two guys on either side of a dark stairway. They didn't look like church deacons, but I decided to call them that in my mind. I left Leonard and walked over to the stairway, looked up it. I said, "What's up there?"

One of the men stepped forward, said, "That's private, sir."

I went back to Leonard. I said, "There's a whole nuther floor up there."

"There's a stairway on the other side of the stage too," he said. "You can see it from here. It's got bookends on either side of it too."

I looked. Sure enough, two more guys. If the two near us were not church deacons, those two were not in the choir. Upstairs could have just been a storage place for hymn books, but I doubted it.

"Buster don't work the brothers," Leonard said. "All white thugs."

"It may not seem that long ago to them that your kind couldn't come in, and it may be they liked it like that."

"That really isn't true," Leonard said. "They did come in here, and you know it."

"They did janitor work," I said, "and they used to come up the stairs at the back and sat up there in the balcony."

"Nigger money was good as any," Leonard said. "I know. I sat up there in the balcony once and spat on a white boy's head."

"You did not," I said.

"No, but now and again I like to dream."

We were whispering a game plan, when all of a sudden the little fellow that had signed us in came over. He said, "The Honey Girls are sick."

"Who?" I said.

"The gospel singers I told you about," said the old ventriloquist, who had come over. "Their adult diapers probably got bunched up and they couldn't make it. Or they heard that young girl come on and sing and left. I know they were here. I seen them, the smug assholes."

"That'll be enough," said the little man.

"Sorry," said the ventriloquist, and he waddled back to his stool.

I had my mind on other things, and hadn't even noticed the young girl, not really. But in the back of my mind I sort of remembered her doing a Patsy Cline number, and not badly at all.

"Honey Sisters say they got sick," said the little man.

"Both of them?" Leonard said.

"It hit them sudden, so you two are on next."

"Oh," I said.

Leonard grabbed my elbow, "Come on, I still remember 'The Old Rugged Cross.'"

"You're yanking me," I said. "We're really going out there?"

"I sing in the shower," Leonard said. "I do all right."

"Oh, hell," I said.

Well, we went out there, and I knew that old tune too. I am an atheist, but I like a good gospel tune now and again. We didn't have any music, but there was the house band and they knew the tune, sort of, though I didn't remember it with a tuba solo. We started out with it. Leonard was good, actually; he sounded way all right. I sort of chimed in when he lifted a hand to me, but after a few lines I forgot the words, so I started singing nonsense. An old lady in the front row in a wheelchair said, "Get the hook."

Leonard finished out while I snapped my fingers and tried to look cool. I think had I had sunglasses, I could have pulled it off.

When we finished, or more or less quit, they were glad to see us go. Someone even threw a wadded-up paper cup at me. Fucker missed.

When we exited on the other side, Leonard said, "Damn, Hap. You fucked it up. We could have won that prize money. Or I could have."

"I didn't make us out as a duet, since we have never sang together even once. I never intended to go out there."

"I've always wanted to do that."

"You sounded all right," I said, "but don't be thinking of it as a second job."

"As for you," Leonard said, "you don't be thinking of it at all. Now, let's see if we can find Tillie."

"If she's alive," I said.

"She's alive, they are going to pay for it. If she's dead, they're going to pay for it, and then pay a dividend."

I didn't even like Tillie, but I sure liked Brett. Brett called her a bent twig. She'd say, "Hap, she's a bent twig, but she's not broken. She can weather the storm and come out on the other side."

She was pretty much still in the storm as far as I was concerned, but if the information we had was right, she didn't deserve this; this was even worse than what should happen to politicians. We headed toward the staircase on the side where we exited, near the choirboys. A man over there pointed us toward an exit. He was a chubby guy in a faded, purple leisure suit old enough to belong in a museum. He said, "That was bad, boys. Real bad."

We ignored him and headed for the staircase.

"Not over there," he said, and he grabbed my sleeve. I shook him loose and kept going. I had a feeling that most everyone here had no idea what was going on upstairs, no idea that the man who ran the Gospel Opry was about as reverent and kind as the business end of a hatchet.

"Those guys don't kid," said the man who had grabbed my sleeve. He was talking about the two boys at the stairs. They stepped out, one toward me, one toward Leonard.

The choirboy on my side said, "You don't come this way."

I kicked him in the balls and he bent a little and I hit him with a right hook. He went against the wall and came off of it mad. I hit him again, a straight right to the jaw. He went to one knee and tried to draw a pistol from under his coat. I pulled mine and hit him in the head with it. He went to his hands and knees, and I hit him again. He kind of bent his elbows like he had failed to do a push-up and lay on the floor. It was then that I noticed my leg where Kevin had hit me with the axe handle was really aching. I noticed this because I was going to kick him again and decided against it.

I looked over at Leonard. His man was already unconscious at the base of the stairs. I think he took him out with one good punch. I rolled my man over and took his gun. I had one in either hand, now. I went up the stairs behind Leonard. Back on stage I heard laughter. Someone had finally succeeded at something. A joke maybe.

When I got to the top of the stairs, Leonard had taken an automatic off of the man he had hit and he had it at the ready. I turned and looked down, wondering if the deacons across the way knew what we were up to. If they didn't, they would soon. I figured the man who grabbed my sleeve would tell them. He might not know what really went on here, but he knew who he worked for.

Of course, if we were wrong, and what we expected was not at the top of the stairs, was really a bingo parlor, we would have a lot of explaining to do. For that matter, we could have a lot of explaining to do anyway.

The deacons figured it out. They came running across the stage in the middle of a dance number with a man and a woman in a horse suit. The man was the back end, the horse's ass. I knew this because I came back down the stairs because I heard running. It gave me a view of the stage. The deacons knocked the horse over and the man and woman spilled out of it. The couple said some words you wouldn't expect to hear at a Gospel Opry. God probably made a big black mark in their book right then.

The deacons didn't have guns drawn, and they almost ran right over me they were coming so fast. When they saw my revolver, as well as the automatic I had taken off one of the choirboys, they stopped up short. They froze like ice cubes.

I said, "Do you really want to get dead?"

One man shook his head and started to run, across the stage again, past the horse, which had been put together again. A tinny trumpet was playing somewhere, and a piano. The horse was dancing. That goddamn tuba was hitting some random notes; that guy, he ought to be put down in the ground with that tuba.

The other deacon, the one that didn't run, put his hands up. He said. "You got to at least take my gun, so I can say I was unarmed."

"That'll work," I said. "But pull it easy."

He did, squatted down and put it on the floor and backed up. "I got no beef," he said.

"That's good," I said, "because I am in one shitty mood."

He backed out and went across the stage walking fast. The couple in the horse suit just quit then. The woman pulled off the horse's head and tossed it into the audience. I hoped she hit the old woman in the wheelchair that said to get the hook.

I picked up his gun, a little nine, and went up the stairs again. Leonard was waiting. "Stop to go to the bathroom?" he asked.

"I was disarming a gentleman."

Leonard pointed with his handgun. "There's one door. Shall we see what's on the other side? Lady or the Tiger."

"I think we might get both," I said.

We moved quickly down the hall and Leonard kicked at the door and it swung back and came loose, hanging on one hinge, and then it came looser and fell. It was a toilet. It was empty.

"They were guarding a bathroom?" Leonard said. "Really?"

There was probably some way to get across, but we didn't see it right away, and we were in a bit of a hurry. We put the guns in our waistbands, under our shirts, went down the stairs and behind the stage. The Gospel Opry folks were not deterred. The action, such as it was, was still going on. It was some kind of comedy act. When we got to the other side, we passed the man and the woman that had been wearing the horse outfit. They gave us the hard eye.

"Were you two part of the disruption?" said the woman.

"No, ma'am," I said, and kept going. We went up the stairs where the deacons had been. We pulled out our guns. There were two doors along the hallway.

"I'll take one, you take the other," Leonard said.

We chose a door, nodded at one another, and stomp-kicked them. My door went back completely off the hinges, old as it was. I could hear Leonard still kicking as I went through.

There was a bed in the room, and a little light to the right, and there was a row of four chairs on that side, and I'm dying if I'm lying, there were four men in those chairs, and the one closest to the light was reading a newspaper. It was like they were in a barbershop waiting their turn. Tillie was on the bed, and a nude man was on her, his naked ass bobbing like a basketball. Tillie wasn't there really. She was in some other zone. She had her eyes open, but they might as well have been closed. She looked skeletal. My guess is she hadn't been fed in a while, outside of what was in a needle. She looked a lot like Brett, if Brett were a concentration camp survivor, and that disturbed me even more.

The four men stood up. They were all dressed, though one had taken off his shoes and placed them under his chair. One of them was wearing a police uniform and had his hand on the pistol in his belt. He was out for a little on-duty nookie and bit of blow it seemed.

By now Leonard had come through the door. The cop pulled his pistol and I shot him. I hit him in the arm and he fell down on the floor and started going around in circles like Curly of the Three Stooges. He was yelling, "Don't shoot me no more, don't shoot me no more."

Blood was all over the place.

The other three men acted as if to run, but Leonard resorted to foul language that had to do with their mothers. One sat back down, as if still waiting his turn, his mother be damned.

I said, "Where's dickhead? Buster?"

Nobody said anything.

"He asked you a question," Leonard said. "You don't say, and we find him, we're going to shoot all your toes off. And then your dick."

By this time the man in the bed had got off Tillie and was standing beside the bed with one hand over his pecker.

Leonard said, "I had a turkey neck like that, I'd keep it covered too. Fact is, I'm an expert on dicks, and that is an ugly one."

"He does know dicks," I said.

The man in the police uniform had quit spinning and had stuck his head up under a chair. He said, "I'm hit. I'm hit."

"No shit," I said.

I went over and saw that Tillie was breathing hard. I pulled the blanket at the end of the bed over her. I looked at the naked man with his hand over his privates and I just went berserk. I don't know what happened to me, but I just couldn't stand to think people like this existed, that they could sit in chairs and wait their turns to top some drugged girl. I kicked the naked man in the balls and hit him in the head with the pistol, and then I went after the other three, but not before I kicked the police officer on the floor once, and heeled his gun under the bed. I started hitting those three guys with the pistols, one in either hand. I was hitting so fast I looked like Shiva. They tried to run for it, but each time they did Leonard kicked them back into play, and I just went to work. I felt wrong. I felt savage. I felt awful, and yet, I felt right.

It didn't take long before all of them were bleeding. Two were on the floor. One had fallen back into his chair. The naked man on the floor wasn't moving. He was lying on his side and had thrown up all over the place, and the air was thick with the stench of vomit.

"Okay," Leonard said. He walked over and put his gun against the shoeless man's nose. He was the one that had sat back down. "Where is Buster?"

The man didn't answer. He didn't need to. A door opened at the far end and two men came in. One had a shotgun. He cut down with it, but we were already moving. I dropped to the floor behind the bed, and Leonard leaped through the door he had kicked down, landed out in the hallway. From under the bed I could see the man's legs, and I shot at them, three times in rapid succession. I hit him somewhere because he yelped and fell down. I shot him again, this time in the top of the head, cracking it apart like a big walnut. The other man had a handgun and he had been firing it all this time. So far he had hit the bed, killed the barefoot man in the chair behind me, and had put some holes in the wall.

From under the bed I saw Leonard's feet as he came through the other door, the one I had kicked down, and then he was on that bastard. I got to my feet and started around, tripped over the policeman who had, without me seeing him, started crawling toward the open doorway.

"Stay," I said, as if speaking to a dog.

He stopped crawling.

By the time I got around to Leonard he had already taken the man down. Somehow the man had shot himself in the foot. I kicked him in the head, just to let him know I was in the game, and then Leonard reached down and took the man's pistol. Considering this guy's aim it was probably best to have left him with it. In time he would have shot himself again, maybe in the head.

"You stick," I said to Leonard.

"All right, but I hear too much gunfire, I'm coming. Right after I kill the lot of them."

I went through the door the two had come through, and by now I could hear yelling down below in the auditorium. The gunfire had roused things up, and was probably more exciting than anything they had seen tonight.

When I got into the room upstairs I saw that it was well tricked out for an old building. Lots of modern furniture, including a big couch. It was pushed back from the wall and I could see feet sticking out from behind it. I walked over there and laid my guns on the coffee table and grabbed the man by the ankles and pulled him out. He tried to hang onto the floor, but this only resulted in him dragging his nails across it. He was a long lean man in a plaid sports coat with hair the color of black shoe polish. I said, "You Buster Smith?"

He said, "No."

I got his wallet out of his back pocket and looked at his driver's license. "Yes you are," I said. "I bet you always got caught when you played hide and go seek as a kid."

He got to one knee. "I did, actually."

I went over and got my guns, said, "I wouldn't try anything.

I shoot you, then Leonard will shoot everyone else, and we'll have a hard time explaining things. But you'll be dead."

We didn't go to jail.

That's the important part. Let me tell you why. So when it was done and everyone was hauled in, including me and Leonard, they waltzed us into the police chief. This is after interrogations, searches, a rubber glove up the asshole, just in case we were hiding hand grenades. He was a nice-looking guy with his black hair cut close to his head and one ear that stood out more than the other, as if it were signaling for a turn. He sat behind a big mahogany desk. There was a little sign on the desk that read POLICE CHIEF.

"Well now, Hap Collins." he said.

I recognized him. A little older. Still fit. James Dell. We had gone to school together.

"It's been awhile," he said. "What I remember best about you is I don't like you."

"It's a big club," Leonard said. "Hap even has a newsletter."

"Me and Jim dated the same girl," I said.

"Not at the same time," Jim said.

"He dated her last," I said.

"That's right. And I married her."

"So, you won," I said.

"Way I like to see it," James said, "you boys raised some hell. And you shot people. And you hit people. And Hap, you killed a guy. I also got word there's two boys with broken legs over in Bullock. They gave themselves up to the sheriff over there."

"Nice guy," I said.

"One of the men you shot was a police officer," said James.

"I know. He was waiting in line to rape a young woman. How is she by the way?"

"Hospital. Touch and go for awhile. But she made it. Apparently she's no stranger to drugs, so maybe she had some tolerance. Hadn't eaten in days. Buster Smith, we talked to him. He came apart like a fresh biscuit. He was only tough when his money worked for him. That cop, by the way, he was the police chief."

"Oh," Leonard said. "Then what are you?"

"The new police chief. I should also mention that the mayor is the one that caught a stray bullet and is as dead as an old bean can."

"Mayor. Police chief. We had quite a night," I said.

To make this part of the story short, we had to stay in the jail till our friend Marvin Hanson could get us a lawyer, and then we got out, and then we got no billed, in spite of the fact we had hunted the bastard down and caused quite a ruckus. The former police chief was dead, by our hand, and the mayor was on the deceased list as well, by a stray slug, and the others that had been in the row of chairs were all prominent citizens. It was best to take it easy on us, let them cover their own dirt in their own way.

Thing was simply this: The crime being done to Tillie was so bad, they let us pretty much skate on self-defense. Hell, after all, it is Texas.

Brett and I climbed into bed and she lay in the crook of my arm.

"Tillie is going to be out of the hospital tomorrow," Brett said.

She had spent about three months in there. She had been in a bad way. I had to say this for the kid, she was tough as yesterday's fajita meat.

"I have to go get her then," Brett said.

"All right," I said.

"I know you don't like her."

"Correct."

"You didn't have to do what you did."

"Yes I did."

"For me?"

"You and her."

"But you don't like her."

"I don't like a lot of things," I said, "but you love her. You think she's a bent twig, and maybe you're right. No one deserves that."

"But she sets herself up for it, right?"

"Yeah," I said. "She does. I don't think she'll ever change. Sometime soon, she doesn't, she's going to be dead. She picks men like ducks pick june bugs. At random."

"I know. I tried to be a good mother."

"I know that too, so don't start on how you failed. You did what you could."

"I did set her father's head on fire," Brett said.

"Yes, you did," I said. "But by all accounts, he had it coming."

"He did, you know."

"Never doubted it."

"I love you, Hap."

"And I love you, Brett."

"Want to lose five minutes out of your life the hard way?" she said.

I laughed. "Now that's not nice."

She laughed, rolled over, and turned off the light. And then she was very nice.

JOE R. LANSDALE INTERVIEWS HAP COLLINS AND LEONARD PINE

Q. Hap, I'm going to start with you. You strike me as an intelligent guy. Why don't you try and make a little bit more of your life?

Hap: Haven't a clue. I keep thinking I will, but I seem to take wrong turns.

Q. Why not back off from the situations you get yourself into? You deserve a little better, don't you?

Hap: I get into them before I mean to. It's like they're kind of lurking out there. I turn left to avoid them, there's more trouble comin' the other way.

Leonard: And he drags me in after him. Can I say something?

Q. Be my guest.

Leonard: Hap's bright, but doesn't fully believe it. He thinks because he hasn't come up with the formula for something like Coca-Cola, or has done him some brain surgery, or cured a disease, he hasn't lived up to his expectations. Problem with

Hap is, he coasts. Ain't sayin' he's lazy. He works hard. When he works. But he hasn't got any rudder.

Q. Now, don't take this wrong, Leonard, but what's your excuse?

Leonard: I don't make any. I'm doing what I want to do. That's the difference between me and my brother here. He isn't entirely happy being him. I'm damn ecstatic about being me. I work hard. I don't worry that much about the future. A little. But nothing serious. Hap, he's nothing but a big ol' bag of worry.

Hap: I thought I was a love machine.

Leonard: You're a love machine can't keep a woman.

Hap: You've had a bit of a problem maintaining relationships yourself, my good man.

Leonard: Yeah. But, you know what? I think I've found a man finally.

Q. That's another thing. Don't the people you guys care about seem to . . . well, you know?

Leonard: Yeah, they seem to give us bad luck. We haven't figured that one out yet.

Q. Well, they're the ones get killed.

Leonard: Yeah. We haven't figured that out either.

Q. This one's for you, Leonard. Do you feel that as you get older you're gettin' your temper under control?

Leonard: What temper?

Q. Well . . .

Leonard: Hey, answer the question. I didn't stutter. What temper?

Q. I was merely sayin' . . .

Leonard: You haven't said anything yet. You asked if I had a temper. I don't have any damn temper.

Hap: Yes you do.

Leonard: Hey, you want a piece of me, brother? You want to wake up with a crowd around you?

Hap: Hey, bubba. You and me get into it, you better brought yourself a sack lunch, 'cause we're gonna be here all night.

Leonard: Yeah?

Hap: Yeah.

Q. Let's change the subject. You guys seem to survive through pure tenacity and a feeling of quarrelsome brotherhood. . . .

Leonard: Quarrelsome. Who you callin'—

Hap: You're right. We do. There's this, Lansdale. You can have all the money there is, every damn thing, and what it comes down to finally, like it or not, you got to have someone to lean on.

Leonard and I aren't brothers by birth. But we are brothers. Like our lawyer friend Andrew Vachss says, "It's the family you choose that counts." We stand by that. It can be your blood kin, certainly, but it doesn't have to be. Way we see it, we can argue and fight with each other, but no one else better think they can. Least not in any serious manner.

Q. All right. Let me ask this: What are future plans?

Hap: Hard to say.

Leonard: Charlie Blank and Hanson have some ideas for us. They've got a little private investigator's agency, and we may be picking up a few jobs from them. Nothing technical. Just little stuff, you know. Hap here, he'll still be looking for a date. Watching his weight. Sticking to nonalcoholic beer and losing his hair. I'll still be cool and calm in my JCPenney's suit.

Hap: You may be calm, but that cheap suit is enough to make anyone else nervous.

Q. I have just a few more questions.

Leonard: Actually, we got to go. We borrowed the truck we're in to get over here, and we promised to have it back. Our junkers are in the shop. Guy needs this one back to go to work.

Hap: And there's a monster movie showing on channel 38 I want to see.

Leonard: Not that he hasn't seen it about a hundred times.

Q. Well, thanks, guys. And be careful out there.

Leonard: Hell, careful's our middle name, man.

THE CARE AND FEEDING AND RAISING UP OF HAP AND LEONARD

CAREERS HAVE PHASES, and I've had a few.

My early career was merely struggling to sell. I managed early on to write some mystery material, and then horror, mostly short fiction. I wrote some books I'm proud of in my early career—*The Nightrunners*, *Dead in the West*, *The Magic Wagon*, *The Drive-In*, and *Cold in July* come to mind.

I remember these were all written in a house on Christian Street. I also wrote there the stories that ended up in my first collection, *By Bizarre Hands*, as well as *Stories by Mama Lansdale's Youngest Boy*.

Shortly after I finished *Cold in July*, we moved to the far side of town, another rural area, to have more room for our kids. Before moving, my study became our daughter's room. She had her crib assembled, amid piles of books, next to my desk, which eventually became covered with baby supplies. I ended up ejected and working on a small, wobbly desk in our bedroom.

Our new house was massive compared to our old one. I had an entire floor for my study, for all my books. With this house came a large desk that I have used ever since, although that is about to change. We are moving. I wrote a lot of books and

221

stories and articles and screenplays and comics on that desk in our middle house, as I have christened it. Our children were raised here.

We are in the process of moving, and as we make efforts in that direction, it occurred to me that this is the house where Hap and Leonard were born. Other characters and stories, and some of my best critically received novels, were birthed here as well, but it somehow seems more significant to me that the boys were born here. There has always been something about Hap and Leonard that has engaged readers in a different way than what I might think of as my more "literary" novels. It's not so much their adventures that keep pulling people back, although that's part of it, but is instead the guys themselves. The way they interact with one another and others. A true odd couple. I feel as if I can hardly take credit for them. They seemed to leap into my skull whole born, like Athena bursting forth from the head of Zeus. And like Athena, their creation was not by design. It was a happy accident.

Let's back up a bit.

I wrote *Cold in July* in the Christian Street house, the one before the house we are about to move from; it was one of a two-book contract I had with Bantam. I wanted, at least then, to write books that I thought would be like modern Gold Medal novels, Gold Medal being a division of Fawcett Books, now defunct. Gold Medal was known specifically for crime books, although they certainly produced Westerns, science fiction, and so on. But it was the crime Gold Medals that hooked me in my late teens, and throughout my twenties. Outside Gold Medal, I was influenced heavily by the usual suspects—Chandler, Hammett, and Cain. But there was a tone in the Gold Medal novels that was quite different. They were an overall collective of hardboiled deeds, capers, thefts, and poor suckers riding life trains to oblivion, with no chance to brake or leap off.

I loved that stuff. I collected Gold Medal books for years,

and still do, when I can find one that isn't falling apart or that I don't already have. And sometimes even if I do have it, I buy it anyway. They are becoming rarer each day. Where they were once stacked in droves at garage sales and used bookstores fairly dripped with them, they are now as unusual to find as the three-toed sloth in your living room.

With my two-book contract at Bantam, I thought it would be fun to riff on the old Gold Medal books, and after a very vivid dream that led to *Cold in July*, I was fired up even more. I thought that one had worked out quite well, and I wanted to do yet another in the same tone. *Savage Season* certainly tasted like Gold Medal, but there was something different about it from *Cold in July*. It was more deliberate, casual, purposely paced, and although it had twists and a dynamic climax, I found I was writing about my past, at least in a symbolic way, about how my life might have been if certain things had gone another direction. They were fiction, of course, but I must 'fess up and say that a lot in the Hap and Leonard books, especially the first three, was taken directly from events in my life, or the lives of others I knew, extrapolated and made a lot more exciting and dangerous.

I was also writing about the sixties, about how that shook out, at least for me. I found a symbolic way of doing that by writing a novel that took place in the late eighties, a reflective book, with Hap feeling the changes, wondering how one morning it was the sixties and early seventies—because much of the time when we talk about the sixties, we're really talking about the early seventies as well—and then, the world was new and more consumer-driven, far less idealistic, and the music kind of sucked. In the mid-seventies, the Vietnam War finally wrapped up and the soldiers came home. All of us who had yelled about civil rights and an unjust war, and so many things—gay rights, women's rights—suddenly felt vindicated. But in the long run, as Leonard says in *Savage Season*, the sixties were just the eighties in tie-dyed T-shirts. I'm not as cynical as Leonard, but there's something to be said, at least partially, for that point of view.

The book I was writing was not then called *Savage Season* but tentatively titled *Ice Birds*. Problem was everyone thought I was saying *Ice Bergs*, so I changed the title to *Savage Season*. It was originally something like *A Strange and Savage Season*, but that was too long and, frankly, didn't quite fit. It sounded a smidgen pretentious. Therefore, the final decision for a briefer and simpler title. I started writing the book, as I said, pulling from my own life, adding things that never happened, and this guy named Leonard showed up. With his arrival at the first of the novel, I knew then it was a buddy story. I love those. But then Leonard surprised me, not only by showing up but by revealing in a sideways manner that he was gay, Republican, a supporter of the Vietnam War, and a war hero. I hadn't known that going in. Hap Collins, my hero of the book, or at least the one who tells the tale, for Leonard is in many ways just as prominent a character, knew that about Leonard, but he didn't tell me until the moment Leonard revealed it. At the time of writing that book, gay characters were uncommon in crime fiction. There were exceptions, but they were rare. Even more rare were black Republicans, and rarer yet, gay Republicans. They existed, of course, but were generally more uncommon than a three-toed sloth in your living room. They were, in fact, as uncommon as a three-toed sloth in your living room wearing a propeller beanie. Also, male gay characters who were, in appearance and action, more masculine were also underrepresented. Yet I knew they existed, so why not represent them as well? I wasn't thinking about breaking new ground, or anything really, just about writing honest characters who weren't all white and straight and middle-class.

Anyway, there I was, writing along, and Leonard showed up, and he and Hap were best friends, and different of opinion in many ways, as many of my friends are different from me, but at the core, Hap and Leonard are one and the same. Honorable men, smart men, who took a wrong boat in life and ended up on the ragged edge of the American Dream.

At the time of that writing, I was not far removed from that very position in life. My wife, Karen, was my saving grace. She directed me in such a way that I moved in a straight line, not in circles. She and I worked as farm field workers, ran a goat dairy, butchered our own meat, and raised our own vegetables. Karen had come from a more middle-class background than I had, but she had dove right in with me, making ends meet as best she could, having faith that our life together would be a good one, and that the American Dream, which I believe in—how can I not? I'm living it—was ours for the taking.

We took hold of it, and have kept our teeth securely clamped there ever since. I know it's an elusive dream, and dream is the right word. It's something we all want, and sometimes it's something, through hard work, inheritance, or accident, that we can have. But, for the most part, it's an opportunity, not a promise. That's all it's ever been, except for the fact that here in our country, that dream is supposedly more obtainable than elsewhere.

Sometimes it is, and sometimes it's not.

That, too, went into the book. In his own way, Hap is, like Gatsby, standing on the pier, reaching out for the green light across the bay. His life is a lot more blue-collar in nature, and the green light represents to him less than it meant to Gatsby. Not great riches and fine clothes and bringing back the past, just less-back-breaking work, a library card, and a TV that gets what was then all three network channels. A home where he can have a good wife and a happy sex life, raise fine kids to whom he can pass along the dreams he holds dear. Fair play. Common sense. A decent bank account. And with a little luck, a quick death in old age without lingering illness, or a tube in his pecker and adult diapers steaming with shit.

So Hap, in his own small, blue-collar way, is my Gatsby. At

least he is in the first few novels. In time, that changes, as all our lives must change.

Leonard, he just wants to be left alone. He doesn't care about anyone's club. He's gay, and he's all right with that. He's black, and if you don't like it, you can ram a stick up your nose. He's a lot less introspective than Hap. He's one of those guys like my dad was. It is what it is. Wish in one hand and shit in the other, and see which one fills up first.

After *Savage Season*, I had no idea that I would ever write about Hap and Leonard again. I didn't intend to, and it was three years before I did. I had moved from Bantam to Mysterious Press by that time, a kind of movement not uncommon to authors, especially in those days when we still had a number of publishers to choose from, and we didn't have computer sales numbers following us around. My then-agent managed to get me a two-book contract at Mysterious, and my first book for them wasn't going so well. I put it aside and very quickly wrote another. When I sat down to write it, Hap started speaking to me, and he took over. Even then, I thought, this is it, two and out. But the book really hit a nerve with the publisher and the readers, and a series was born. And boy, did I love Hap and Leonard.

Savage Season, the first, has its funny moments, but compared to the others in the series, it is a little more dour. It was followed by seven others, funnier on the whole, although still dark in places, and variable in tone and themes. The first was my caper book, or as close as I'll get to that; the second was the mysterious murder that is tied to the heroes; the third was the Bad Town novel; and the fourth was . . . well, wacky. The fifth was a road novel, the sixth a fish-out-of-water novel. I left the series for eight years to write other things at yet another publisher, Knopf, and for one of their paperback lines, Vintage.

At that time Mysterious Press had the original Hap and Leonard novels, and Knopf wasn't interested in carrying the series forward because of that. That's why the eight-year wait. Finally, the Hap and Leonard books went out of print, and Vintage picked them up. I wrote two new Hap and Leonard books back to back for them. One was a kind of mysterious assassin novel, the other was a dangerous cult book. The latest, *Honky Tonk Samurai*, forthcoming in 2016 from my current publisher, Mulholland, is what I call putting the crew together for one big event. It will be followed by *Rusty Puppy*. The definition of that one is yet to be decided. I never know until I'm finished, and frankly, even then I'm not absolutely certain. What remains in all the books are those guys, their close friendship, their personal histories, and the adventures.

I mention all of this to show how long Hap and Leonard have been with me. After the first six novels, I ceased aging them except when they were having books written about them. So the eight-year wait between number six, *Captains Outrageous*, and number seven, *Vanilla Ride*, is in my mind only a few months later, and so on. If I didn't do that, my guys would be in wheelchairs right now, fighting it out in rest homes with villains who were trying to take their desserts and piss in their bedpans.

But between all that waiting, now and again, I wrote shorter pieces about them. After *Vanilla Ride* and *Devil Red*, numbers seven and eight in the series, I wrote a novella, *Hyenas*, about them, and a short story that is among my favorites, a dark piece titled "The Boy Who Became Invisible." I followed this with *Dead Aim*, another novella. Some years before these, however, my brother Andrew Vachss and I collaborated on a Hap and Leonard novella that to my taste is one of the oddest pieces I've been involved with, unique because Andrew is unique. He added a character to the Hap and Leonard mythology, Veil, and he appears in *Veil's Visit*, also included here, and although it's not exactly rare, it's a story that, until now, has been hard to capture. Veil, like my brother Andrew, is smart and unpredictable. A man couldn't ask for a better brother and friend than Andrew Vachss, whom I love and admire, as does my entire family. He thinks outside the box as a writer, as a lawyer, and as a protector of children. For my own children, he is Uncle Andrew, and they love him and think the world of him. Of course, they should.

What else is here?

I also had a promotional piece I had written to advertise *Bad Chili*, the fourth book in the series. It was "cleverly" called "Death by Chili." It went out to reviewers and whoever received galleys of *Bad Chili*, part of a promotional package that included the story and a hot pepper glued to the page. I still have one or two of those promotional packets somewhere.

"Death by Chili" is the lightest of the Hap and Leonard pieces. Something to cleanse your palate. It's a kind of locked-room mystery, and it's Leonard's story, for the most part.

Anyway, all the Hap and Leonard stories to date, plus some related material, are collected here, including an interview I did with the guys and, better yet, an intro by Michael Koryta. To have a fine writer like Michael write about Hap and Leonard, and about me, is humbling indeed. I'm honored to have him here.

I am also grateful to have Rick Klaw, my editor on this book, as a friend. I have known him for many years now. He was nothing but an energetic kid with a lot of plans when I met him. Now he's an energetic adult who has fulfilled many of those plans and is in the process of fulfilling others. Fortunately, I have been a part of those plans, and I owe him a lot for helping put this book together.

I hope for Hap and Leonard fans who might have missed these when they first came out, this will be a small treat. For those who have yet to discover Hap and Leonard, perhaps these short visits will encourage you to come on over and visit them in their truer habitat, the novel.

I would also like to thank SundanceTV; my friend and director, Jim Mickle; and my good buddy, actor/screenwriter Nick Damici, for all their hard work on developing these characters into a series. A special thanks has to go to Lowell Northrop, my friend and co-collaborator, for organizing and presenting this series to Jim and Nick, and for all his hard work and relentless pursuit of a series about Hap and Leonard. He knows the characters better than I do—I think they talk to him more than to me.

I should also mention, with great pride and respect, James Purefoy and Michael K. Williams, two fine actors and equally fine fellows who have brought Hap and Leonard to life on the small screen. Thanks, guys. It has been a treat.

And thanks to my pal Bill Sage, as well as the always game Jeff Pope, the wonderfully intense Neil Sandilands, the remarkable Christina Hendricks, as well as Jimmi Simpson and the sweetly tough-as-nails Pollyanna McIntosh. She's what we in Texas call "a pistol." You need her to climb through a window, she'll do it. Wrestle a bear, she's ready. Kick someone's ass, where the hell are they?

Thanks to all the crew and actors and everyone involved in the television show for braving mosquitoes; all manner of huge, crawling bugs, including fire ants; alligators; snakes; tornadoes; windstorms; rainstorms; and blistering heat to make this series a reality.

Special thanks to my niece and assistant, the smart and lovely Pamela Lansdale, aka Pamela Dunklin. She kept me focused, provided granola bars when I looked as if I might be losing blood sugar, and made certain things went smoothly. And, of course, thanks to my lovely wife, Karen, for letting me go on a two-month long adventure into TV land. And to my children, Keith and Kasey, thanks for supporting your old man with kind words and humor.

Finally, thanks to the Baton Rouge, Louisiana area, and all

ABOUT THE AUTHOR

Joe R. Lansdale is the author of more than forty novels and four hundred shorter works, including stories, essays, introductions, and articles. He has written screenplays and teleplays, including for *Batman: The Animated Series* and *Superman: The Animated Series*. He wrote the script for the animated film *The Son of Batman*. His works have been translated into numerous languages, and several novels and short stories of his have been filmed, among them *Bubba Ho-Tep*; *Cold in July*; *Incident On and Off a Mountain Road*, for Showtime's *Masters of Horror*; and *Christmas with the Dead*, which he produced with a screenplay by his son, Keith.

Lansdale is the recipient of numerous awards and recognitions, among them the Edgar Award and ten Bram Stoker Awards, one of which is for Lifetime Achievement. He has received the Grandmaster of Horror Award; the British Fantasy Award; the Inkpot Award for Lifetime Achievement; the Herodotus Award for historical/crime fiction; the Golden Lion Award for his contribution to the works of Edgar Rice Burroughs; the Grinzane Prize; and others.

Lansdale is also a member of the Texas Literary Hall of Fame and the Texas Institute of Letters, and he is Writer in Residence at Stephen F. Austin State University. He is the founder of Shen Chuan Martial Science and has been recognized by the International Martial Arts Hall of Fame as well as the United States Martial Arts Hall of Fame.

Joe Lansdale lives with his wife, Karen, in Nacogdoches, Texas.